I0823191

THE BODY

Also by Bethany C. Morrow

Cherish Farrah

Mem

for young adult readers

So Many Beginnings

A Chorus Rises

A Song Below Water

THE BODY

BETHANY C. MORROW

TOR PUBLISHING GROUP
NEW YORK

This is a work of fiction. All of the names, characters, organizations, places, and events portrayed in this work are either products of the author's imagination or used fictitiously.

THE BODY

A Nightfire Book
Published by Tom Doherty Associates / Tor Publishing Group
120 Broadway
New York, NY 10271

www.torpublishinggroup.com

Nightfire™ is a trademark of Macmillan Publishing Group, LLC.

EU Representative: Macmillan Publishers Ireland Ltd, 1st Floor, The Liffey Trust Centre, 117–126 Sheriff Street Upper, Dublin 1, D01 YC43

The Library of Congress Cataloging-in-Publication Data is available upon request.

ISBN 978-1-250-39212-1 (hardcover)
ISBN 978-1-250-39213-8 (ebook)

First Edition: 2026

Printed in the United States of America

10 9 8 7 6 5 4 3 2 1

To Amy/Ambrosia/Amtrak/Amsterdam,
who has now named one of my books
and one of my main characters

These people draw near to Me with their mouth,
And honor Me with their lips,
But their heart is far from Me.
And in vain they worship Me,
Teaching as doctrines the commandments of men.

Matthew 15: 8–9 (NKJV)

THE BODY

I

Mavis was afraid. She was biting back panic, hands tightening around the leather steering wheel and then loosening again. The corner of her lip was between her teeth and any minute she would bite through. It was clockwork. A thought would occur to her, something hypothetical and only mildly catastrophic. The kind of thought that other people would let pass by. Thoughts were like birds, they said, and you couldn't help which ones fluttered through, but you could help the ones you allowed to nest.

Mavis's thoughts must have been the only ones that came with talons. They didn't flutter through. They didn't even snag the corner of her brain; they sank deep. They gripped and gored. There was nothing she could do to make them leave, either by will or inattention. Once they were there, they were there, and she had no say in how long they tormented her. *Mildly* metastasized into *terrifyingly catastrophic* as the thought took on texture and weight. Soon, it was too robust to be hypothetical, and Mavis might lose anywhere from an hour to half a day playing out torturesome scenarios against her will, her mind held prisoner until the thought ran its course. Afterward, her body often felt battered and bruised, and always, she'd given herself a vicious canker sore on the inside corner of her mouth.

Mavis had tried to get in front of it this time. She'd gotten what she considered insurance—something to counteract the worst of her imagined catastrophes. Not even an hour later, she knew it hadn't worked. She was still just as terrified as she'd ever been. Worse. She wasn't afraid of losing Jerrod; she was certain that now she would. That she already had, and there was no undoing it.

The traffic light wasn't changing. It was never going to change. She'd be stuck at this red light forever, and she wouldn't get home before Jerrod, at least not in time to shower and weave a sophisticated dinner out of the contents of their kitchen. She was a good cook, and they always had leftovers on league night—but today "good" meant the beginning of the end. Today, Jerrod would wonder why she hadn't thought to do more. Why his wife didn't think he deserved better than bowling-alley food on Thursday nights.

The light was going to cost Mavis her entire life.

Her teeth sank into her inner lip just as the red flicked to green, but she barely felt the sting. It was relief, not pain, that made her chin tremble. Relief sent a swift tear straight from her eyelashes to her blouse. Relief made a vacuum to replace the taloned thoughts threatening to shred Mavis to pieces. Thanks to relief, Mavis didn't see anything but what was directly in front of her. She was focused on the road home when the other car bludgeoned her passenger door like a battering ram.

She heard the impact before she felt it, and then it was a violent lurch in her guts as her momentum shifted from forward acceleration to sideways careening.

The sound was devastating. Metal changed shape by deafening

force. Before the pain began to register, Mavis knew the crash was fatal by the shrieking, crushing, screaming whines of the three vehicles involved. The car that sent her sideways didn't brake. Even when it'd pinned Mavis against the nose of a vehicle on the other side of the intersection, it drove them back even farther until the driver's foot fell off the accelerator.

She didn't believe it when it stopped. It was too sudden. Her eyes clenched shut, Mavis's body communicated a litany of concerns to her brain. Her legs felt broken. Her skin was burning under the seat belt and down her exposed arms. She hadn't realized she was speaking, but her voice trembled in a string of hushed pleas.

Pleas, not prayers. She'd thought she was going to die and she'd only whimpered pathetically. She hadn't prayed for deliverance, or the courage to face the end. Mavis would live, but she'd have to live with the knowledge of who she really was: deep down, her conscience damned her in a voice very much like her mother's.

Mavis reached up to scrape at whatever was coating her tongue and found that her lips were wet. There was something in her mouth. Sand. It was burning her throat.

Mavis opened her eyes and saw the blood on her fingers. Her nose or mouth must be bleeding. More concerning than that was her surroundings.

The air was pink, and visible. Granular. Something was floating all around her.

She'd died.

She was dead.

"You're not dead, sweetheart, I can hear you!" Someone was speaking to her through the pink. They were a strange silhouette, shapeless and swaying. "You were in an accident. Can you hear me?"

Mavis tried to answer and instead began to choke.

"It's okay, sweetheart, help's coming!"

"Where am I?" Mavis called through a cough. "Where am I?"

"You're still in the car, sweetheart. We can't get you out."

"Where am I?" Mavis asked again, choking this time on the adrenaline rushing in. Her body was shivering. "What's wrong with the air?"

"You're in the car, sweetheart," the voice cooed. Whoever it was, they were on the verge of tears. "I think you're concussed. All of your airbags deployed. It's just the dust from the airbags."

Mavis studied the walls around her. It was airbags protruding from the driver's and passenger's doors, more spreading like an apron from the dash. The windows were behind the airbags. That's why it looked like Mavis was inside a bulbous pod. Like she'd left her world and landed in another.

The bag coming out of the steering wheel looked like a deflating lung, and on it was a Rorschach stain of blood.

It'd hit her in the face at some point. That she had no memory of it scared her most. The full-body shivers became rolling tremors.

"Jerrod," she said aloud.

"My name is Casey, sweetheart," the voice outside her car said. "I'll stay with you, okay?"

"My husband," Mavis called louder. "I have to call Jerrod."

"Okay. Can you reach your phone?"

When Mavis looked at the well in the middle console where her phone usually sat, she realized her vision was blurry. Like looking through a rain-streaked window.

"It's not there."

"Okay," Casey answered. The young woman was still swaying, if Mavis's eyes could be believed. "Is it connected to your car? Can you voice command?"

"Call Hubby!" Mavis cried.

She still couldn't believe she was in her car anymore, but a familiar automated voice echoed Mavis's command and then a loud tone rang out around her.

"Hey, baby," Jerrod's deep voice boomed inside Mavis's pod. "You home?"

At the sound of his voice, Mavis crumpled forward. She was sure he could be heard outside the car, too, but for once, she didn't care. Relief, again.

"Mavis? Baby, are you okay?"

It wasn't the shower she'd planned, but from the mangled center of what could have been her coffin, her husband's disembodied voice washed over her. Her conscience quieted.

"Jerrod, I'm hurt."

"There was a car accident," Casey called out. "She's trapped but help is coming."

Jerrod was on the move. Mavis could hear him panting, keys jangling, and his own car beeping when he unlocked it and let himself in.

The sound of his breath pulled away momentarily, and he cursed before he brought the phone back to his face.

"Baby, something's wrong," he said. The concern was warping his voice. Jerrod had always been a startingly calm man; it made his fear evident by comparison. "I can't see where you are. Your location sharing isn't on."

His breath pulled away again, and the next curse was an exclamation.

"Mavis," he said, the mic too close to his lips on his return. "You have to tell me where you are, baby."

"She's in the intersection of Ross and Fifteenth Avenue," Casey answered when Mavis frantically tried to beat back the deployed airbags to check.

"She's *in* the intersection?"

Approaching sirens blared, but Casey shouted the location a second time and Mavis heard her husband's car rev.

"Drive careful," Mavis told him, mostly out of habit, and in response, Jerrod choked out a laugh. A moment later and he was crying.

"I'm coming, baby."

Mavis was the last person left in the wreckage.

Casey had been driving the third car, the one Mavis's was pinned against, and she'd been able to get out without assistance. She'd crawled onto what was left of her hood to check on Mavis while a group of passing motorists attended to the car responsible for the accident.

Mavis had been sure Casey was standing, somewhat unstably, right outside her door, but that was impossible. There was only mangled metal and pooling fluids, no place to stand or sway.

"Mavis," a firefighter called to her. "We're gonna separate these cars so we can get you out of there, okay?"

"Okay," she replied, tightening her already closed eyes to try and rein in her impatience. She needed to move, to get out of what was left of her car and see if she could still walk, if she was bleeding anywhere but her face. She was just now realizing that her body was numb and panic was creeping back in.

"It's gonna be very loud," the firefighter said. "It might sound scary again, but it's just us getting this mess detangled."

The accident had sounded like screaming, in a way, and it was seared into Mavis's memory. The way metal and glass sounded when they shattered or when collision broke them into new forms. At the first responder's warning, it started up in her mind again. An abbreviated five-second soundscape abruptly played, and Mavis's breath caught. She was never going to forget it.

The responders only detached Casey's car. After that, a pair of hydraulic scissors severed Mavis's door from the rest of the frame, and the world was still there, on the other side. The air wasn't pink and granular. It didn't burn.

Mavis's breaths came faster then. Something about the bright blue sky, and other cars still intact in the intersection. The people clumped on the two corners she could see from the now unobscured driver's seat. It made her arms tremble so much that her hands danced in her lap.

The world shouldn't look the same way it had before the light turned green. It was too much to process that the sky was bright and blue while a paramedic stood close enough for their uniform to graze Mavis's face while they pressed gloved fingers against her neck and down her back. That the sun shone beautifully while they spoke calmly, softly telling her what they were doing, why she was shaking, that it would pass.

She could feel everywhere they touched her, and the relief resurfaced. When her seat belt was unbuckled, they helped Mavis turn in her seat, then slowly stand with assistance. Attempting to sit her on the gurney revealed that Mavis's tailbone was bruised. Badly. Every movement had caused some discomfort, but this was worse. Despite being seated a moment before, it took Mavis several tries to get on the gurney. Taking it in painstaking increments, the paramedics guided her breathing, too, though it was frequently interrupted by Mavis's involuntary yelps.

She hadn't wanted to be loaded into the ambulance without Jerrod, but there was concern. They needed to give Mavis something for the pain and to assess her for more serious internal issues with some degree of privacy, but they wouldn't leave the scene without further discussion, they promised.

When Jerrod arrived, no one had to tell her; Mavis heard him. Even from inside the closed ambulance, among the dozens of voices, her husband's was as distinctive as any physical attribute. She would recognize him in any crowd, from a distant glimpse of his particular curl pattern, or his gait, or the exact register and tone of his voice. She could've stood up in one painful feat if the paramedics hadn't stopped her, collarbone, tailbone, knees, and shins be damned.

They opened the doors, and Jerrod leapt onto the rig like his body was coursing with adrenaline, too.

"Baby," he whispered into her hair, one hand cradling the back of her neck, the other snaking between Mavis's back and the gurney. It hurt—her whole body hurt—but she latched onto him and didn't let go.

She'd almost lost him. She'd convinced herself she had.

"I love you," she whispered in reply.

Jerrod parried fear with a flurry of rhetorical questions. Was she okay? he asked, while he embraced her in an ambulance. Why hadn't he been there? Was she all right? Why today, when he was across town? Why, at all?

He apologized for things outside his control, made promises he couldn't keep. He'd protect her. He would never let something like this happen to her again.

Mavis soaked it in. She buried her forehead in her husband's chest like the paramedic wasn't standing close by. Like the doors weren't open, and the whole world couldn't see them.

She believed him.

Everything would be okay now. Anything she'd done before someone ran a red light and hurtled her sideways into a different solution didn't matter now.

Jerrod was afraid of losing her, too.

Everything was going to be okay.

II

Everything was going to be okay.

Jerrod was afraid of losing her, too.

The knowledge soothed her better than the paramedic's Tylenol #3. When Jerrod stepped backward out of the ambulance, his dark eyes wet ever since their brief and whispered prayer, Mavis didn't collapse into panic. The taloned thoughts didn't return. They might, at some point. There was nothing saying this reprieve was forever, but for the ride from the scene of the accident to the emergency room, Mavis felt at peace.

Her husband was close by, weaving through traffic, riding the ambulance's wake. Her car was totaled, but Jerrod couldn't leave his behind. She'd be okay until they were reunited at the hospital.

By the time she was wheeled through the second set of automatic doors, he was back at her side.

"Middle car?" some member of the ER staff asked during the trade-off.

"Yes, this is Mavis, the driver. Her husband met us at the scene."

"One more?" they asked as the parties separated.

"No, third car walked it off. She refused transport."

There was no goodbye, the paramedics simply doubling back

the way they came once Mavis was off their gurney, and the ER staff taking over as though accustomed to their ongoing conversation.

Mavis and Jerrod were left alone in a room made up of cloth on three sides. The sound of hospital curtains being yanked back and forth formed a constant chorus, their hooks attached to wheeled rollers that clattered across the tracks. They were either impossible to move quietly, or no one on staff felt inclined.

It was unreal, how abruptly the venue and atmosphere changed. If her position had been precarious at the scene, half a dozen people attending, as soon as she was in the emergency room, the urgency disappeared. It was comforting. It meant she was out of the woods. There were people who needed medical attention more than she did.

"I'm sorry, sweetheart," she said when Jerrod had tucked her beneath the light hospital blanket and sat facing her on the bed. He'd taken one of her hands—the one with bloodstained fingertips—and was squeezing it at odd intervals in a way Mavis could tell was automatic.

"Mavis." Jerrod said her name like it was delicate. "Why would you apologize, baby? I'm the one who feels guilty. I can't believe you went through that by yourself."

Before she knew it, her lip was between her teeth again. Mavis winced.

"I feel guilty, too," she said, weakly. She confessed it like it would let the slightest bit of air out of a balloon. Only so as to make it easier to tie off. To avoid eruption and stop any more from leaking free.

"You have nothing to feel guilty about." He was standing again, coming to her side to pull her into his abdomen. His head rested on hers.

"It feels like it's my fault," she told him.

Mavis was caught off guard when her own curtain was snatched aside before she or Jerrod saw the shadow on the other side. She reached up to flick away her tears, her chin tucked toward her chest.

"Hi Mavis," the intruder said. He was wearing a stethoscope around his neck and a photo ID clipped to the pocket of his scrubs. He glanced up from his tablet and made meaningful eye contact with her husband.

"Jerrod Dwyer," Jerrod complied.

The other man glanced at Mavis, Jerrod's hand in his. "Husband?"

"Yes," she said, and nodded.

"Okay." He pointed to himself with the tablet stylus. "Doctor." The corner of his mouth ticked up when the couple gave anxious laughs. They were more like grunts, pressure releasing at a welcomed sign of mirth. "What the heck did you get yourself involved in today, Mavis?"

The tears resurged despite her smile. She tried to hold on to it, but first her eyebrows buckled, and then her face collapsed. Mavis sobbed. The two men sprang toward her, her husband and the well-meaning doctor flanking her on either side, a hand on each of her shoulders.

"I'm sorry, Mavis," the doctor said. "Gallows humor certainly isn't fun for everyone."

"No," she insisted, shaking her head and casting out a tearful laugh. "It's not your fault, that's totally fine! I'm just overwhelmed, I think."

It wasn't taloned thoughts torturing her now. Nothing hypothetical. It was shame. It was relief and gratitude trying to breathe beneath the suffocating weight of regret.

Mavis had been so consumed with fear, with how undeserving she'd been made to feel, that she'd focused on all the wrong worst-case scenarios. She hadn't gotten around to considering this one. The one where everything was going to be okay, but she would never be. The one where she couldn't take back what she'd done, both because it had happened and because it had been in service of her marriage.

"I'll start over," the man said, and he sat down in the chair that hadn't been close enough to her for Jerrod. "I'm Dr. Moore. I'm really glad you're just overwhelmed, and I hope that's all the damage you're gonna take from what I understand was a very terrifying car accident."

Mavis took a deep breath. She nodded, a smaller, more natural smile flickering in and out.

"I'd like to get some scans of your chest to make sure there's nothing more serious than seat belt bruising, and then your pelvis for the same reason, and—" He glanced back at his tablet. "We should probably just look at your tailbone and your knees, too. Is there anything you're worried about?"

"My throat," she said, touching her neck. "It was burning."

Dr. Moore stood, drawing an instrument from a front pocket and sanitizing it before having her open her mouth.

"Your airbags deployed, I assume?" he asked.

"All of them," Jerrod answered while Mavis's tongue was still depressed.

"Yeah. You probably noticed a lot of dust. You probably *inhaled* a lot of it."

"Is that serious?" Jerrod asked.

"No, it should be fine."

"But it burned?" Jerrod pressed.

"Well, the throat doesn't really like dust." Dr. Moore calmly concluded both his examination and Jerrod's inquiry. "I'll have someone bring you something to drink before the scans."

Dr. Moore wrenched the curtain aside in preparation to leave, but he turned back to the couple, mouth open to ask or say one more thing.

Beyond him, an older woman shuffled into the open space between curtained rooms. She didn't look like she should be walking on her own; she was barely making progress. She could be stopped with very little effort, if anyone but Mavis seemed to notice her. And the longer Mavis looked, the more reason she had.

The older woman's short hair was white, except where it was red. And wet. She wasn't wearing a hospital gown, or any outer clothing. It took a moment for Mavis to realize that beside the woman's bra and underwear, the color against her sallow skin was various concentrations of red. It was smeared across her chest and shoulder, and all the way down her side. Somewhere between her rib cage and the lip of her high-waist panties, the red was more alive. It was a deep, more vivid color where it hadn't been spread out, and it moved. Like a forgotten faucet, it bubbled up and over the fabric while the woman trudged.

"What's she doing here?" Mavis said just above a whisper. The men in her makeshift room quieted. They'd been in conversation since Dr. Moore turned back, but Mavis hadn't heard a word. Now she was grimacing and sputtering against the pain of getting out of bed.

"Lay down, baby," Jerrod said even as he gave her room, steadying his wife as she stood.

"Help her," she told him, and her husband followed her finger to the bloody woman losing steam in her great escape.

"Mrs. Spencer!" Dr. Moore bolted toward the woman, calling for a nurse.

At his touch, the older woman screamed. She swung away from him, one of her hands flopping at the wrist. It was discolored and swollen, a blackening balloon that seemed barely attached to the otherwise wiry, pale arm.

Mavis was standing at her open curtain when the hospital finally erupted into noisy chaos.

"She's undressed everything," Dr. Moore was relaying to nurses showing up empty-handed and rushing away. He didn't mean her clothing; her injuries had been attended to, and the older woman had undone the staff's efforts before trying to flee, her fingers tipped with blood.

"I can't just leave him there!" the woman cried. "You can't just leave him in the street!"

"Mrs. Spencer, you have to stop moving." Dr. Moore was pressing against her bubbling abdomen.

"Sister Rose?" Mavis asked, when she'd accepted who the woman was.

Everything stopped.

"Sister Rose! It's me. It's Mavis Dwyer." Jerrod helped Mavis to the center of the chaos, relieved staff taking the opportunity to procure a wheelchair and whatever they intended to administer once the woman was no longer on her feet. "I'm Daniel and Marie Carson's daughter?"

Rose Spencer was an upsetting sight. The last time Mavis had seen the woman, her white bob had been freshly cut. Gaudy diamond cluster earrings bulged below the blunt edge in chocolate and white, one stunning red diamond at the center. She'd been wearing a shade of eye shadow Marie Carson had found unbecoming, a dark blue settling deep in the wrinkled fold of Rose Spencer's eyelid. It looked like a bruise, Mavis's mother had noted, discreetly.

Mavis hadn't thought the eye shadow quite as indecent. Now, Mrs. Spencer was standing before her covered in nothing but blood and undergarments. It couldn't be the same person. One of the older woman's eyes was smashed deeper into her face, and the effect was much worse than an ill-chosen cosmetic. It made her look lopsided, her features asymmetrical and mismatched. A deep gash on the bridge of Rose Spencer's nose made Mavis worry the appendage would dislodge and slide off the woman's face. Everywhere, her skin seemed paper-thin, blue veins etching like electricity beneath it.

"Mavis," Mrs. Spencer moaned, her one working hand gripping Mavis's blouse tight. Jerrod stood close, as though worried what the older woman might do. "They left Bill in the street. I've got to go get him."

Dr. Moore glanced at Mavis while he redressed Mrs. Spencer's abdomen. He nodded.

"What happened?" Mavis asked the woman.

"I don't know," the woman replied, and her chest seemed to cave in. Her good fist tightened, Mavis's shirt taut in her grasp. Her black balloon-hand bounced against Mavis's other arm, and Mavis winced, afraid the thing would pop. "I don't know. We were going to dinner. Bill wants a hanger steak. I've got to call the restaurant and tell them we'll be late."

Nothing seemed outlandish about her claims except that she was making them in the middle of an emergency room with hospital staff attending to her wounds for a second time.

"How did you get here?" Mavis asked, shaking her head to clear the confusion. She was beginning to feel her own injuries again, her lower extremities pulsing so intensely she was afraid her shins would split down the middle.

"First car," Dr. Moore replied quietly, his expression more solemn than it'd been since they met.

"What?" Mavis turned to Jerrod as though he could offer clarification.

Dr. Moore stood, and, in a seesaw effect, Rose Spencer seemed to deflate. She sank into the wheelchair, aided by several nurses.

"I've got to find Bill," the older woman whimpered as she was wheeled away.

"Her husband was driving the car that hit yours," Dr. Moore confirmed when the rest of the staff was out of earshot.

"I know them!" Mavis insisted as he began herding her and Jerrod back into the curtained room. "I've known the Spencers all my life. They go to church with my family."

"You know the people that hit you?" Jerrod pointed where Rose Spencer had been and then at his wife, as though to confirm a connection.

"That is"—the doctor pushed air between his lips—"wildly unlikely. Which accounts for at least half the cases I encounter in this ER."

"Why is Sister Rose saying they left Brother Bill in the street?"

Dr. Moore looked at Mavis. He held her in a steady gaze, the way he did whenever there was destabilizing news to deliver.

"Mr. Spencer was pronounced at the scene. I'm very sorry, Mavis."

The pink pod exploded around her. She was back inside of the car, dust burning the air and the inside of her mouth. The belt tightening against her chest, cutting into her belly. Metal screaming. Or maybe it had been Mrs. Spencer she'd heard. Maybe the woman had known and then forgotten.

"No one told her?" Mavis asked, softly. "When she woke up, no one told her he was dead?"

"Mrs. Spencer never lost consciousness. She was awake at the scene, and she would've seen—" Dr. Moore cut himself off. "I confirmed it to her, as well."

The three stood in respectful silence for a moment more.

"I'd better go see about her." Dr. Moore moved the curtain gently this time, and then he was gone.

Mavis sat on her hospital bed, and Jerrod followed. She turned and studied her husband's face. His dark eyes and wide nose. The brown pigment of his top lip. She reached up and massaged his coily hair, careful not to disturb the part on the right side. Everything was in its rightful place, unblemished. Every part of him was whole. He was here.

"I don't know what to say," Jerrod began, his deep voice a quiet rumble. He touched his wife's face. "I'm so glad you're okay."

"Me, too," she replied, nodding slightly enough not to disrupt his touch. "I can't believe that was Sister Rose. Do you remember the way she used to look?"

"I don't think I've ever seen her before, but . . . she looked terrible."

Mavis pulled back from resting her forehead against her husband's chin.

"You've met the Spencers before, sweetheart."

"Have I?" he asked.

"Yeah, they were at our wedding."

Jerrod's eyes drifted while he tried to access a memory, but he didn't find it.

"Oh. That's news to me."

III

Mavis didn't enjoy her wedding. When she'd confessed as much to her mother the next morning—at the brunch she and Jerrod were obliged to attend before leaving for their honeymoon—Marie Carson had scrunched her nose and shaken her head.

"That's certainly not something a new wife should say," her mother said, the sparkling laugh no match for the sharpness of the chide.

"You asked how I enjoyed my day," Mavis replied, hushedly, her apologetic defense intended only for her mother.

"Yes, and I meant for you to gush over this handsome new husband you've been blessed with," Marie Carson informed her with less discretion. "Everyone said it went off without a hitch."

It hadn't, but Mavis didn't ask who'd said that, or how they would know. She didn't ask why it mattered, the opinions of the many guests her parents had required despite that they were virtually strangers to Mavis.

"Your father and Jerrod's parents were very generous," her mother continued, as though she and Mavis were alone at one of their mother-daughter luncheons. She'd always taken those opportunities to impart wisdom on which Mavis would depend as a future wife. Always in the chiding tone of someone correcting a flaw, rather than simply informing. It was sharp but routine, shallow pinpricks like precise acupuncture. Whenever she suffered the process in public, it straightened Mavis's posture and weakened her brow. "You wouldn't want to sound ungrateful, that's all."

"I think there's room in gratitude for a little disappointment," Jerrod had offered, holding his wife's hand atop the table linen. He didn't usually interrupt the private asides Mavis and her mother shared in public. Mavis's father didn't—he didn't seem to hear them at all—and Jerrod had learned by example.

Mavis thought she'd be relieved when there was finally someone on her side, but she lowered her eyes at Jerrod's insertion. She set her teeth on top of each other and tightened, as though to see whether or not they would break. She kept the inside of her mouth clear of them, lest she accidentally make herself bleed in front of her parents and her new husband. They wouldn't know it—unless she bit too hard, the blood pooling on her tongue, staining her lips, lacing her fruit fork.

Jerrod might've tried being on her side the day before. Regardless how it'd worked in their favor, he hadn't been on her side when he'd caved to his mother, who'd insisted they amend the wedding ceremony.

It had been uncomfortable enough reading the vows she hadn't wanted to personalize.

"*What will people think, the two of you reciting impersonal vows?*" her mother had asked. It was an accusation, not a question. Mavis knew because she knew her mother—and because of what the woman said next. "*You've wanted to be married since you were a little girl; it's all you talked about.*"

Mavis had felt herself shrinking, the embarrassment compounding with every validating memory rushing to mind. The sheets she'd made into veils. The Sundays she'd waited impatiently for service to end so that she could practice walking down the aisle. The adoring approval she'd received, even when still pantomiming the bridal procession in middle school. It would've been humiliating enough if her mother had stopped there.

"And to have wasted all those years with Cyrus."

"*Mom,*" Mavis protested.

"No, I think it bears reminding that there was a time you hoped to make vows to him."

Mavis's shoulders had inched closer to her ears, her face so hot she feared it must be glowing.

"You tried everything you could to convince him you were ready. Daddy could only do so much."

It wasn't talons Mavis felt digging, goring into her gray matter while her mother regaled her with the most demoralizing five years of her life. They weren't hypothetical thoughts, but memories. Pleading with her father to speak to Cyrus, to insist that Mavis *was* wife material. That there were some things that couldn't be perfected outside the covenant of marriage, some faith required on Cyrus's part, too. Shouting at her mother that it was her fault Mavis needed Cyrus to love her this much. Screaming that she hated the man, that she didn't want to be wife to a man who'd already been unfaithful and said she was to blame. Sobbed that it was her parents' fault she'd believed him.

It wasn't fair. They didn't despise Cyrus's sin. The second time Mavis mentioned it by name, they accused her of keeping a record of wrongs. Cyrus hadn't asked forgiveness; he hadn't expressed remorse for his repeated betrayal, but she was expected to blot it from her mind. That's why she'd fallen apart. Because sin had to be dealt with harshly. It had to be met with unsympathetic disdain.

But not his. Never Cyrus's.

There was no use asking whether this trip down memory lane served a purpose. Besides reminding Mavis of her stunning self-debasement, and her lack of wisdom, not to mention faith. Her parents' failed attempt to secure Cyrus's proposal could be forgiven; they'd despaired at the sight of the daughter they'd poured everything into being so thoroughly unmoored. They'd recovered long before Mavis had. Even before Cyrus had informed her who he was "supposed" to marry, breaking up with her a week after their fifth anniversary, her parents had withdrawn. They'd informed Mavis that they couldn't permit her to shed another tear in their presence over the relationship, or in any way perform her idolatry in their home. They'd taken a stand, and it felt very unfair to Mavis.

"I'm not trying to press into old wounds, daughter," her mother had said, when Mavis was engaged to Jerrod and hesitant to read aloud vows meant for him. *"But you owe it to him to say things you never hoped to say to someone else. Your husband deserves that."*

Mavis could understand that. She'd felt herself softening.

"You're far too old to still be this lazy."

She'd written her own vows, as her mother instructed. She'd delivered them before an audience of hundreds, though several times her voice dipped for privacy. Each time, her mother gestured to the pastor, who raised Mavis's elbow to bring the microphone closer to her mouth. No one missed a word.

When Jerrod read his, Mavis panicked. No one knew. Her

eyes were heavily camouflaged in lashes and liner and contouring shadow. The tears made them glisten, but that was to be expected. His own nerves kept even Jerrod from properly interpreting his bride's wide, frantic stare. The unnatural repetition of her blinks. The way the muscles in her face jumped, so that expressions flashed across her face too briefly and were replaced too quickly to be sincere.

Jerrod was promising to study her. To marvel in how his new bride had been fearfully made—and he didn't specify *for him*. He promised to give her space and encouragement to grow.

There was throat-clearing from the audience, both sets of their parents included. If Mavis had glanced at her mother, she knew the woman would be bulging her eyes and glancing away in a show of secondhand embarrassment and genuine disapproval.

That wasn't why Mavis had panicked. She'd panicked because the vows that Jerrod had written were beautiful and kind, and totally unrealistic. He was declaring before what felt like the whole world that he had no idea what marriage was. Mavis panicked because, in that instant, she awoke from whatever spell she'd been under for the duration of their nine-month courtship.

The man she was marrying was literally too good to be true. It meant he'd turn out worse than men like Cyrus, whose transgressions became common and forgivable. It meant that when Jerrod inevitably faltered—when the biological needs she'd been taught to accept and to protect men from overwhelmed him—it would be disastrous. The disparity between the man who was making these vows and the man who'd inevitably betray Mavis would be so stark, there would be no way to reconcile them. She would be destroyed and he defeated. He wouldn't remember that a husband's sin, though devastating, was also a wife's greatest opportunity. He wouldn't encourage Mavis to move from strength to strength, to grow in grace and humility, and be a testimony to others. He'd believe the damage he'd done too great and—out of pity—he would leave her.

Onstage, Mavis smiled back at Jerrod. He was vowing to devote himself to this life, his eyes welling up either at the sight of his bride in tears, or because he knew that they were doomed.

And then something remarkable happened. Something galling, and startling—and maybe wonderful.

After Jerrod and Mavis finished reading their vows to each other, the pastor asked the congregation to stand. It hadn't happened during rehearsal; the pastor hadn't reminded them of it during the run-through because it wasn't supposed to happen. Mavis had discussed it with Jerrod, and he'd understood why she didn't want to include the congregation vow in their ceremony.

The bride and groom making outlandish claims toward one another and future-casting a perfect union was setting themselves up for disappointment, but disappointment was part of marriage. They were expected to believe a life of bliss and consideration and compromise and grace was something they could agree to during one ceremony and for the rest of their lives. They would have heavenly mercy and aid in the endeavor, and so it was a noble aspiration, no matter how panicked it made Mavis.

The congregation was another matter entirely.

There were hundreds of them. When they stood, whether uniform or not, the sheer number of participants sounded like a military company coming to attention. And then they were instructed to pledge an allegiance to a pairing they'd had no say in. A pairing about which at least one or two that Mavis knew of had expressed doubts. The majority of them had very limited knowledge of either Mavis or Jerrod; they were coming from afar to witness the union out of duty to Daniel and Marie Carson. If they'd only invited people they actually knew, Mavis could've had the small wedding she'd wanted. But her parents warned against letting shame dictate the start of her real life. They said that she was still hiding, that ever since Cyrus she'd wanted to slink out of sight. To avoid her church family, the people who had encouraged her at one time to lay claim to her future as Cyrus's bride—and who later admonished Mavis's "obsession" with marrying him. Everyone knew when Mavis crossed from faithful longing to selfish ambition but her. They knew the threshold after which she'd stopped being prayerfully hopeful and begun trying to force her will. They knew both that marriage was the greatest need and sweetest fulfillment, and that Mavis had taken all their instruction and encouragement too far.

But there was something worse than that. If Mavis wanted to escape them, she had good reason. They'd also whispered Cyrus's criticisms of her back and forth under the guise of soliciting prayers, despite knowing what he'd done. They somehow knew not just that he was an authority on Mavis, but that *his* conduct didn't define or disqualify him.

She hadn't wanted them to stand and vow on her behalf. She didn't want them to promise to hold her and Jerrod up. Together. Accountable. And Jerrod had agreed. His mother had cried when he mentioned it over the phone—Mavis had known better than to tell her parents, unprompted—but he'd explained that they wanted this ceremony to reflect their identity as a couple. So while the pastor was explaining to the standing crowd the vow they would momentarily echo, Mavis tilted her chin, quizzically.

Surely, Jerrod hadn't gone behind her back to satisfy his mother.

No one in the wedding party participated, mostly because having attended the rehearsal, they weren't expecting it. Mavis's collection of bridesmaids included a few girls she'd gone to college with, and the photographer captured them playfully cringing.

Her maid of honor simply blinked through the ambush, as far as photo albums would tell. She was the former Stephany Leonard, with whom Mavis had gone to school from kindergarten through twelfth grade. It was less of a feat given that it had been the same school the entire time, but regardless, Stephany and Mavis had been friends—or in friendly proximity—from the age of five. Stephany had been married for a handful of years by the time Jerrod proposed to Mavis, and at first the distance that developed between them had hurt. Eventually, Mavis understood the necessity of Stephany surrounding herself with other married women, but the relationship never really recovered. If not Stephany, Mavis would have had to ask a cousin to be her maid of honor, and then she doubted Stephany would have attended the wedding at all.

There must've been others who didn't participate, even if they stood when directed. There could hardly be any gathering of totally compliant hundreds. But Daniel and Marie Carson did so emphatically, and beside them, Bill and Rose Spencer did as well.

Jerrod wasn't too good to be true, after all. That night, while he helped his new bride out of her gown and all the trappings underneath, he was quiet. The faucet was echoing in the bathroom, the oversized jacuzzi bath filling in preparation for their first night as man and wife.

They were in a splendid suite in the hotel where the reception was probably just beginning to wrap up. It had been the Spencers' wedding gift, coordinated with Mavis's parents when they were paying the balance on the reception. It was a silly, thoughtful extravagance that would make the next morning's brunch all the more convenient.

Jerrod immediately began rubbing his wife's back once it was bare and bowing, the weight of the dress and the day removed but Mavis still folded on the bedroom's dimpled sofa.

"Are you going to make me the bad guy?" she asked, her voice slightly muffled by the proximity of the upholstery.

"I'm not going to make you the bad guy. I'll start." Jerrod sighed. "I should've told her no."

Mavis sat up, her brown cheekbones flushing.

"I thought we already had."

"I know." Jerrod nodded and sat in the space she'd freed beside her.

"So?"

"I'm sorry, Mavis. As soon as the pastor said it, I knew I was starting out this marriage all wrong."

She had to suppress a grin, keep her face from cracking into a smile. She felt a little guilty, letting him think his betrayal was a bad thing, but she had to. It had to be a mistake if it was going to save their marriage. He had to have been thoughtless, to have put someone before her. Then she got to be gracious, when it seemed she was too much in love to stay upset. When she collapsed toward him like she would fold herself in half again, caught his face in her hands, and let the smile break, his shoulders dropped in relief.

"You don't want an annulment? To start over, at least?"

"No, silly," she said, kissing him first. "I do not want to start over."

"I *am* sorry, baby," he insisted. "Nothing like this will ever happen again."

She nodded before pulling him closer, letting her tongue slip into his mouth gently, and then letting him take over.

Everything would be okay now. Jerrod wasn't too good to be true.

Everything would be okay, until it wasn't.

Until seven years later, when Mavis panicked again.

IV

Six hours after Mavis was blindsided by Bill and Rose Spencer's luxury sedan, she and Jerrod arrived home. She'd heard both her parents' outgoing messages several times by then. Daniel and Marie Carson were on sabbatical in the Mediterranean. They planned to be for the next two weeks, and Mavis wouldn't interrupt just to tell them she'd survived a fantastically frightening car accident, except that it had involved close friends of theirs. One of whom had died.

"Are you sure you want to deliver that news, baby?" Jerrod asked while they carefully traversed the brick steps leading to their front door. He'd already made one trip to unlock the house and put the hospital folder and prescriptions on the mantel. Now one of Mavis's hands was in his, and he cradled her lower back as though afraid she'd lose her balance. Perhaps now he thought her accident-prone. There were worse things in the world than a doting, protective husband.

"Of course I don't *want* to tell them," Mavis confessed. "And certainly not in a voicemail."

"You don't have to. You know that, right? You were in the accident, too, baby." His face went occasionally slack, distracted by the task of navigating their home with a newly compromised wife. "It's tragic, but the Spencer family has probably started making notifications themselves."

He was probably right. Mavis wanted him to be. Still, she felt responsible. Bill Spencer had died today.

Mavis felt her guts churn.

She couldn't tell Jerrod why she felt like the accident was her fault. Bill Spencer had inexplicably barreled through a red light and straight into the passenger side of her vehicle, but if Mavis had been at home, the Spencers would've traveled safely through the intersection. The traffic camera would've caught his plate and a fine would've been the only penance for what might've been a lapse in the older man's cognition or focus. Maybe Bill had been lost in conversation with his now widowed wife. Or maybe they'd been arguing on the way to dinner. Mavis couldn't decide which was worse, and she tried to put the thought out of her mind.

It happened everywhere, every single day. Millions of people died and Mavis didn't blink, but that rationalization felt cheap and nihilistic. Mavis didn't know millions of people, and her inability to grieve them properly didn't mean no one else did. Every day, someone somewhere was out of their mind with grief. Today it was Rose Spencer's turn.

"Mavis?" Jerrod was watching her carefully. "Baby, are you all right?"

They'd made it up the staircase and into their room. Mavis had never gotten into the habit of making the bed until just before climbing back in, so Jerrod had tried to mimic the hurried exercise while keeping one arm around his wife. It hadn't been as difficult to get situated, the medication holding Mavis's pain at bay.

"You look far away," Jerrod said.

"It's still light outside," Mavis answered. They both looked toward the gable skylight above the bed. The sun was somewhere outside the gridded glass, but it wasn't far. There was a hint of white in the pale blue sky, as though clouds had been there and then faded away, or burned off.

"Summer's almost gone." Jerrod sighed. "Enjoy it while it lasts."

"What?" Mavis asked at the slight smile playing on the edge of his mouth.

"Just relieved that's all that was on your mind. Nine P.M. sunsets."

She smiled back. She didn't tell him why the light in the sky disturbed her. Her brain kept tripping over the daylight, insisting that this was not the same day it'd been before the car accident—let alone the same life. There weren't enough hours in the day to contain so many events. But she wanted Jerrod to commit to his uncertain smile. All she had to do was stop trying to force things to make sense. Let the day splinter into different lifetimes if it needed to. If that's what kept her here, with a doting and protective husband, certain of his love, and each grateful for the other, it was worth it.

"I'm sorry you missed league night," she said to justify any lingering traces of guilt she might betray.

"That is the absolute least of my worries, baby." Jerrod kissed her forehead. "Are you going to call your parents?"

Mavis shook her head, eyes sliding low. Rose Spencer would tell them. In fact, the woman probably had the phone number of the Carsons' resort. She and Bill had probably been invited to meet them abroad the way they often did when Mavis's parents were away.

Mavis had been given no such invitation, had no such contact information. Children were meant to be seen and not heard, but Mavis was an adult now. She was meant to be neither. Unless she needed her parents—and the strict definition of that need was unilaterally determined—she would only embarrass herself. Or invite scrutiny she couldn't afford.

"I should call my parents, though," Jerrod went on. "Right?"

Mavis's face must've made him second-guess himself.

"It feels a little bizarre, no one knowing what's happened today," he explained.

"I know," she said, adding emphasis to contradict whatever expression she'd made.

"I guess it feels a little bizarre to call just to inform them, too."

"You should call them, sweetheart," Mavis told him, squeezing his hand. "It'll make you feel better. But can you let them know we'll see them in a couple of days?" She knitted her brows in exaggerated earnestness.

"Yeah, of course," Jerrod agreed. "Can I get you anything first?"

"No," she answered. "I think I just want to rest."

"Okay." He kissed her forehead again, both of them giggling when he tucked her in before closing the door and heading downstairs.

The laughter disappeared with Jerrod. Mavis tried to hold on, but her hands only tightened around the blanket. Her pulse felt like it was sputtering in her veins, hiccupping frantically in her neck, her chest, her wrists.

People might ask where she'd been when the accident happened. They'd know where she was headed, but not where she was coming from. It wasn't a necessary piece of information—it wouldn't tell them anything or explain why the collision had taken place—but people were demanding. Blame was so easy to assign. It was so readily shifted. It felt wicked to hope that tragedy would temper their judgmental brand of curiosity, but Mavis did. She was glad at least for the bruises developing on her skin.

She'd wanted a shower before the accident, and now the smell of a hospital emergency room was clinging to her. While Jerrod was probably downstairs, already on the phone with his parents, she threw back the covers and got out of bed. Chose the handheld rather than the rainfall showerhead. She didn't have time or energy to wash, condition, hydrate, and then straighten or twist her hair before Jerrod was ready for bed. She just needed to scrub the day away.

Mavis remembered Rose Spencer's hair, wet with blood, and released a slow breath. She let the water course over her body, and turned as though away from the woman. She closed her eyes while the shower filled with steam.

Baby. She remembered the sound of Jerrod's voice when he got to her at last. The way he'd pulled her into his arms in the ambulance. The way she'd melted into him.

Her stomach tumbled down.

Her husband had always thought her fragile. It didn't normally send excited chills through her thighs. In fact, very recently the idea of what he'd think she couldn't survive had sent Mavis into a panic. But this was different. A welcome change. She'd earned his delicate touch with pain. She wasn't weak, she was a survivor. She'd sustained a hurt that wouldn't drive him away; it had brought him close.

Mavis let her hot forehead rest against the cool tile.

She meditated on Jerrod's perfect skin. The brown of his lips.

He was afraid of losing her, too.

Baby.

"Baby," Mavis whispered back when she felt herself melting again.

Tingling, she washed quickly, wincing through her hurried movements. She'd done a haphazard job on her lower extremities, and had forgone the back scrubber completely. They weren't the areas she'd been concerned about.

She felt exhausted all over again by the time she was drying off in front of the bathroom mirror. Another dose of Percocet should allow her to sleep a bit early and through the night.

Mavis stilled. Waited.

She squinted, as though her eyes were antennae and the gesture would clarify some signal.

She moved deliberately through the bedroom, careful not to land on the small area of the floor prone to whining.

At the door, she listened. There were voices. Jerrod was talking to someone, and he was agitated. Mavis strained and made out the hum of a much higher voice.

Jerrod's mother was in the house. Deborah Dwyer had imposed again; Mavis had no doubt in her mind. The woman had insisted on coming to the house, regardless what Jerrod told her, and now she was hushing her agitated son, speaking with enraging calm while she reminded him of his sleeping wife upstairs.

Their voices pulled away, as though they'd been in the entry, perhaps at the base of the stairs, and had moved toward the kitchen or living room.

Mavis dressed quickly but cautiously. She held on to the dresser while stepping into clean underwear, pulling on a pajama dress before creeping back to the bedroom door to listen. She'd considered texting Jerrod, but as far as her mother-in-law knew, she was asleep. That was the only thing sparing Mavis. She didn't want to see anyone, least of all their parents.

When someone began gingerly up the staircase, Mavis heard them. It wasn't Jerrod. He'd have no reason to sneak, and if he did, he knew which stairs to avoid. Deborah Dwyer did not.

She also wore a cascade of bracelets on her right wrist. Mavis's mother had once commented on the collection, not quite innocently asking whether or not Deborah re-accessorized daily. Jerrod's mother had been unoffended. She'd proudly extended her arm, the lengths of Figaro dangling from one of her bracelets clattering against the stones and various trinkets of others.

"I've made every one of these," Deborah had said, oblivious and beaming. *"I never repeat myself; they've each got to be inspired. I've begun using so many bits and pieces I'd never even seen before."*

She'd pointed out a stainless steel nut, flanked on both sides by small, round wooden beads. On the other side of the same bracelet, populated mostly of gold and brown baubles, were the corresponding flat and lock washers.

"I'd hardly set foot in a hardware store, Sam'll tell you," Deborah had carried on. *"But with art, you invent new uses for things. That's creativity."*

Mavis had cringed, not just at her mother-in-law, but at the way Mrs. Dwyer had expected a theologian academic married to a second academic to be impressed by her crafts.

"You must save quite a bit of money on jewelry," Marie Carson had replied, turned Deborah Dwyer's wrist one way and then back, maximizing the brash melody the bracelets produced. *"Although I don't think tiger's eye is quite expensive enough to warrant acrylic synthetics, do you?"*

Mavis had interjected that she wouldn't have known the difference, and her mother had shrugged as though not enticed by low-hanging fruit.

Now she heard her mother-in-law's bracelets skittering against the oak railing as the woman snuck up the stairs. Deborah Dwyer had stolen away from her son and was coming to ambush her daughter-in-law.

Mavis retreated. She sprang away from the door, only thinking to lock it when it was too late; she was already halfway to the study. The room directly next to her and Jerrod's bedroom was adjoined, accessible from both the hallway as well as a door beside her walk-in closet. Mavis ducked inside and shut the bedroom behind her before moving to the door leading out into the hall.

She felt silly. She was playing hide-and-seek with her husband's mother, but it was the only option available to Mavis if she didn't want to endure her probing, intrusive brand of concern. She had a right to rest.

Mavis lay against the door a moment. Across from her, the study's great Palladian window wildly overshadowed the underwhelming backyard below. The yard was in a purgatorial holding pattern while she and Jerrod decided how they wanted to use the space, so inside the study, Mavis had crowded the extravagant window with her favorite plants. There was a Meyer lemon and a rubber tree, and three monsteras because she couldn't look at their leaves without marveling. Mavis was always awed at the empty spaces. That something could be incomplete by design.

The walls of the study were lined with arched built-in bookcases to match the Palladian design and, in the center of the room, Mavis's favorite piece of furniture: an oversized daybed sofa. Bathed in light and accented with throw pillows and a plush blanket, it was a delightful place to rest. She'd have no problem explaining why she was napping here instead of her bed, if questioned.

On the other side of the hall, Mavis heard the bathroom door open, the pipes gurgling from recent use—or as decoy. Any minute, Deborah Dwyer was going to lightly knock on the master bedroom door, as though that hadn't been her intention all along. As though there wasn't a full bath on the first floor, next to the guest bedroom.

Mavis listened for Deborah's footsteps. They should be moving slightly away.

They did, briefly. Then they stopped.

Mavis knew her home. She and Jerrod had lived in it all seven years of their marriage.

Deborah Dwyer had only taken two steps. She was standing in the middle of the hall.

Mavis paused her breathing, as though to reduce the clutter. She listened.

It sounded like her mother-in-law hummed something. Some short refrain. Mavis had just barely registered the sound and couldn't place it. It was strange. Strange enough that, were Mavis not intentionally hiding in a different room to avoid the woman, she'd open the door and ask Deborah what she was doing.

Why didn't the woman just go to the bedroom door? It was the entire reason she'd come upstairs, Mavis was certain.

Deborah took another step.

Mavis's head tilted. That time Deborah had definitely approached. She was moving toward the study, unless Mavis was misinterpreting the sound.

She wanted to burst out of the door. Surprise her mother-in-law in the hallway. Confront her, if Mavis wasn't allowed to hide. She knew why *she* was tiptoeing around; she'd demand to know why Deborah was. Mavis was the one on pain meds, who'd been jostled and blindsided, and trapped in a pod. It wasn't unreasonable for her to be less than reasonable today.

It wouldn't be unreasonable to consider all of those things were impacting her interpretation either.

Deborah might be on her phone, distracted and not paying attention to the precise trajectory of her steps.

The bracelets clattered and clinked, the way they had when Deborah extended her arm toward Mavis's mother.

She was standing in the hall with her arm extended. Pointing.

Mavis didn't think. She just slowly pinched the lock between finger and thumb and turned it. It didn't matter that she hadn't made a sound. It didn't matter that no one knew she was in the study, or that she hadn't thought to lock the door until she was already doing it. Once it was done, Mavis's heart galloped. Her nervous system understood what the action implied, and a cold alertness she hadn't felt before crept up the back of her neck. It triggered every hair on its climb until Mavis was afraid she'd shudder against the door.

This was silly.

But in the hall Deborah didn't move toward her son's bedroom. She came right up to the study, as though she could divine her daughter-in-law on the other side of the door.

Mavis looked down at the handle a moment before it began to move.

Her brow crashed low. What was Deborah Dwyer doing?

The handle rotated only as far as the lock allowed, then slowly it rotated back.

Mavis closed her eyes to listen, letting her forehead sink toward the door without touching it.

When Deborah hummed again, Mavis heard her.

Here comes the bride. Just the first line of the "Bridal Chorus."

Mavis drew back, staring quizzically at the door as though she could see the woman on the other side.

The door jolted, and Mavis jumped, her hands flying. She stopped herself before she could clasp them over her mouth and the sound of skin on skin could give her away.

"Mom!" Jerrod whisper-barked from the stairs. "What are you doing up here?"

Mavis heard Deborah whirl to face him. "Jerrod, you scared me!"

"What are you doing?"

"Is Mavis in the study, dear?" she asked, impervious to chastising.

"Mavis is resting, Mom, I told you that. I asked you not to come up here."

Deborah moved in his direction and lowered her voice, though not enough.

"The door to the study is locked, honey," she said.

"How do you know?" he asked, forgetting his whisper.

"What?"

"How do you know it's locked?" he insisted.

"Jerrod, I may not be one of your brilliant in-laws but I know when a door is locked. I thought you said Mavis was resting."

"Just tell me why you're testing handles in my house, Mom."

That time, Mavis did cover her mouth. It was more a reminder not to laugh than a constraint. She was impressed, the way Jerrod refused his mother's bait and kept the attention on her behavior for once.

"I don't appreciate that, Jerrod," Deborah was saying when

she retreated to follow her son back down the stairs. "Help me find your father; we've got to get home and take our evening pills."

Their voices drifted, dissipating in the distance, and Mavis felt her shoulders relax. It was confirmed. Her pain had made all the difference. She laughed to herself, now that she wouldn't be overheard.

"I *do* appreciate that, Jerrod," she snarked, coming to trace a finger inside the hollow of one of her monsteras leaves.

Standing in front of the Palladian window, shrouded by her greenery, Mavis looked down into the backyard and saw Samuel Dwyer staring up at her. The sun was finally setting but it was still high enough to crest the roof of his son's house and shine directly into his unblinking eyes. Her father-in-law just stood there, arms deadweight on either side, staring into the second-story study like he knew she'd be there.

V

For the first year of her marriage, Mavis dreamt about Cyrus regularly. She didn't want to, but she didn't know how to make it stop. Going to her mother for counsel had proved a mistake.

"How long before you let that man go?" Marie Carson had asked. Even over the phone, Mavis heard the disapproval and disgust.

Mavis wasn't holding on to Cyrus. She felt like he was holding on to her. He'd marked her, and his leaving without ever looking back wasn't going to change that.

"You're married," her mother had felt it necessary to remind her. "Whether you deserved it or not. Despite that you don't."

A familiar fissure at Mavis's center reopened.

"How can you say that? What makes me unworthy?" Her voice was too emotion-laden. She knew while she was still speaking that she'd lost any chance at being heard. "Wasn't I supposed to want love? Marriage? Wasn't I *taught* to?"

As expected, Marie Carson didn't dignify her daughter with acknowledgment.

"Dreaming about another man is a betrayal," she said. "It

means you're devoting your thought life to someone other than Jerrod, and it will destroy your marriage."

Mavis couldn't tell if it was a warning or a wish. She hadn't bothered describing taloned thoughts. She hadn't told her mother how upset the dreams made her feel. How frustrated she was upon waking. When she slept, her mind reinstated the man whose memory shamed her. Against her will, it was Cyrus standing beside her. He was often just outside her periphery, but she could always sense that it was him. She knew exactly who was orbiting her just out of sight, and Mavis always resisted. It was familiar—believing she was in a relationship with Cyrus—but she always knew something was wrong. Even though the facts of the dream made sense, Mavis's heart couldn't be fooled. There was a calm, a steadiness, that didn't match the man she knew so well. He couldn't be responsible for the fact that, at the start of each dream, she was happy, and she was smart enough to know she hadn't gotten there with him.

She wasn't tormented enough for him to be the man she'd married. As soon as she told Cyrus she wasn't his wife, she woke up.

She'd wanted the dreams to stop, but not enough to try describing them more clearly to her mother. Not enough to confess them to Jerrod when he might misunderstand them, too. The idea that he'd just as easily characterize them a betrayal became a taloned thought of its own. Mavis had learned from Cyrus how dangerous her faults could be. That the real harm in her missteps was not the way a man's feelings could be hurt, but rather the way a man might be given license to misstep himself. If she betrayed him in her thought life, she had to be prepared for the sin to compound. For it to escalate. Wives—and women who hoped to become one—had a terrible amount of influence, for better or worse. If Mavis opened a door, even timidly, curiously, naively—even if she never crossed the threshold—she had to know her husband would. By the time she married Jerrod, Mavis had the emotional scar tissue to prove it.

She'd kept the dreams a secret, and it meant that with every occurrence, she was more upset. She felt helpless. Terrified. Finally, she felt angry. In her dreams, Mavis began terrorizing Cyrus back. As soon as she sensed his presence, she turned on him. She whirled around so that he couldn't occupy her periphery, spinning like a tank gun turret when he tried to duck back into a blind spot. She'd gotten good at tracking and then attacking him. She'd knock him backward and dig her knees into his chest while she screamed into his face that she was not his wife. That he was not the man she married.

When Jerrod and Mavis had been married seven years, Cyrus invaded her dream again, and she pounced. She sprang at him immediately, despite that it had been years since he'd appeared. She dug her knees into his chest, grinding against his rib cage before leaning close enough to feel the warmth of his breath. She remembered the exact bristle of his tightly shorn beard. The distance and angle from his jaw to his earlobe. The hyper-specificity of intimacy. Mavis ignored all of it.

"You are not the man I married," she growled through gritted teeth.

Beneath her, Cyrus smiled, his teeth like porcelain.

"Yes, I am," he said back. But it wasn't his voice.

Cyrus was a tenor. There was no velvet rumble from deep in his throat. Not like in Jerrod's.

Mavis had recoiled too quickly, and lost her balance, but Cyrus didn't get up. He just lay there, where she'd mounted him, and chuckled. It wasn't forced or villainous. The laugh wasn't full-bodied, as though he took any particular pleasure in what he'd said. It was the way he used to laugh at her when she misspoke. When she over-seasoned the food, and couldn't salvage it. When she needed his help with something she'd tried to accomplish on her own.

The hyperventilation that started in the dream had followed Mavis out. She'd woken up already upright, struggling to regulate her breathing, and afraid to look at the man beside her.

She'd known it would be Jerrod, the way it had been for seven years. Once awake, her sense of Cyrus's presence was always gone. She knew he couldn't really be lurking in any corners—but his words were still in her head. They were sharp talons sinking into her brain, where they would stay.

"Yes, I am."

Things he'd said in the dream.

"The seven-year itch is biological."

Things he'd said years ago, while they were together.

"A good woman can make infidelity the furthest thing from a man's mind."

The contradictions she'd spent five years trying to unravel.

"A man who hasn't failed in his faithfulness has succeeded in lying."

Cyrus was why Mavis hadn't asked Jerrod if he'd ever been unfaithful in a relationship. She'd been afraid of him confessing something, and terrified of him denying it. Throughout their nine-month courtship, Mavis had resisted, knowing she couldn't be reassured regardless of his answer. Instead, she'd sent a message to Stephany Leonard and suggested coffee. The two women hadn't been in contact since Stephany's wedding, but with Mavis's engagement, perhaps that would change. It would be good for Mavis, having a churchgoing, marriage-minded friend who was a few steps ahead to tell her some of the pitfalls to avoid.

Even better that Stephany didn't go to *her* church, where confidences were sometimes sacrificed for the higher good, and memories seemed unforgivingly long.

"Don't ask questions you don't want answered," Stephany had flatly advised her. The young woman hadn't smiled, the unflatteringly pale pink not jovial enough to distract from the sharp cut of her thin lips. "Do not."

A brief titter of a laugh escaped Mavis, but she cut it short when Stephany's blank expression held.

"There's a lot of marital advice thrown around, but for a wife," she'd told Mavis. "That's scripture."

"What if you suspect something?"

Stephany'd blinked. "Don't."

Don't. It was as useful to Mavis as imagining thoughts were birds fluttering by.

"It's not worth it." Stephany had picked up her coffee but only to stare at the lip of the container. "I'm not interested in being miserable for the rest of my life."

Mavis hadn't dared ask whether Stephany had suspected anything against her will. It wasn't fair to assume the worst, Mavis was sure, but the other woman's distracted pessimism had seemed telling. In the end, it had served to confirm the inevitability Cyrus asserted, and after seven years of marriage, when attacking Cyrus didn't end the dream, all Mavis's suffocating fears returned.

Jerrod wasn't perfect. It'd comforted her on their wedding day, and dozens of times in the seven years since. He lost his composure, walked away when frustration got the better of him. He easily became accustomed to the thousands of services Mavis provided, and while he was quick to praise her, it didn't seem to occur to him that he should relieve her on more than special occasions. He vacillated between affirming her in the face of often complicated relationships with their mothers and unnecessarily involving Deborah Dwyer in the particulars of their life.

"A married woman shouldn't be running the streets."

Early on in the marriage, when Mavis was afraid of smothering Jerrod—the consequences of which had been convincingly proved to her in her past relationship—she'd suggested he take two evenings a week to himself. Jerrod hadn't interrogated his wife's concern for his independence at the beginning, or in any of the years since. He'd joined a bowling league and spent the second night at the gym, or in various activities with friends, and he'd never given it a second thought. When he was going to be late, he always let Mavis know. He was thoughtful enough.

"A wife is a wife whether her husband's at home or not."

She'd gotten accustomed to boredom. Mavis might make a coffee run, as a treat, but she didn't make a habit of being out on Jerrod's alone evenings. She lost the will to cook a new meal after awhile, but she was usually at home, in case he called it a night earlier than expected. Sometimes, he did. Sometimes he came straight home from work, told her he'd been missing her all that day and would see the boys the next time. She'd felt a cold pang in her core. Worried he'd regret it. Misremember it as something she'd asked for or insisted upon.

Mavis loved Jerrod. She'd rather he take the necessary time off from her than exhaust his desire for her completely. So when she stumbled into their closet the night of the car accident, she panicked.

They'd been in bed for hours, Mavis stirring because the air-conditioning had made her too cold to sleep. She'd gone into the closet to trade her pajama dress for a pant set when she saw it.

Jerrod's league shirt, on its hanger.

Where it shouldn't be.

The bowling alley was on the other side of his office, and Jerrod took it with him on league night. When Mavis called him from the site of the accident, he was leaving work, walking through the business park to his car. He'd rushed to meet her in the ambulance, and followed her to the hospital, and when they'd gotten home, he'd taken her things inside and then helped his wife, but he'd left his briefcase and his work phone behind. He said he'd get it in the morning, to let the office know he'd be taking the next couple of days to look after Mavis.

His league shirt should've been in the car. It should've been hanging in the back seat. Mavis should've seen it on the ride home from the hospital. Instead, it was in the closet.

Mavis stood with the long-sleeved pajama top bunched around her wrists, her skin goose-pimpling. She'd meant to quickly pull it over her head before grabbing the bottoms, but she was staring at the yellow-and-red collared shirt on the hanger, picturing a short and shapely woman named Djidji in her head.

The morning after the car accident, the bruises had surfaced. Both of Mavis's swollen knees were a red-ringed deep purple. There was one on her calf, inexplicably. Her chest was riddled with them, as though she'd been in a boxing match, and her nose and the skin between her eyes were discolored, too. The pain medication had tapered in the middle of the night, and Mavis couldn't sit up without yelping.

"Hey," Jerrod cooed, coming back into the bedroom. He was hurrying as much as one could while holding a tray. He set it on the empty side of the bed before studying his wife's face, one hand against her cheek.

Mavis couldn't think straight, let alone hold a conversation, until she took something. On the tray, Jerrod had a dose of her prescription, a bottle of water, a mug of tea, sliced lemon, honey, a small spoon, saltines, a glass ramekin of washed grapes, and two sandwich cookies. She smirked through washing down the pills.

"What?" Jerrod asked, but he looked down at his assortment of offerings like he already knew. "Is it all wrong?"

Mavis shook her head, tucking her chin before she spoke because she hadn't brushed her teeth.

"It's darling."

She meant it. Even though she'd been battered in a car accident, and it looked like her husband had googled how to care for a wife with morning sickness.

Jerrod was holding a lemon slice, waiting for Mavis's approval. After she nodded, he did the same with the honey, then stirred her tea and offered it to her. It wasn't until she'd accepted that she realized the mug was lukewarm. She should've noticed the lack of steam curling over the water. The honey he'd stirred was tornadoing in the bottom of the mug, the water not hot enough to quickly dissolve it.

He must have seen her watching it.

"I didn't want to make it too hot to drink," he said, but it was sheepish. "It made sense at the time."

He tried to take the mug and Mavis pulled out of his reach, tongue between her teeth, cheeks high in a grin.

"I always think, why does she make steaming, scalding cups of tea that are too hot to drink right away?"

"Because tea needs steeping, dumbdumb," Mavis said, the two of them laughing as Jerrod reached again for the mug. "And honey needs dissolving. Careful! You'll get tepid water everywhere!"

"Please let me make it again, this is embarrassing," Jerrod begged through a laugh.

Mavis relented, handing back the tea.

Jerrod sighed dramatically at his failure, his back to Mavis as he trudged toward the door.

"Get it together, Jerrod," he admonished himself, before turning on his heel and continuing out of the room backward. "But on the bright side, I'll have the kinks worked out before I'm responsible for a pregnant wife!"

Alone in the bedroom, Mavis's face was frozen, the genuine smile she'd given her husband painfully adhered even after the mirth soured. She'd forgotten the piercing hurt radiating from her damaged tailbone, but now the pinpricks stabbed anew. It was one thing to overlook the small signs and signals that her husband had succumbed to the seven-year itch. She'd been cataloguing the things Stephany Leonard told her not to suspect ever since the Cyrus nightmare. Putting them away as inconclusive when Jerrod continued being a loving husband to her. Trying to put them away. The week before her car accident, she'd seemed to unravel, all the years of stasis undone after overhearing one phone call. What was worse were the small signs and signals that her husband wanted children. The hints he dropped when they accidentally walked down the baby food aisle at the grocery store. The way a growing percentage of the videos he forwarded her throughout the day involved infants.

Mavis didn't want to have children. She used to. The idea had been tangled up with her fantasies of marriage since she was a child herself. But that was before her body had developed into a pear-hourglass figure, and before Cyrus had told her what that meant.

"*It's gorgeous,*" he'd said, almost purring, his hands squeezing her hips in a way that made her remember him chastising her immodesty the week before. *"It's gonna be impossible to manage after the babies start though."* He'd slapped one hip.

"I know I'll have to prioritize fitness," Mavis had tried to agree.

"No, it won't matter. Women with your shape widen at the hips. It's sexy right now, but it makes it impossible to see them as wives first once they're mothers."

It was another hinderance to fidelity, she'd surmised, and it sounded like it was totally outside her control. She'd joined a dance-aerobics class at the church not long after that conversation, but the timing had been wrong. It'd seemed self-centered rather than a way of habituating regular, dedicated exercise.

Now, Mavis had been married seven years, and the acute fear had proved not to be merely of unfaithfulness, but of being divorced. Of the devastation that came from being altogether rejected. Stephany Leonard's "don't" wasn't enough. It wasn't enough not to suspect if the affair meant a man was done with the life they'd vowed to share. And, with a man as well-intentioned as Jerrod, Mavis was convinced that's exactly what it'd mean. Only more swiftly if she became anything other than a wife in his eyes.

She couldn't be a mother. Even if it was the only way to earn a modicum of her parents' very valuable attention, to prove she was doing anything worth their involvement after years of failing, Mavis Dwyer could not risk it.

Her hips must signal an enticement, always; never a birth canal.

There was a hole in the backyard. It wasn't accidental; the dirt wasn't haphazardly blended, sun-blanched topsoil mixed with the darker earth underneath as though accomplished by the mindless scuff of a shoe. Samuel Dwyer had been standing right in front of it, but that didn't mean anything. Of course, neither did the hole, as far as Mavis knew.

She hadn't told Jerrod about his father standing in the yard, staring up at her in the study. She hadn't told him about his mother's strange behavior either.

For that matter, she hadn't mentioned his league shirt hanging in the closet. She hadn't spoken Djidji's name or asked where he'd been headed when the Spencers plowed into her. Whatever had happened—whatever either of them had done—Jerrod had been taking care of her ever since. Mavis felt full, and constantly on the verge of lightheadedness. It was overwhelming, the way he lavished care and consideration on her. He'd always been a dream come true, but it was like nothing she'd ever experienced. She'd never felt assurance the way she did recovering from a devastating accident. All day, Jerrod was a satellite. Never far, always circling back to her. At night, despite her wounds, they were tangled up in each other, whispering their relief. Nothing—no suspicion or guilt—was worth as much as knowing Jerrod was afraid of losing her, too.

Still. The hole was strange.

"Does that look intentional to you?" Mavis asked when she'd gone stir-crazy being in the upstairs of their home and asked Jerrod to help her down into the garden. She'd wanted to stand where Samuel Dwyer had been, to investigate whether or not he could see into the window. Whether it had only seemed like he was watching her.

"How long has that been there?" Jerrod asked, in reply. He settled into a squat, arms resting on his knees, head at a tilt.

"It's got to be new. Right?" Mavis stood at Jerrod's shoulder, careful not to shade his view. "A ground squirrel, do you think?"

"Not unless they've learned to use garden spades." Jerrod answered, grabbing the tool neither of them had used since Mavis had repotted a plant in the study. She hadn't noticed it lying nearby, but it was dirty from recent use.

"Dad was back here," Mavis offered. "Maybe he was . . ."

"Digging in the dirt?" Jerrod finished her thought. "Like a weirdo?"

Mavis remembered her father-in-law's limp arms and the vacuous, glazed expression on his face while he stared up at the study, the sun in his eyes.

"Do you think he's weird?"

Mavis hadn't meant to ask. It sounded like she was making a general inquiry about a man she'd personally known for years, when she was only trying to gauge whether her husband would entertain the idea that his father had made Mavis uncomfortable.

Jerrod looked up at her, tossing the spade toward the hole.

"I think it'd be weird for a sixtysomething-year-old man to randomly dig in someone else's backyard, yes. Plus, I'm almost certain the spade was in the garage, with the gardening stuff." Jerrod looked back at the hole. "So what was he doing in the garage?"

Finally, he stood.

"You don't think that's odd?" he asked.

Mavis wasn't going to tell her husband that she thought his father was odd any more than she would tell him his mother was a nightmare. That wasn't fair. *Her* mother was a nightmare. His mother was insufferable.

"He did give us the down payment for the house," she said with an uncertain shrug.

"What?" he guffawed. "So it's free rein? You don't think that, Mavis." Jerrod pulled her into his arms. "I'm not gonna say anything to him, don't worry. We don't confront our parents. I know."

"He might just be dropping hints about the state of our landscaping." Mavis let her forehead rest against her husband's lips until he puckered.

"Note taken." Jerrod took Mavis's hand and led her back toward the house.

VI

She heard the spade crunching into the earth.

In the middle of the night, from the dead of sleep, Mavis heard the digging recommence. Without the ambient sounds of the day, the tinny echo of the garden tool carved noisily through the packed dirt. It bounced off the house and the nearby trees until finally Mavis batted her eyes open.

It hadn't been part of her dream.

Someone was in her backyard.

Mavis heard the tip stabbing the ground, the blade sinking in behind it before whoever was digging up her backyard twisted the tool and heaved it out.

Mavis was wide awake.

"Jerrod," she whispered at her husband's back. When he didn't rouse, she waited, but the sound of trespass only got louder.

Jerrod's white T-shirt glowed under the skylight. Mavis had never interrupted his sleep. She'd gone out of her way not to, and as usual, it had nothing to do with him. Cyrus had responded poorly, and Mavis had faced almost unanimous reprimand upon seeking the counsel of their church community, and she'd adjusted accordingly.

She did not disturb Jerrod.

It was beginning to sound like an assault. The metallic point was piercing with more aggression. Mavis imagined the digger's grunts of exertion. She imagined her father-in-law hunched, his back a bridge. The man turning over the earth and then scattering the excavated dirt through the sometimes sparse grass.

Mavis got out of bed. She didn't make a sound, just briefly closed her eyes and took a deep breath to overcome the pain she was starting to accept as permanent.

The digging kept on while Mavis moved through the adjoining door and came into the study. There may as well have been a spotlight, the way the room was illuminated. The Palladian window seemed larger, more imposing, when she might not be the only one looking through it. The shadows of her plants were cast across the furniture and the walls and the bookcases. Mavis moved slowly so that her own shadow wouldn't draw attention. If her father-in-law looked up the way he had before, she didn't want him to see her. Though she didn't know why.

Mavis hugged the wall and slid toward the overlarge opening.

The sound of metal and earth, over and over.

Mavis turned her head askew so that she could peek with one eye without half her head being visible.

A hunched back, the way she'd expected.

They were hovering over the hole they were digging, holding themselves up with one hand while they plunged the spade back into the ground. Their body was heaving, exhausted but lurching on.

Mavis flinched back several times. Her limbs felt heavy, leaden, and her mouth was spontaneously dry. She felt like she should cough, but she was afraid of who might hear her.

It wasn't Samuel Dwyer in her garden. Whoever was hunched

over was too small to be her father-in-law. They were barefoot, barelegged, a long shirt covering them from shoulder to thigh.

It was a woman. Her peach skin glowing like Jerrod's T-shirt.

Mavis watched her rest, both palms on the ground, the spade set down.

The woman stood, her back still to Mavis's window, and studied what she'd done.

What was going on? Who was in her back—

The woman swiveled to face her and Mavis threw herself out of frame. Her shoulder and head hit the edge of a bookshelf, and Mavis crashed to the ground.

"Baby, you should've woken me."

It was something he said after the fact, when the threat of interrupted sleep and outsized rage and berating was out of reach. When the need had already gone unfulfilled, but Mavis was meant to feel silly for not trusting that her husband was always available to her. She didn't answer it.

"What is going on around here?" Jerrod asked rhetorically. He was kneeling on the floor of the study, Mavis sitting with her back against the bookcase that had felled her. "Should we take you back to the hospital?"

"No." Mavis shook her head, lacing her eyebrows to demonstrate how ridiculously unnecessary it was.

"You hit your head."

"Barely."

Jerrod closed his mouth and exhaled through his nose.

"I think we both know I'm no warrior princess, honey," Mavis told him, fingertips tracing circles in the curls on her husband's thigh. "If I were hurt, I'd go."

He relented, nodding and running a hand down her naked arm. For a moment, Mavis didn't say anything more. She started to, but hesitated. She only glanced over Jerrod's head, at the window. He'd turned the light on when the sound of Mavis colliding with the furniture woke him, and from the floor, the glass looked a murky indigo, the outside too dark by comparison for her to see anything. Or anyone.

"Is she gone?" Mavis finally asked. When he looked at her, his forehead a labyrinth of creases, she flicked her eyes back to the window. A moment more, and Jerrod had scuffled to his feet. He had to turn the light off and look again before he could see the yard below.

"Did you see someone?" His voice was strained, as though his vocal cords were just as tight as his shoulders had suddenly become.

"The hole-digger," Mavis answered from the floor of the now dark study.

Jerrod bolted. He bounded down the stairs, and almost too quickly for the distance he had to cover, Mavis heard the back door open and the chime that alerted when the perimeter of the house was breached. She stood, but by the time she was at the window, Jerrod was somewhere in the many shadowy pockets of their backyard. Occasionally, he zipped out of one and into another, visible for a moment and then quickly gone again. Eventually, he came back to the hole. He picked up the spade, and turned to look up toward the study.

It was only Jerrod, but Mavis felt her chest clench, her breath halt sharply.

He looked away, into the shadows again, and then he headed back toward the house.

"I think I know her," Mavis blurted out when they reunited in the bedroom.

He was barely over the threshold, and still holding the spade in a tight fist.

"I do know her," she clarified, only to correct herself again. "I used to."

It felt like déjà vu, telling him this. But there was something about his silence this time, the way his furrowed brow could be abject confusion or complete incredulity. Both were more than warranted. But the possibility of his skepticism made Mavis feel unsteady. Like it was her first time on a BOSU ball all over again and one wrong move might tip her over. It meant something, to have had someone on her side for seven years. One person she hadn't had to convince of her worth or credibility. Mavis's chest clenched again at the thought that perhaps she'd taken that for granted until right now, when it seemed maybe her husband was having doubts.

Mavis had told Jerrod about Cyrus, to some degree. It would've been impossible to avoid, since it was her only substantial relationship. Any answers to questions about previous courtships or intimacies of any kind would have to reference the man she'd been with before Jerrod. Then there were the emotional wounds he'd left. Those, she told Jerrod about more sparingly, otherwise she might've lost credibility. After all, she'd stayed with Cyrus for five years, and when it was over, it hadn't been her choice or desire.

Mavis hadn't told her husband anything about the years

between Cyrus's departure and meeting Jerrod. In her memory, they were simultaneously a slog and a blur, and both for the same reason. Her mind was wholly occupied, singularly focused on just one thing. There was one route to happiness. To wholeness.

Marriage.

The time blurred because of days and months spent in pursuit of that one desire. Regardless how many forms the pursuit had taken—how many classes taken, how many small groups joined, how many conventions attended, how many journals kept—the busyness revolved around one goal.

The time slogged because, despite the corroboration received that this goal was worthwhile, a deception had to be enthusiastically maintained. Mavis had to pretend to thrive in her singleness. She had to testify to its value, to the blessing of it.

A year before meeting Jerrod, Mavis had gone on a retreat. It was called Victory in Vacancy: Flourishing as a Single Woman. It was an inaugural gathering, with the coordinators reaching out to several local congregations. When the opportunity was introduced during Sunday morning announcements, there were eight slots advertised. The demand far exceeded the availability, the attendee list expanding to sixteen participants with plans for another retreat the following season. By the time Mavis saw a woman digging in her backyard, the retreat was nearing its tenth anniversary and boasting hundreds of attendees four times a year.

Havilah Greene had been Mavis's roommate at ViV. She was something of a celebrity for the five days and four nights the group lived together in a beach house on the Carolina coast. Havilah had been engaged the month before the retreat, but she'd had a restless spirit and finally realized she wanted the man too much. He was dominating her heart in a way she knew would spell trouble, and she'd made the difficult decision to step intentionally into a season of singleness to refocus on her individual calling. Despite coming as an attendee, Havilah had become a de facto counselor, slipping away one-on-one with several of the sixteen to offer an ear and wise counsel. She offered a perspective no one else had seemed to consider—that the enemy might dangle a proposal to distract the women from the blessing of marriage.

Everything could seem right and actually be wrong. Or vice versa. It would take a multitude of confidantes to properly assess which was which, and an ever-growing slew of motivational speakers to keep the path illuminated. Havilah Greene would pick up that mantle almost immediately after attending ViV.

She'd been much more modest at the retreat than she looked digging up Mavis's yard in a nightshirt. Every night Havilah had slept not just in a loose pair of jersey pants and long tank top, but in a coordinating cardigan. She was the first white woman Mavis met who wore a silk scarf to bed, and once Havilah's contacts were swapped out for glasses, she was much less self-conscious than the other women.

"One day a man will have the honor of seeing me at peak relaxation," she'd said, her slippered feet against the naked wood coffee table while the group enjoyed a nightcap of mulled wine. "Everyone gets to see my hair done up and my heels on. Only my husband gets to see my hair in a braid and my glasses sliding down my nose."

Amid the pleasant sighs and relieved burrowing into the oversized sectionals, Havilah's outlook welcomed and received by most others, Mavis couldn't help but wonder whether her future husband would have preferences a few of the other attendees didn't have to consider. For instance, would braids be desirable so long as they were one or two and a single-day style on straightened hair? Were box braids or passion twists considered natural, if that was the preference, or something else? As for lazing around in loungewear, she'd gotten the distinct impression that the range of her femininity was not quite so broad as Havilah's; she wasn't certain whether or not dressed-down relaxation would be considered an honor or a failing on her part.

Nine years after ViV, Mavis didn't know whether she'd be able to find her former roommate. She couldn't imagine she still had the card in which all of the retreat attendees had written and exchanged their phone numbers. Mavis didn't remember Havilah's married name despite attending her wedding, in a tradition Havilah herself had started. Every time one of the sixteen moved into matrimony, they should invite the whole group. They'd shared so many tears and vulnerable admissions and prayers, it didn't feel like an imposition when Havilah suggested it in the note included with her own wedding invitation. It only briefly felt like braggadocio when Mavis sat with the handful of fellow ViV ladies not seven months after their tearful goodbye.

Havilah Greene had hyphenated her last name, at least online, and on her event flyers. Online, she was nowhere in her profile picture. Instead, her three children represented the woman who had been leading retreats on everything from singleness to wifedom to savoring seasons of pregnancy. Her page was a hybrid, showcasing what could be considered aspects of her personal life but carefully curated, and ones from which she clearly drew for her professional career. It also had a contact tab that included an in-app audio call option.

The next morning, in the kitchen, her phone on the table between her and Jerrod, Mavis pressed call.

"This is Havilah!" The woman's voice was bright and energetic, in the way it might be if, just before answering, she'd been asleep or agitated. A wondering about her consistent assumption that everyone was the opposite of what they portrayed threatened to talon Mavis's brain.

Jerrod tapped her wrist, and Mavis lurched toward the device.

"Havilah, it's Mavis!" Her voice was equally enthusiastic, and definitely disingenuous.

On the other end of the call, the woman held her breath, her eyes no doubt roaming whatever room she was in. Havilah Greene didn't remember her.

"Mavis Carson, originally? We were roommates at the first—"

"Victory in Vacancy, Mavis, oh my gosh! How are you?"

"I'm blessed," she replied. It was automatic. She hadn't even considered her answer before it passed between her lips, and now a barrage of images and sounds from the preceding days played like rapid fire while she smiled. "It's been so long!"

"It has!" There was a sharp amusement lacing Havilah's reply. Perhaps she was accustomed to the unprompted calls of people she'd known before her name became a logo, a thick, curvy font complete with liaising flourishes between several of the letters quickly synonymous with her personal brand. People must appear out of the woodwork often, hoping to rekindle a connection or receive preferential access to the woman who strutted stages miked and recorded. "What can I do for you, Mavis?" the woman asked.

Mavis had to admire the way Havilah cut to the chase. She didn't allow the fact that she'd once insisted that Mavis consider her a mentor stop her from establishing a boundary in the present. She communicated her unavailability and passed the ball back to Mavis's court.

For her part, Mavis wasn't as versed in anticipating linesteppers or confronting community celebrities who'd trespassed on her private property eight hours prior. She looked at Jerrod. At first he offered her a blank stare, then flashed an uncomfortable, shrugging grimace.

"I think I saw you yesterday," Mavis said, her commitment to the approach dissipating before the last syllable. Her eyelids drooped.

"Oh goodness, was it at HomeGoods?" Havilah sounded genuinely delighted at last. "Do you go to the one on Emerson, too?"

"No, it was last night. Late."

Cell phones didn't crackle the way landlines used to, so when both women stopped talking, there was nothing but the background noise of whatever program Havilah was using to distract her young children so she could take what she'd assumed was a business call.

"It was actually early this morning," Mavis barreled on. "In my yard."

"I'm—" Havilah interrupted herself with a chuckle. "A little confused, Mavis."

"I saw you in my backyard in the middle of the night."

Silence.

Mavis couldn't imagine being accused of something so outlandish without immediately asserting her innocence. If she was, in fact, innocent. She didn't know how to interpret Havilah's lack of response. And then the woman was speed-whispering to someone in her home.

"Mommy's gonna step into the other room. Patience, can you keep an eye on your brothers, please?"

A small, delicate voice agreed, and the background noises pulled away as Havilah moved.

"Mavis, I'm just a little confused."

"Are you?" Mavis asked, careful to strip her tone of any firmness. "Because you haven't said you weren't here."

Silence again. If the woman was anything like Mavis, the inside corner of Havilah's mouth was drawn between her teeth.

"I don't even know where you live," Havilah said, the words deflating as soon as they were uttered.

"Havilah," Mavis ventured after another quiet spell. "Is everything okay?"

The woman sniffed, a telltale static betraying her.

"What's going on?" Mavis pressed.

"I never remember my dreams," Havilah said, hushedly, and then she sniffed a second and third time. She was moving around whatever room she'd gone into. "If I sleepwalk."

She found the box she'd gone in search of, and must have been wiping her top lip and beside her mouth, the tissue brushing against her phone.

"It hadn't happened in so long, I just thought . . ." Havilah swallowed hard, the sound of her breath filling the hollow of her open mouth afterward. "I thought I'd gotten victory over that."

"Can you remember your dream from last night?" Mavis asked. When Havilah began sniffling again, Mavis looked at her husband. Jerrod shook his head without meeting her gaze, a distressed expression etched into his face.

"What happened?" Havilah asked, her voice thick with congestion now. "What was I doing?"

"You were digging," Mavis answered. She made every effort to be gentle, though there was no way to undo how disturbing a scenario it was. "In my backyard. I don't think it was the first time."

"How did you know I was there?" The woman must've been wearing some manner of jewelry; there were sounds like clanging chimes as Havilah snatched another series of tissues from the box and cleaned her face more vigorously.

"I heard you. It woke me out of sleep, and when I looked down into the backyard, you were on your hands and knees in a nightshirt."

"That isn't possible," Havilah said, clearing her sinuses one more time. She was finished crying, and despite the lingering congestion, when she spoke, it was with more certainty.

"Havilah, I saw you."

"From where?"

"What?"

"You said you looked down into your backyard. From what distance?"

"From the second floor, in my study, directly overlooking the backyard."

"In the wee hours of the morning when you'd just woken up." Havilah attached her sentence to the end of Mavis's.

Jerrod's eyes widened by a magnitude.

"Havilah, you turned and looked up at me."

"I have no idea where you live, Mavis. We haven't seen or spoken to each other since your wedding, and if memory serves, you didn't even speak to me *that* day."

Havilah Greene had attended her wedding. Mavis hadn't recalled.

"I've faced a lot of attacks on my ministry and calling—"

"Havilah," Mavis tried to interject.

"And believe me, I know we can all be unwitting vessels for distraction and discouragement, so I don't keep ledgers, but this has to be rebuked."

"Havilah, I saw you in my backyard, and it scared me to death."

"I'm sorry you were scared, Mavis, and I'll hold you up in prayer, but I know what I've been freed from and I won't let a sudden accusation hurl me off-track into a season of doubt."

Three atonal vibrations marked the end of the call.

VII

Mavis and Jerrod stole the security camera. It wasn't planned, but Mavis knew as soon as the call with Havilah Greene took a turn that the day was not going to improve.

Jerrod didn't ask her whether or not she was sure it had been Havilah. Mavis would've been relieved except that she was too busy waiting for the question, for the indication that her husband had a very reasonable uncertainty. He hadn't seen Havilah himself, and just like with Rose Spencer, finding out the woman had been at their wedding would be news. At least the Spencers had been introduced to him; Mavis had a specific recollection of the procession after the ceremony, and then Bill and Rose had visited them at the bridal table during the reception.

Whatever lies Havilah was telling—to herself or anyone else—she'd been telling the truth about Mavis not speaking to her at her wedding. It hadn't been a slight; there were hundreds of people at the wedding, and instead of feeling like the guest of honor, Mavis had been a marionette. Her mother had instructed her on everything from when the ceremony should begin—too punctual and guests wouldn't have an opportunity to mingle—to how best to adjust when her smile had gone stale during the extended photo interlude between services, to which tables she should visit and in what order while the reception guests were dining. In the end, Mavis and Jerrod had obediently and effusively thanked and conversed with everyone the Carsons had invited. There had to be dozens of people Mavis had not only not spoken to, but also wouldn't have known were there at all if not for Marie Carson's toast. It'd become more a series of acknowledgments to her and her husband's peers and loved ones followed by a veiled discouragement. She hoped everyone understood the effort and attention that went into a veritable gala of a wedding, and that no one should feel hurt if they didn't get a chance to see or speak to the bride amid her various responsibilities. Instead, Marie Carson instructed everyone to pour their congratulations and best wishes into the mini guest books at each table, with the promise that Mavis would read and respond to each of them individually once she returned from her honeymoon.

Havilah had left a bubbly if generic felicitation, but not an address for Mavis's thank-you cards.

"If you weren't sure, you would never have called her."

Mavis startled. She was standing in the center of a hardware store aisle wide enough to accommodate two hand trolleys side by side and only vaguely remembered walking from the car to here. The sharp warehouse lighting was gentler here, the next aisle over a long boulevard of ceiling fans ranging from elegant and decorative to high-powered and industrial. They were outfitted with warm bulbs whose light blocked out the harsh panels above the fan canopy.

In the home security aisle, Jerrod was standing in front of mostly keypad dead bolts and comparing the specs on the side of two camera packages.

"Are you talking to me?" Mavis asked, and her husband glanced at her.

"You've been quiet ever since the phone call," he said, a stern look of concentration crushing his eyebrows. "I know you're second-guessing yourself."

"I wasn't," Mavis answered, honestly.

"Then you're worried *I'm* second-guessing you."

She didn't answer, which was answer enough.

"You would never have called that woman if you didn't know for sure," Jerrod repeated, locking eyes with his wife. After a beat, he turned back to the package in hand and his voice drifted distractedly. "I am not second-guessing you."

"Thank you." Mavis walked over and wound her arms around one of her husband's while he read. She laid her head on his shoulder and closed her eyes, listening to the thrum of the nearby fan blades.

It had been Havilah in their backyard. It was strange, maybe a little creepy, but it was better than any alternative Mavis could imagine. Havilah was an untreated sleepwalker whose grand nighttime adventures involved digging holes. Mavis could handle that. They were buying cameras to mount on the house, facing the woman's preferred workspace, and then, if it continued, Mavis could show them to Havilah. She might actually help the woman who'd clearly become accustomed to dispensing truths, not receiving them. There wasn't anything shameful about needing intervention. It was a sentiment Mavis had heard over and over since fading away from her parents' congregation, but in all honesty, one she struggled to believe. It was all well and good to *be* the hands and feet, to have something essential to the lives and afterlives of others. It was another thing entirely to be a beneficiary of those valorous saints in the here and now.

Mavis felt a closeness. Half her body was pressed against Jerrod, but she felt someone behind her. A sense that what had recently been empty space was occupied. There was less room for the sound of air moving on the next aisle over.

Mavis lifted her head from Jerrod's shoulder and opened her eyes. By the time she turned to look, a man was walking away. Had he really been standing close enough for her to feel him? She looked at the bay of cameras and dead bolts just behind her and Jerrod, and found that there were only two unstocked spaces. Both those boxes were in her husband's hands. But maybe the man had gone for a closer look and ultimately changed his mind.

"I can monitor this one's feed from my phone," Jerrod said, his voice a sudden intrusion for the second time.

Mavis glanced back at the boxes in her husband's hands. They looked indistinguishable, but she nodded.

At the far end of their aisle, the man was climbing an employee ladder, three large boxes balanced one on top of the other in his hands. He must work here. Mavis let out an audible breath. Maybe she *should* be second-guessing herself. She'd been accused of narcissism before.

"I'll go to Saturday evening service from now on," she'd told her mother, years ago.

"Sunday morning is the appointed time for worship," Marie Carson had replied. Mavis's father, Daniel, nodded big but didn't lift his eyes from his magazine. *"Careful what compromises you make, especially for your pride."*

It wouldn't do any good to retort that the church her parents held so dear *offered* services on Saturday evening. This was merely her mother's ring walk, an early showcase meant to establish the conflict before she landed a spectacular blow.

"To think that people would wake up, consecrate themselves,

make their journey to the sanctuary, lift their hands in praise, and have Mavis Carson and her broken heart on their minds has got to be the height of vanity."

"Why are you pretending people don't gossip?" Mavis had shouted, already in tears. *"They're your friends, and they aren't discreet!"*

"Lower your voice."

"You tell them things I've confided in you! You tell them things he said to me, the ways he mistreated me, and still they all stare at me*! Like I did something wrong by getting hurt! Like it shouldn't be obvious that Cyrus was a monster, and no one—none of you—ever tried to rescue me!"*

Marie Carson's lips had been sealed shut, and Mavis'd thought that meant she was hearing her.

"If falling for a monster makes me a woman of weak discernment, what does sitting idly by while someone terrorized me make all of you?" She'd been screaming by the time she was done.

Her mother had lifted her chin, watching her daughter's chest heave as though the young woman had run a marathon instead of losing her temper.

"Mavis," the woman had begun, and Mavis felt herself shrinking. *"I will not speak to you when you are being disrespectful."*

The man she'd thought was hovering behind her had been an employee. The person digging holes in her yard had been a woman refusing to accept that she was struggling. Her mother had at least been right about people having more on their minds than the sins of Mavis Dwyer.

"Can I ask you a question?" Mavis hooked her chin over her husband's shoulder, staring down at the boxes he still held as though comparing their weight. "Those are identical cameras, aren't they?"

"They are not."

"You can tell me. I'll still let you cradle them for a few more hours."

"There are very key and minute differences—they're almost identical, I think, yes." A closed-mouth laugh rumbled in Jerrod's chest cavity, Mavis letting hers tumble out.

"But you have to do the dance," she said.

"There's so much pressure, as a husband, to make big decisions." Jerrod alternated lifting one hand and then the other higher.

"Or to make decisions big," Mavis offered.

"The painstaking deliberation is what infuses it with gravitas," Jerrod confirmed. "It's important be*cause* I'm taking it this seriously."

"Too quick and you don't love your family."

"You get it." Jerrod nodded, his composure persisting despite the way his wife's laugh delighted him. "Whoa!" He'd barely turned to watch Mavis, her face still perched on his shoulder, before turning and gripping his wife's arms. He only dropped one of the camera packages, so the sharp edge of the other dug into Mavis while her husband twirled her to his other side. It was an odd time to relive the impressively tight turn from the couple's first dance, and Jerrod was squeezing her to the point of pain.

Where Mavis had been standing, something crashed to the concrete floor, what looked like shards of a giant eggshell exploding outward. They had been the circular lampshade that wrapped around the enclosed fan blades; now one of them protruded out of

Mavis's shin, a trickle of blood beginning to run toward her shoe. She didn't feel anything.

The fan was destroyed, the bronze ceiling mount tilting toward her atop the half-crushed remains, wire leads reaching toward Mavis as though desperate to escape what was already finished.

"Watch out!" someone cried, but Jerrod was already pulling Mavis behind him, pinning her between his wide back and the shelves on the opposite side of the aisle.

The man Mavis had seen climbing the employee ladder was standing on the top shelf, above the dead bolts and cameras, and he was holding an unopened box the size of the destroyed fan over his head.

"Hey!" Jerrod yelled, throwing his hands in front of him as though to stop the man from heaving it toward them. It didn't.

Mavis screamed, ducking behind her husband when the man released it. Jerrod crushed her against the shelves in an effort to shield her, his misleadingly slender frame still too heavy for her to escape. He'd turned his face away to minimize injury, but Jerrod tried to bat the sealed box with his raised forearms, a pained grunt escaping him on impact.

There were two men bounding up the ladder toward the attacker now. They were wearing orange aprons; he wasn't.

"Sir!" one of them yelled as they approached him from behind.

They shouldn't have warned him. The attacker whirled, grabbing the protectively outstretched arms of the employee closest to him and hurling him from the landing. He fell what had to be two stories, bouncing off his shoulders as though the concrete were rubber. His apron flew to cover his face like a veil while the man went backward, heels over head, before landing on his stomach. There wasn't any blood that Mavis could see. He'd tumbled over concrete like a rag doll but there were no outward signs of injury, except that when he finished his somersault, the man didn't move.

On the landing, the second employee had taken a step back in retreat, watching the overthrow in shock. Now the attacker lunged. The employee collapsed beneath him, inventory from the shelves tumbling to the ground.

There were so many people screaming, Mavis couldn't hear the sounds of impact. Somehow that made it worse. No one else went up the ladder while the attacker mauled the second employee. The man Mavis had felt behind her was straddling the employee, using fists, elbows, and forearms to pummel him. There was no hesitation. No mercy. While the employee's legs quaked and his arms flailed, color changing as blood and fluid released from his face, the attacker had the stamina of a gorilla tirelessly mangling a helpless victim.

Someone screamed for the police, for anyone to save the man Mavis could not hear. He must be begging, too, if he could still speak. But there were other sounds: inhuman noises that could've been from the employee or the man gripping his head before bashing it against the shelf plank.

The attacker stood up. He didn't sway. He moved as if the violence had cost him nothing. He left the employee limp and retrieved something from the last box he'd carried up the stairs. Returning to his victim, the attacker raised an industrial fan overhead, the tilted blades visible behind the steel grilles, and then he brought it down. He didn't drop it. He held the machine while he bashed it over the employee's face repeatedly, the other man's body jumping with each blow.

Jerrod had been stunned still, Mavis sheltered behind him and watching the carnage from over his shoulder.

"Run," he told her now. As if she'd been waiting for permission, Mavis took off, her husband behind her. There were people running toward the exit and back the way Mavis and Jerrod had come, but they didn't stop until they were in their car, peeling out of the parking lot, the shard still in Mavis's shin and the camera still in Jerrod's hand.

They sat in silence, Mavis on the living room couch with her legs pulled up against her chest, Jerrod in an armchair. He looked like a besieged king, his weight against his forearms on the polished cherrywood frame, his head sagging toward his chest. The stolen camera in one dangling hand.

Mavis slowly loosed the shard from her leg and then held the blood-tipped glass. She studied it. It hadn't gone deep, thanks to her shin bone, but the blood was running again. She shouldn't let it stain her couch, or drip onto the living room carpet—but she couldn't move.

"I'd better get this thing installed," Jerrod said. His voice escaped like a grumble, like getting away from the hardware store and back home, and inside, and safe from harm hadn't solved everything. They both felt wrecked. Exhausted. Confused.

"I think I'm cursed," Mavis whispered.

"I'm not so sure it's you," Jerrod said, equally quietly.

It wasn't what Mavis had been expecting. She thought he'd ask what she meant, and then she'd have to figure out a way to explain everything to her husband. Now she held him in an unsteady gaze, her vision shivering as a horizon of tears rose. Maybe Jerrod would explain things to her instead.

"I don't know," he mumbled, lifting his head without opening his eyes. "I don't know. But something is very wrong. Something is very wrong."

Mavis felt her lip between her teeth.

"With us?" she asked. She meant between them. In their relationship. She wanted to know if Jerrod meant the series of unsettling and frightening events they'd suffered lately or if he was talking about what had been wrong before that. She wanted to know if he was saying that recent events made that wrongness undeniable.

Mavis felt fear coil tight around her heart. A sharp pain darted across her chest. Waiting for her husband to assuage her panic was worse than standing on the other side of the study door while her mother-in-law loomed. It was worse than seeing a half-dressed woman dig up her yard in the middle of the night. It was even worse than watching a shocking attack at the hardware store. Those things had come out of nowhere, were incongruous with the rest of Mavis's life. On some level, she didn't feel obligated to make sense of them, because individually they were startling, together they felt like a supernatural haunting, and in neither case could she imagine what came next. She didn't know why they were happening, or whether they were connected in the first place, so she couldn't fixate on their trajectory, if they had one. There were no taloned thoughts about worst-case scenarios, and how the world would feel or treat her when it was done and exposed.

The fear she felt about Jerrod was different. She knew exactly what she was afraid of.

"Do you think something is very wrong with us?" Mavis pressed.

He wasn't listening. Mavis's blood was pounding in her ears, her leg bleeding, her body still sore with more ache settling in, and Jerrod's eyes were closed. He was rolling his head on his neck, laying it against one shoulder and then the other.

She wanted to scream for him to hear her, to pay attention. She wanted to yell everything she'd thought and never said, explode the way she had only ever done with her parents. But she had been so careful never to lose control with Jerrod. Her parents were immovable; they were an impenetrable wall she could break herself against knowing they would suffer no damage. Nothing would change.

She'd been careful with Jerrod so that he'd know she was worthy. That she was wife material. Then she'd found that getting engaged compounded her worries. To have been offered the first promise only to lose it would be far worse a fate than what she'd suffered with Cyrus. And then they'd gotten married, and Mavis knew she would not survive losing it. She couldn't let the people that had known her every grief and misstep poison Jerrod against her, so she'd slowly created distance. She'd scheduled things on Sundays, suggested outings rather than that they stop attending church. Slowly, casually, it simply wasn't something they made a habit of. Jerrod didn't seem to mind.

Mavis couldn't afford to scream in front of Jerrod. She couldn't insist that he attend to her. That he answer her burning fears and questions.

Don't, she heard Stephany say.

So she didn't.

"Do you want to get the camera installed?" she asked, and Jerrod slowly opened his eyes.

"Yeah," he said through an exhale, and pushed himself out of the armchair.

VIII

Mavis heard digging. It started in the middle of the night again. The sound of the toilet tank refilling echoed loudly as Mavis climbed back into bed, but once the noise abruptly stopped, she heard the spade cut through the earth.

Havilah Greene was sleepwalking again.

Mavis stared out the skylight overhead, counting three distant stars in a net of black sky while she listened to Havilah work.

She sat up sharply, like a mummy reanimated. Unlike the undead, various regions of her body screamed in protest.

Jerrod had brought the spade inside. The tool Havilah had used before was sitting on his bedside table.

Had she really brought her own equipment this time? Was it sleepwalking if she came over, couldn't find the spade, went home, retrieved one of her own, and came back?

Mavis opened her phone. Jerrod had downloaded the app to both their devices expressly so that, if Mavis refused to wake him, she at least needn't get out of bed when Havilah returned.

After a moment, the live feed played. From her bed, propped against the headboard, Mavis stared at her backyard, bathed in the light affixed to the camera. It was almost the same vantage point she'd had standing at the Palladian window, but slightly lower and zoomed on the hole Havilah had made.

Except Havilah wasn't there.

The feed had no audio, but Mavis could definitely hear digging. It wasn't as dainty a sound as it'd been before. She hadn't realized she could tell the difference between a spade and a full-sized shovel, but Mavis was almost certain that now she was hearing the latter.

She zoomed the camera out. The un-landscaped yard wasn't lit throughout, and tree canopies made it so that both corners were swallowed up in shadow. The feed adjusted the murky pools of dark, but the white balance didn't actually illuminate anything.

Still, the sound of a shovel excavating.

Finger against her phone screen, she rotated the camera as far as it would go in one direction, and then back the other way. Wherever Havilah was digging, Mavis couldn't see her.

How would a sleepwalker know to avoid a brand-new camera's range?

The next time the shovel cut into the earth, the sound of metal reminded Mavis of an industrial fan. The only part of the hardware store attack she'd been sure she'd heard was the tilted blades vibrating inside their grille enclosure as the man smashed the machine repeatedly against the employee's face.

He couldn't have survived. She wasn't sure about the one who'd bounced against the concrete floor. Mavis hadn't looked for news of the attack, not to find out the identity of the attacker or of the victims. She'd been surprised how quickly the visuals had vacated her mind, honestly. She felt weak, exhausted, like every muscle in her body were turning to petrified stone, but she'd almost immediately stopped imagining the second employee's body jolting beneath his attacker. Until now.

Mavis was suddenly aware of the darkness in her bedroom, and the way the light from her phone deepened it. She turned off the screen and squeezed her eyes shut for a moment to help them adjust. Once open, they darted from one corner of the bedroom to another, her breaths forceful and clipped, as if she'd been sprinting.

Metal piercing packed ground.

Jerrod's soft breathing, his back expanding and contracting evenly beside her.

She'd been sound asleep minutes before, but Mavis couldn't relax now. Anything could come out of the black around her. Anything could happen in the harsh light of a warehouse, or in an intersection under a bright blue sky. Anyone could come within a breath of her, or onto her property in the middle of the night. Cameras didn't stop them.

She couldn't catch her breath. She couldn't stop the tremor coursing through her, a coldness wrapping around her arms and chest, sweat gathering above her lip.

Mavis listened to the shovel. Hours passed before—exhausted—she must have fallen asleep.

It rained the next day. Mavis stood in her study, fingers absently caressing a monstera leaf while she studied her backyard through the window. Somehow overcast and rainy weather only made it more stunning, the drama of the sky beautifully framed in the great arch of the center window, the white grid a sharp contrast against the deep gray outside.

She'd meant to search out Havilah's new workspace, but been

deterred by the downpour. When Jerrod finished his call, she'd decide whether or not to tell him what she'd heard the night before. She had nothing to point to, since the camera hadn't captured anything, but maybe they'd go search the backyard together.

Mavis was curled up on her daybed sofa, watching rain glide down the window when Jerrod joined her. He didn't say anything, just gingerly lifted her legs onto his lap, careful not to disrupt the large rectangular bandage on his wife's shin, and stared into the gray. Mavis winced discreetly, adjusting slightly to reduce the pressure on her bruised tailbone, and waited.

They'd been married seven years. Mavis could hear the absence of conversation. She could sense the pre-discussion tension, the way Jerrod inhaled and then held his breath before letting it out. He hadn't decided how to begin before coming. Or he'd lost his nerve. Or, Mavis suspected, he was depending on how well she knew him. Waiting for her to ease the pressure, the way he had the night of their wedding.

"You want to talk about something," Mavis said. She didn't say how upsetting it was, being made to accuse him.

"Yeah," Jerrod said, one hand curled around her ankles to keep her legs atop him, the other absently caressing the unblemished one. After a moment his eyes followed his hand, as though just now realizing what was beneath his fingertips. His head tilting, his stroke becoming light enough to send a shiver through Mavis.

"What is it, baby?" she asked.

"I just got off with work," he began, the preamble a frustrating delay after Mavis's assistance. She emptied her voice of impatience.

"And?"

"And." He paused. "I need to get back to the office, baby. I don't want to, but I'm getting some pretty unsubtle pressure about working from home, not being available for field appointments." Jerrod's voice collapsed.

His hands came to a rest, and Mavis looked between them and his face. He turned to her.

"I know it probably feels like it's too soon, baby."

"Then I don't have to say it," she responded, quietly. "There's so much going on, I just . . ."

"I know." Jerrod abandoned one of his wife's legs to take her hand. "I wish there was some way to explain that to the office. I intended to today, just to let them know the accident isn't all we're dealing with. And then I had no idea how to explain why these weird, disjointed, unrelated instances constitute a family emergency. I mean, they don't."

"They don't?" Mavis asked, blinking back tears.

"You know what I mean, baby. They've caused us distress, for sure, but people go through weird things all the time."

"If you hadn't pulled me behind you—" Mavis began.

"I don't even want to think about it," he interrupted. "I'm just glad we weren't seriously hurt."

"Jerrod." Mavis's eyes darted to her bandaged shin.

"Baby, you wouldn't even go to the ER. You wouldn't let me call our doctor."

"So I'm not hurt?"

"Mavis, you know that's not what I'm saying—"

"You're saying I'm not hurt *enough*."

"What are you doing?" Jerrod asked, his face creased in confusion. "Why are you putting words in my mouth?"

"Don't blame me for hearing what you're telling me."

"Do you want me to take you to the ER?" Jerrod asked, a sharpness in his tone.

Mavis snapped her mouth shut.

"I could justify asking for another week out of the office if you'd gone for any follow-up care, so do you want to do that? Should we fabricate an emergency?"

"We already have an emergency," Mavis cried. She couldn't help the way her voice rose, and she pulled herself out of Jerrod's reach, abandoning the daybed sofa despite the way the throw blanket momentarily tangled with her legs. She only went as far as the window, the unseasonable chill from the rain permeating the glass.

Mavis's emergency hadn't happened in the intersection of Ross and 15th Avenue, or in their backyard. It hadn't been the scene in the hardware store, but Jerrod didn't know that. His wife knew him well enough to interpret the breath before he spoke, but Jerrod couldn't sense when, in the middle of a conversation, the couple splintered. When whatever he had been talking about, his wife was talking about something else. There were small tells. The way Mavis crushed against the cold glass of her favorite window. Her shoulders slumped, as though she regretted what she'd done. As though she regretted the way she'd spoken, but she collapsed, discouraged by guilt.

Jerrod wasn't too good to be true. He didn't study her, like he'd vowed. Not the way she studied him. He didn't investigate the why of her behaviors, not to recognize when her doting was borne of panic, let alone to suspect her. He didn't know it, but thus far Jerrod had adhered perfectly to Stephany Leonard's "don't."

"I think it'd be a good idea for us to see someone," he said.

Mavis was sealed against the window, the rain trailing as if the glass was crying. The first hole Havilah had dug an infinity pool in the yard below.

"I know how your parents feel about it," Jerrod said carefully. "But I hope you'll really consider it."

Daniel and Marie Carson felt every marriage could benefit from pastoral counsel, with the possible exception of their own. Part of distancing herself and Jerrod from the church in which she'd been raised was escaping the expectation that she would share her most intimate worries. Details of her marital insufficiencies. It was more than just exposing both herself and her husband to scrutiny. Even if there was wise counsel and care, Mavis didn't want to know what the person behind the pulpit might have been thinking about—and who—when they prepared their sermons. What subtext might be tailored specifically to her.

"I wish it was everything it's made out to be," Mavis began without knowing how honest she would be. "I wish admitting our struggles to one of them was actually the answer."

"I don't know that talking to them will be a magic bullet," Jerrod spoke at last. "But I don't think we can just go on like nothing's happened."

Mavis felt her heart faint. He wasn't leaving her an alternative. There was no way to refuse counseling without appearing callous about her marriage, regardless how far it was from the truth. If she said she didn't want to enroll in that counseling at the last church they'd attended, she'd have to give a reason. She'd grown up there; they'd been married there. The only explanation would be her pride.

"I wish I'd ever felt worried over, instead of just watched," Mavis said, her lips suddenly parched. "Maybe I did, and I just couldn't tell."

Her husband stared back at her from the sofa but he didn't speak. If she stopped now, she'd have to interpret him. Decode his body language. Count the seconds between breaths, and blinks.

"I know we're supposed to trust them, but most of the time 'community' only shows up when there's punishment to exact. They want their pound of flesh. They're not interested in taking back the prodigal son."

Even as she said it, Mavis knew why. She understood. Empathy had to be preserved for the perfect, otherwise forgiveness encouraged repeat offenses. That might not have been the message from the pulpit—it might have been the complete opposite—but it was the culture of the pews, and no one denounced it.

There was no such thing as redemption, not really. It meant that confession and repentance were too great a risk.

Don't.

Mavis swallowed hard, and said no more.

"I don't get what you mean about the prodigal son," Jerrod told her. "We haven't done anything wrong. We witnessed something completely terrifying, baby. The therapist wouldn't have any reason to judge us. I just don't want to go back to work and assume we're gonna be okay. Mentally."

He wasn't talking about marriage counseling. Thank heavens.

"Will you think about it, Mavis?" Jerrod asked, and she turned from the window to face her husband. His brown skin was warm and inviting against the sofa's radiant mustard-hued upholstery.

He was so handsome, the gray from outside the window still bright enough to shine against Jerrod's cheekbones and the lips she loved so much. Cyrus had been handsome, too. Mavis had been taken in by beauty before.

If this wasn't about marriage counseling, then wanting her to talk to a therapist had to be a diversion. Something to distract her while he slipped away. Jerrod wasn't used to being constantly in Mavis's company. She'd gotten him accustomed to a great deal of time apart, doing whatever made loving her sustainable, and he was trying to wriggle out of her clutches.

"Will that make you feel better?" she asked. "About leaving me alone in this house, after everything?"

Jerrod snorted, forced an exhale out through his nose, and shook his head. He folded forward and, pressing his hands into his knees, stood up.

"You can be so selfish," he said.

Mavis's mouth gaped.

"Everything is only happening to you, right?" He waited, but Mavis remained struck. "I *want* to go from being terrified for my wife, to worrying about some lunatic trespassing on our property, to watching a madman—who was at least momentarily focused on *us*!—destroy another human being. None of that hurts *me*. Right? I'm not exhausted. I'm not constantly aware that I don't get to fall apart, because I'm the one responsible for making sure we have a home for you to hole up in."

Mavis should have collapsed into tears. She should have covered her face in her hands and wilted. That would've been the end of it. Jerrod would know he'd crossed a line, and the care and doting attention he'd been showering on her the past few days would've been renewed. Instead, she felt heat wash over her in waves. Her shoulders coiled tight, her fists pinning to her sides as though every action was necessary to keep herself contained.

"What a provider," she barked. "Keeping a roof over my head—the way *you* promised—so you can leave me alone with a *lunatic* in our backyard!"

Jerrod's jaw tensed and released. If Mavis let him, he would quickly regain his composure and then it would just be her out of control.

"She was here last night, and you didn't even notice! Again! I sat up half the night, in terror!"

His expression shifted and Jerrod came to the window in two large strides. Mavis could see the concern gathering between his furrowing brows. She let her voice lilt, let it soften so he could hear her worry.

"I don't know why you never hear it."

Jerrod's eye roamed the backyard briefly before locking on the first hole Havilah had made.

"She was digging somewhere else, so the camera wouldn't pick her up. I was so scared I couldn't even get back to sleep."

"Did you see her?" he asked, one hand on the glass like it would allow him to lean or see further.

"I told you, she avoided the camera. I could just hear her digging. All night."

When Jerrod's eyes dropped, Mavis saw it.

Don't, she heard Stephany say.

"What?" she asked anyway.

"Did you take your pain meds before bed?" he asked.

Mavis didn't answer, and Jerrod didn't turn to face her. The cold was bleeding through the window, chilling one side of Mavis's body and turning the nail beds of Jerrod's hand purple.

"Did you find the new hole she made?" he asked, redirecting. He was trying to undo the first question. The way he'd implied there hadn't been any digging the night before. That the sound might be easily conjured by Mavis's mind now. That Havilah hadn't been there.

"No, Jerrod. I was looking for it from up here, but obviously I can't see everything."

"And there was no one on the feed."

It felt like a blow to Mavis's chest. It felt like the wind being knocked out of her. Her throat felt raw, instantly sore, like she'd been screaming for too long, and no one had heard her.

"Baby." Now it was Jerrod collapsing a shoulder into her favorite window. It was cold, but he let his temple rest against it, too. "I'm not saying . . ." He didn't know how to finish what he'd begun. "I'm just saying why did we get the camera if we weren't gonna trust it?"

"Every time I think you're perfect," she began, his hand falling away from her chin. "Every time I think you'll take care of me, you prove me wrong."

"I never claimed to be perfect, Mavis." Jerrod's voice was a deep rumble. "I didn't know I was supposed to be. You aren't."

There was a rush inside Mavis's head, like water cascading down a storm drain. It left her lightheaded.

"You should go back to the office," she told him. "Today."

"You're impossible," Jerrod rebutted, without hesitation. "It's impossible being with you."

Mavis nearly choked, a cry broken into hiccups that jostled her head and shoulders.

"There's no right way to tell you anything you don't want to hear. I don't have a right to reasonable questions—"

"I—heard—digging!" Mavis screamed so violently that her entire frame shook.

Jerrod didn't snap. His eyes didn't flare, his posture didn't jerk rigidly to signal that he might respond in kind. Instead, he snatched his phone out of his back pocket and opened it, his thumbs tapping the screen.

"What are you doing?" Mavis asked, her chest heaving. "What are you doing!"

"I'm looking for the new hole. Because Havilah was in our yard last night."

It was worse than if he'd yelled back. Instead, he was trying to humiliate her, to shut her down, the way Cyrus did.

Mavis shifted from one foot to the other, her weight jerking while her fists tightened. She was panting while Jerrod studied the feed, moving his fingers against the screen so that the nearby camera tilted and turned.

She could snatch the phone from his hands. Smash it against the glass of her Palladian window. Shatter both. Fall with the broken pieces to the stone pavers below.

Instead, she tore out of the study, through the bedroom, and into the walk-in closet.

She doubled back, her panting exacerbated, spittle escaping her lips by the time she was standing in front of her husband. She hurled his league shirt into his chest, covering his phone.

"That's why you want to go back to the office," she spat. "I know, Jerrod. I've known for months."

He was holding the shirt in one fist, his other hand hanging at his side now, and his phone with it.

"You've known what? What are you talking about?"

"You didn't even bother taking it this time."

He was just staring at her, pretending not to understand.

"It wasn't in the car when you drove me home, Jerrod. You didn't take it when you left for the office. You weren't going bowling. If I hadn't been in that accident, you would've been somewhere, with her, and I would've been at home, like always. Waiting."

"You're always at home because you don't have a life, Mavis. You've got me, and you've got your paranoia, and eventually you're gonna have to choose because I'm not doing this with you." He closed his eyes and half shook his head before starting again. "I have never secretly met up with anyone. I shouldn't have to say that. Just because you're hurt doesn't mean I did something wrong. I had to figure that out a long time ago."

From her spot frozen beside the window, Mavis listened to her husband's angry plod down the stairs. The house rattled when he slammed the guest room door.

IX

Mavis couldn't remember the last time Jerrod actually slept in the guest bedroom. She was intent on not remembering this time either.

They'd let the sun go down on their anger plenty of times, but committing to sleeping separately meant something catastrophic. It cemented the conflict as important. Impactful. Devastating.

Mavis cracked the slow-release tablet between her teeth, washing the broken pieces down with a swig of lukewarm tap water before she could change her mind. The twenty milligrams of melatonin she took next felt petulant. It was dramatic—four additional pills—but hopefully harmless. She just didn't want to lie there, longing. She wanted to feel herself drift away. She wanted that tug at the base of her brain, like life was a whirlpool and sedation was a quick escape down the drain. When Jerrod came back into the bedroom, she wanted him to find her sound asleep. The small terror of not being able to quickly rouse her. He'd see the pill bottles beside the bed and remember everything she'd gone through in such a short time. He'd force himself to relax and then watch her, study her face in repose. Caress it. Whisper an apology before kissing her. Smile despite himself when his closeness disturbed but couldn't interrupt her rest.

Mavis moaned when she felt him get in bed later, but she couldn't open her eyes. There was more than the tug of melatonin. Her body was leaden. A weight pulled down through her middle and into the mattress, like an anchor tied to her sternum. She was a small boat and she rocked one way and then the other, like a storm had descended on dark waters.

Mavis felt Jerrod twisting and tilting her, felt his hands on her shoulders and her hips and her ankles all at once. Maybe he was more afraid than she'd expected him to be. She opened her mouth to comfort him, to tell him that she was here, on the turbulent ocean, but still in his arms, in their bed. From where she was, it made sense. She could calm him and stay here in this in-between place a while longer, if she could just speak without waking herself.

Something sutured around Mavis, the entire length of her body crushed. Confined. Her limbs sealed against her sides. The boat and the water were gone. Now she was being consumed, constricted as though by some great snake who would soon ingest her whole.

Mavis blinked, a flash of her bedroom visible for a matter of seconds before her eyes sealed shut again.

There had been hulking shadows all around her. Dark entities hovering above and beside her, silent except for muffled and distorted grunts.

Mavis blinked again.

She wanted the dream to end now. She hated when this happened. She'd almost wake, but her unconscious mind would follow her back. It would hold on to her, make it so she couldn't get free. Impose images from the other side onto the room around her. It was only frightening because she didn't have a choice. When blinking didn't bring her out, she knew screaming wouldn't either. She'd tell herself to cry out, and she'd think she had, but it would be on the wrong side. Only her unconscious imagination would hear it. Her vocal cords would still be at rest.

Sometimes she'd think she succeeded. She'd feel groggy and slow, but she'd drag herself upright and swing her legs over the side of her bed, her hands gripping tight enough to feel the mattress pattern beneath the fitted sheet. She could always feel Jerrod behind her, his back to her, expanding and contracting quietly. Even when the sun spilled down through their skylight and the real Jerrod must already be at work, his sleeping avatar never proved that Mavis must still be dreaming. Nothing did, until she'd stood beside the bed, the hardwood floor familiar and exact beneath her feet.

The picture didn't adjust. Despite being upright and out of bed, the image in front of Mavis remained a horizontal view of the items on her bedside table. And then she snapped back into place, lying down, her back to her husband's sleeping avatar—whom she now understood that she shouldn't be able to see.

She would sit upright, swing her legs over the side of her bed, stand up, and find herself lying down again, facing her bedside table.

It never helped to scream, but Mavis did it anyway. This time, something was different. She heard herself—and not just between her ears. She heard her voice careen into her surroundings, ricochet off the walls and furniture. These things were real, and suddenly she was alert. Her eyes were still closed but she felt her bed beneath her back, felt her fingers against her thighs, her arms pinned to her sides.

When something pressed against her face, Mavis knew it was a pillow. Jerrod's. She could smell her husband on the pillowcase. A moment more and it was suffocating her. It was being held against her face with an intentional force, muffling Mavis's cries.

Then it was gone. A gust of fresh air rushed in to satisfy her terrified gasp, and Mavis's eyes flew open.

She was awake, in her bedroom, and she wasn't alone. The hulking shadow people hadn't been her imagination. They hadn't followed her from a dream. There were intruders in her house.

Mavis screamed again. In response, a staff grew above her head. A pole of some kind, and at the top, between the skylight and Mavis's face, the pointed head of a shovel. It wasn't the garden spade. What reared back above her was the full-sized tool she'd heard the night they'd installed the camera. Havilah had given up on digging holes in the yard and was about to break Mavis's face.

The shovel stopped, then yanked back the other direction as though possessed.

Jerrod grunted and growled, and then he'd taken it. He barely wound back before slamming the shovel into the intruder's face, the force sending the back of their head into the wall with the speed of a freight train. Something hot rained on Mavis's skin and, screaming, she rolled away.

Someone grabbed at her while she rolled, but she hurled herself until she'd gone over Jerrod's side of the bed, narrowly missing his nightstand on her way down. When she landed, the wind was knocked out of her, but she didn't stop. She was swaddled in her own top sheet and blanket but the compression loosened in the fall, and she rolled back the other direction and under her bed.

All around her, grunts and the sound of violent collision. There were three sets of legs on one side of her. Jerrod was grappling with a second person, the intruder he'd pummeled with the shovel collapsed across the space Mavis had vacated.

A fourth set of legs stood at the foot of her bed. The person sank down into a squat and looked at her. They reached for Mavis and took hold of her ankles.

There'd been no boat and no boa constrictor. She'd left the door open for Jerrod and instead, three intruders had come inside her bedroom and bound her up. Now Mavis struggled against the hands gripping her ankles, wriggling an arm free from the blanket and taking hold of a thick wooden beam above her head. The beam was almost too wide to keep hold of, especially while someone tried to pry her free with the weight of her own body.

The hands gripped her leg higher, tightening around her wounded shin and activating an onslaught of torture through her limb. Mavis cried out, bucking in a vain attempt to undo their grip.

"Havilah, get off of me!" Mavis screamed. "Jerrod!"

At her plea, Jerrod doubled his efforts. Mavis heard his growling exertion, the thud of flesh pounding flesh, and then his own gust of breath leaving his body. His feet stumbled back toward the hall as though he'd lost his advantage, and Mavis screamed for him again.

The shadowy outline that'd taken hold of her ankles was climbing Mavis's body. Mavis dug her fingernails into the wooden beam, thrashing her body as violently as she could, but the intruder didn't stop, even when their back cracked against the bed frame.

Mavis struggled to free her other arm, to draw it up and out of the swaddling blanket. Her second hand emerged as the dark figure crested her chest. They wrapped their hands around Mavis's throat and she gagged despite that there wasn't space and clearance enough to straddle and properly choke her.

"Havilah!" she screamed, both arms flailing, her nails catching their skin as she slapped and scratched at her attacker.

Someone was lying on top of her, under her bed, their hands around her neck. Jerrod was fighting, but he was hurt. He wasn't going to save her. The way no one had saved the employees at the hardware store. The way no one had ever saved Mavis.

She reached up toward the face hovering over her chest, felt her fingers slip inside a mouth, felt her nail scratch at the inner rim of a nostril before she found it.

Mavis drove two fingers into an eye. It sank back into its socket until there was no more room for retreat and then Mavis used her nails to pop the surface, a warm, viscous deluge rushing over her knuckles amid rabid screams.

The hands released from her neck. The intruder tried to recoil, but Mavis had curled her fingers toward the palm of her hand, the thin bone of their skull between. They wrenched away, and Mavis felt something fall out with her retreating fingers.

They were screaming, scuttling backward to curl themselves against the far wall and hide beneath the window. It didn't sound like Havilah Greene. It didn't sound human at all.

Mavis didn't wait for them to come back. She rolled onto her stomach and turned herself around, pulling her way down the length of the bed. She kept her cover until the last moment but there was another pair of legs to greet her when she emerged, Mavis transferring the goo on her fingers to the pants leg that did not belong to her husband. She looked up into a dark face and screamed.

"Mavis." Jerrod was stumbling in the hallway, trying to come back inside.

While Mavis watched him, willed him toward her, a large hand buried itself in her hair, fingers digging at her scalp to grip.

She fought, hair ripping audibly. She kicked, the blow landing on the man's knee. He moved his leg protectively and Mavis pushed off with her hands and toes, skidding toward the study's adjoining doorway.

He hadn't let go of her hair, and when she lurched, Mavis felt her scalp separate before she got free. She felt the blood swell out from the crown of her head, pool until it was thick enough, and then run down her head and behind her ear, collecting into a jewel at her earlobe. It swung free when Mavis twirled to slam the door behind her.

A man's hand broke between the faceplate and the frame. The bones snapped as he kept the door from latching, and then it exploded back open, knocking Mavis hard against the trim of her daybed sofa. She curled into a ball and closed her eyes so she wouldn't see the man barreling toward her.

He never arrived. Mavis opened her eyes when she heard Jerrod intercept the intruder, both their bodies colliding with the Palladian window. The sound of glass breaking was more destructive than it looked, the window splintering but not falling apart. Two men lay huddled on top of each other in front of the broken window, but one was pushing the other off him and preparing to get back on his feet. Jerrod would not be the victor.

Mavis rushed back through the study door, through the bedroom, and out into the hall where the shovel lay.

In front of her extravagant window, surrounded by the wide leaves of her indoor garden, the last intruder was stomping on her husband's back.

Mavis screamed, and the man turned back to face her, the pointed head of the shovel leading her charge. At the malleable resistance of his abdomen, Mavis pushed forward with all of her weight. She carved his abdomen open, intestines like wet rope tumbling from the gash and onto the metal while he watched, open-mouthed. Mavis drove the shovel deeper, impaling him before he finally broke the glass and the man fell from the study. The motion sensors tripped the light from the installed camera as he passed and when he landed in Mavis's backyard, she could see the shovel shooting out of the intruder's broken body, straight as a planted flag.

The world was quiet except for Jerrod's labored breathing, and the whimpering cries of someone huddled beneath Mavis's bedroom window wondering where they were.

The ambulance felt familiar, even though it was Jerrod lying on the gurney, Mavis holding his hand from the airway seat. The scene at her home had been jarring, just like the day of the car accident, when the driver's side door and its airbag armor had been removed. There were dozens of people congregating in groups in every space of the property, from the front yard to the backyard, some at the kitchen table, more upstairs in the bedroom and the study. Every light in the house had been turned on in the middle of the night, making the place feel foreign.

It shouldn't be so bright.

There shouldn't be so many people.

There shouldn't be a lifeless, disemboweled man on the stone pavers in her backyard.

That night, the alarm hadn't been set and Jerrod hadn't been sleeping in the couple's bedroom. The first fact was explained by the circumstances that'd led to the second. The couple had had an argument. But coincidences were suspicious to people paid to investigate them, especially when someone died. In the hours after the invasion, they said Mavis saved herself. They said it with relief, at first, acknowledging that had it gone any other way, she'd be under the sheet, and Jerrod, too. By the time the ambulance pulled away, Mavis heard it said incredulously.

Let them disbelieve. Mavis could hardly believe it herself. She kept replaying every injury she'd sustained in what had felt like a marathon of pain. Thank goodness she'd taken her medication in excess. Thank goodness she'd numbed her body with sleep aids. Thank goodness for adrenaline, and the clarity to accept what people had shown her time and again: Mavis was on her own.

Knowing that had made the difference. It'd saved her life. It'd helped her take someone else's.

Knowing *that* lulled Mavis to sleep before the ambulance reached the hospital.

"What the heck are you doing here again?"

"Good morning to you, too, Dr. Moore." Mavis was the only one awake when he came in.

"I'm trying to be gentle because I know you don't like my sense of humor, otherwise I'd seriously suggest you get a life. The ER is not as fun as it seems, Mavis."

"Notice how I'm not bursting into tears."

"I know. I'm impressed." Dr. Moore dropped onto a stool and rolled himself closer to her. "I always feel like Fred Flintstone when I do this. How are you feeling?"

Mavis hesitated. She glanced away when a once-taloned thought snagged her brain.

Be humble, it said.

Be small, is what it meant.

She lifted her eyes without raising her head, and Dr. Moore's eyebrow ticked.

"I feel amazing," she told him. "I feel better than I have in a long time. In as long as I can remember."

Dr. Moore shrugged. "I'm not gonna argue with that. They tell me you might've saved Husband's life."

"Is he gonna be okay?" Mavis asked, whatever bravado she may have been guilty of melting into worry.

"Yeah." Dr. Moore nodded big, as though to overwhelm her concern. "Everything looks worse than it is. It's nothing more serious than if he'd had a bad boxing match. And was too old to be boxing, and hadn't sparred in a long time. He's gonna be fine."

Mavis dropped her chin, a wave of relief making her feel just a little bit fragile. She shook her head instead, staved off the prick of tears with amusement.

"Your bedside manner is awful," she told him. "Everyone thinks so."

"Again. Cannot argue that." Dr. Moore pointed to the white bandage on Mavis's shin. "Is that from tonight?"

"Oh." She sighed. "No. That's a day old."

"So between the car accident and tonight, you found some other way to get hurt." Dr. Moore gingerly removed the dressing to reveal the scabbed shin. "And how did you accomplish that?"

Mavis winced when a fiber from the bandage snagged the thick crust on her injured leg. She'd meant to reapply Neosporin at least once since attending to the wound, but life had insisted on propelling her mercilessly forward.

It felt like a dream now. It felt far away and far less real now that worse had happened in her own home. Now that she'd killed a man. She hadn't knelt over him and used a piece of machinery to change the curves and contours of his face. She hadn't thrown him from a high shelf onto a concrete walkway before he could get his bearings. Mavis had been proud of what she'd done. That she could. She'd been invigorated in a way she'd never experienced before, not even when Jerrod had begun doting on her. But remembering that anything had come before—that there was a before and would be an after, that her self-defense wasn't a one-and-done exhibition and there might be a next time, that she might have to rally all over again and there could be a different outcome—drained Mavis of adrenaline.

Dr. Moore was waiting for her reply, watching Mavis's demeanor shift. It rewound, her neck shrinking into her shoulders, her fingers clawing at the pleather beneath her. Like a time elapse in reverse, she relinquished the newness of confidence and returned to a shivering anxiety.

"I don't know if it was in the news," she began, deflated at being her former self. "I mean, it must've been."

Dr. Moore waited, shoulders relaxed, hands on his legs. He didn't brace himself. He didn't tense. He probably heard bad news every time he came to work, saw terrible things on a regular basis. He'd learned to let them come to him. He didn't try to anticipate what horror Mavis might describe; he just waited. To Mavis, it was a remarkable feat. She didn't bother hoping she could learn to replicate it.

"Something happened at the hardware store," she told him, because she still didn't know exactly what.

"You were there?" Dr. Moore's brow jumped.

Mavis nodded slow.

"He's here," he told her.

Her breath cut so sharply, her chin ticked upward.

"*Someone* is here," Dr. Moore amended his HIPAA violating

disclosure. "And is on the psych ward." He pointed up as though the facility were just above their heads. "What are the chances?"

"I don't know," Mavis said as though confessing. She hadn't tried to estimate them, hadn't really tried to make sense of the nature or frequency of the sudden deluge of tragedies she'd been involved in. She hadn't watched the news or read about the scene at the hardware store, not even to find out the identity of the man who'd stood too close to her before probably killing at least one person.

"If I had a *really* awful bedside manner, I'd ask if you're cursed, Mavis Dwyer."

They locked eyes.

"Is that the only explanation?" she asked as though simply wondering aloud. As though she weren't desperate for someone to know the answer.

"I mean. It's either that or you're an ER doctor, too."

"That would explain all the accidents in my vicinity, wouldn't it?"

"That would explain all the accidents." He nodded. "Pro tip: you shouldn't actually be *involved* in them."

"Okay," Mavis agreed. "That's a good note."

"Just helping out." Dr. Moore wore a half grin when he pushed back on his stool as though concluding his visit.

"Did they bring the victims here, too?" she blurted out.

Dr. Moore's face softened without breaking. Another remarkable feat.

"Just one."

Mavis nodded at too quick a pace. She looked a bit like a toy that'd lost a screw.

"The assailant claims to have no memory of it," he continued.

"That part they're reporting on the news. He won't accept that it happened. He thinks everyone's lying to him."

"People do that." Mavis nibbled at the corner of her lip.

"Dissociate?"

"Lie." Mavis let the moment fall into quiet before starting again somewhere else. "And mine?"

Dr. Moore was confused.

"Did they bring the people who broke into my house last night here, too?"

He didn't answer, his expression still gentle.

"Just one?" she asked.

The doctor shook his head.

"Two?" Mavis asked, surprised enough that it came out a whisper.

Dr. Moore nodded.

Mavis's relief escaped in a gust. Jerrod hadn't killed the intruder he'd incapacitated with the shovel. They hadn't regained consciousness even after the violence ended. While Jerrod was wheezing next to the gaping mouth that used to be her Palladian window, Mavis had gone back into the bedroom. She'd ignored the hysterical intruder still beneath the window, their arms wound around their head to preserve their surviving eye, and watched the body strewn across the bed. She hadn't thought they'd moved, not even to exchange poison for lifegiving oxygen, but Dr. Moore said they were alive. Despite that their blood had splattered like a pointillist painting on her bedroom wall. They might be in a coma, but they were alive.

"I killed one of them," she said, softly, Dr. Moore glancing down as though he already knew. "There were three. I blinded one, and I killed one with a shovel head. I carved out his intestines."

The man in front of her didn't pale or faint.

"It didn't sound anything like the digging," Mavis told him, though he hadn't heard her backyard being pillaged during the night. "It sounded wet."

Dr. Moore nodded again.

"The sounds will be hard to forget," he confessed.

X

When he woke up, Jerrod was ravenous. After pulling Mavis into his arms and onto the hospital bed, he'd held on to her for half an hour. It would have been silent except for the sound of material crumpling between their pressed bodies and Jerrod's guts churning from hunger. After their meditative hug, he'd eaten one plate and then requested another. While he ate the second, Mavis opened the surveillance camera feed on her phone. It had no audio, but she silenced the device anyway. Made sure to hold it perfectly straight, despite that her chair was across from her husband's hospital bed and it was physically impossible for him to see the screen.

The footage wasn't set up to record or be stored. Mavis had no way of watching the man she'd disemboweled trigger the camera before landing on the stone pavers in her backyard. She would never be able to replay the moment of impact. The way his pelvis and lower back landed first, the upper and lower halves of his body snapping against the hard ground like there had been magnets embedded beneath him.

All Mavis could do was watch a live feed of the place where the man had fallen. Mentally reconstruct him in the scene. Place his back over the impact cracks in the stone. Match the dark stains with the various openings in his body. Some stains were blood, some must've been whatever variety of fluids occupied a human torso.

From the hospital a dozen or so blocks away, she watched a raccoon cross the yard, coming out of the shadow of one of the tree canopies and slowing as it approached the exact spot Mavis studied. The creature moved as though it knew, as though it could smell what had happened here. Maybe an animal's sense of smell functioned like sight because when it was near, the raccoon reached out as though expecting to touch a body that hadn't been there for hours by now. It moved around inside the phantom man, touching and smelling each stain, sometimes scratching at a dark spot and then tasting it.

"Was it Havilah?"

Mavis dropped her phone in her lap.

"Sorry, baby," Jerrod said. "I didn't mean to startle you."

"That's okay." Mavis closed the device without picking it back up.

"I don't know if you saw all of them," Jerrod continued. "I just wondered if Havilah was part of this. And why she would . . ."

He trailed off, chewed the small bite more than was required.

"I only saw the man and only after he tripped the lights," Mavis answered. "The other two were in the dark."

"Did you know him?"

She froze, the pinpricks at the corners of her eyes a warning.

"Baby," Jerrod pressed.

Her phone vibrated against her lap.

"Did we know him?"

Mavis was afraid she wouldn't be able to move. She pulled her head back by imagining Jerrod swinging the shovel in their bedroom, and for a moment she couldn't put it right again. She studied the hospital ceiling while hot tears streamed down both sides of her face. Closed her eyes.

She'd meant to nod. Yes, she knew the man she'd killed. Yes, Jerrod had met him, though a very few times, and not in seven years. They hadn't kept in contact after Mavis pulled away from what by then she considered her parents' church.

"Baby," Jerrod's deep voice crooned. "Talk to me."

If she searched her memory for the man's name, she'd find it. She'd be able to recall something about him, even if she'd learned it secondhand.

Her phone vibrated again, and Mavis rushed into the en suite bathroom before Jerrod could push the overbed table aside and get to her.

She locked the door because the last time she'd gone into the restroom, a nurse had informed her the toilet was for the patient's use only. Jerrod had been asleep, so he hadn't heard the reprimand, or the nurse's claim that it was hospital protocol. He hadn't heard Mavis's voice echo slightly when from inside the bathroom she'd turned and responded.

"I didn't know hospitals had protocol for where the other victim of a very bloody home invasion could pee. I guess I should've pissed at home, after the man who tried to kill me was dead."

That was before, when Mavis felt strong. When it felt like she'd won. Like she'd ended whatever curse had befallen her. She'd almost convinced herself that her guilt didn't matter. That all of this hadn't been condemnation after all.

Then Mavis opened her phone.

She had a message request from herself. Or from a pictureless account under the name Mavis Dwyer. Inside, an attachment was blurred for security purposes. She couldn't see the thumbnail without accepting the request.

Mavis hesitated.

This felt like the "next time" she'd been afraid of. When during Dr. Moore's visit she'd regressed into her former self, into the real Mavis, the one whose thoughts had talons, it had been because her victory was not the end. There were no rolling credits. No promise that this resolution would last.

Her thumb tapped the request, accepting before Mavis had exhausted her fears.

It was inevitable. Mavis understood that even when shushing emojis bubbled up from the bottom of her screen. Little yellow faces held a finger in front of their lips and swam upward before fading. Mavis understood that there would always be a next thing from now on, even when the thumbnail was too dark to make anything out. Even when she drew in a breath and tapped the screen again and a video began to play.

It was night. Outside. There was a cone of light somewhere beyond what was being captured, but it didn't illuminate the foreground.

Rosebushes, maybe. Some row of flowering bushes, well maintained.

The camera hovered down, as though whoever was holding it got down on the ground. Now Mavis could see something else was growing between the bushes. A strange, bulbous orb, like a dark gourd planted in the wrong garden.

It moved. Rolled forward, but not far.

Mavis squinted, instinctively pulled the phone closer to her face.

Another light flicked on, this one shining down from immediately above.

The gourd was a human head.

Someone was growing out of the ground.

No.

Someone had been buried neck-deep.

Cyrus had been buried neck-deep, in front of the rosebushes he'd always said he'd keep.

Mavis started to tremble, but she didn't drop the phone. She didn't yelp or scream. Her mouth didn't gape, though her eyes did.

At first she thought Cyrus was dead. The apparent rolling was his head falling to the side, after which Mavis saw blood trickling from one corner of his mouth.

What was this? Mavis didn't ask the question aloud. She didn't look away, or blink—but she still didn't see what flew into frame and cracked against the side of Cyrus's head.

His eyes took turns opening and closing before they stabilized. Cyrus twisted his neck, eyes squeezed shut when the light shone into them. That's when he seemed to realize that he couldn't move.

He was alert now. His eyes tracked between multiple points. He was looking at someone. Several people, standing in front of him. His gaze dropped, locked with the person lying on the ground, holding the camera.

He barked something. A question, maybe. The video had no sound but Mavis still heard him. It was a demand. That's where he began, bearings be damned.

Cyrus struggled against the dirt packed against him, threw his shoulders hard on one side and then the other, and there was give. A gap appeared, loosened earth collapsing down. It emboldened him. His jaw flexed and then he let loose a second tirade of threats. The finger he'd thrust into Mavis's chest on too many occasions to recall was trapped below the surface, but she could see the muscle in his shoulder that always tightened in the moment before. She knew that he was cutting them down, whoever they were. That he was making promises he was absolutely committed to keeping. That whatever he was bellowing at his audience was tearing into their flesh so deftly that a physical weapon would seem a gift. A gracious reprieve.

Maybe for them it wasn't so bad. If the unseen targets of Cyrus's anger had never felt his affection, maybe they weren't wrecked by this. Mavis had pulled her shoulders forward, wrapped one arm across her front as though to protect her chest, but maybe that was because she knew him. Maybe words were only effective weaponry when the target had been primed to receive them. To be destroyed by them. To live or die by them.

Even muted, Cyrus dispensing what Mavis was certain were devastating verbal assaults was difficult to bear. She felt something curdling in her stomach. A queasiness brought bile up into her throat. She was sitting on the toilet, worried she'd need to kneel in front of it soon, when something hit Cyrus in the face.

Mavis stood.

Cyrus was quiet. His mouth hung open, blood pouring from it like a faucet.

He'd always taken pride in his teeth. They were pearl statues, perfectly aligned along the bottom, none too broad or narrow. He'd remarked once that if he and Mavis ever had children, they'd have to put money aside to make sure her eyeteeth didn't ruin the children's smiles. Now Cyrus's front teeth were jags. Whatever had struck him bowed his once gorgeous smile and knocked Cyrus into a stupor.

Another stone was cast. And then another. Now they collided

not just with Cyrus's head but with each other; some ricocheted to the ground where Mavis could identify them.

A stone knocked Cyrus's face to the side sharply, his eyes rolling, a large knot visible on the back of his head.

Another.

Cyrus spasmed, a red spray escaping his mouth when two rocks simultaneously struck his temple and his cheekbone.

His face was changing. Warping. Growing and splitting and gushing. Blood flowed like a sheet now, while a final barrage of stones flooded the frame.

And then it wasn't Cyrus anymore. There was no sign of him left. The indignation had dissipated. The beauty was erased. The head growing between the rosebushes was swollen and disfigured, and the video ended.

XI

One week before the Spencers sideswiped Mavis at Ross and 15th, she'd overheard Jerrod on the phone. Or rather, she'd heard the woman who'd called him.

Djidji Patton was an executive assistant in Jerrod's office. She was five foot four in six-inch heels and had a figure out of a campy cartoon, with surprisingly understated hair and nails.

At the company Christmas party, Mavis had flushed at the sight of the woman, and then made a fool of herself.

"Lovely to meet you, Gigi," she'd said, and smiled until she felt the skin around her eyes crinkle. It was a valiant effort, ignoring the crushing pain in her chest, offering her hand to a woman who worked closely with Jerrod and smelled like bergamot and amber.

"Not Gigi, baby," Jerrod had corrected her. "Djidji."

His arm was snug around Mavis's form. It draped behind one shoulder and crossed her back, his hand tangling with the one she always crossed in front of her when she was anxious.

"Gigi," Mavis had almost whispered, confused by the slight difference she could detect but couldn't replicate.

"Jerrod's the only one in the office who says it the way my

parents do," Djidji had said, excusing Mavis's failure with a friendly wave of her small hand.

She wasn't his work wife, according to Jerrod.

"That's not a real thing, baby," he'd assured her. "Work spouses are a sitcom trope."

Then, a week before the accident, Jerrod had answered his phone while carrying groceries, the device in hand but not pressed to his ear when Djidji's voice spilled from the speaker.

"Home yet, babe?"

Jerrod had let the heaviest bag fall the short distance to the ottoman and rushed the rest of the load into the kitchen, the phone sealed to the side of his face. He hadn't said a word.

Don't.

Mavis didn't retrieve the heaviest bag and follow Jerrod. She didn't race up the stairs and lock herself in the study or in the bathroom, back against the door, palms flat against the cold tile.

Don't.

Mavis had to do something, she couldn't stand in the entry all day, but she didn't do anything to let on that she'd heard. She went back out to Jerrod's car and retrieved his briefcase and travel mug before locking the doors.

If Djidji had ever been in Jerrod's car, Mavis would've smelled her. That didn't mean they hadn't gone to lunch—or somewhere else—separately on occasion.

The talons had been merciless. They sank so deep so quickly that it physically hurt. Mavis was in bed early that night, the migraine making her sleep restless. Hours before sunrise, she was wide awake.

It had been remarkably easy. That was one benefit of knowing someone as well as Mavis knew Cyrus. She knew how to lure him without seeming to. Plausible deniability, at least for a while.

Sometimes they weren't villains. Sometimes they were called to teach a lesson you weren't mature enough to learn.

It would've been too much if they were Mavis's own words. Especially since she tagged her mother in the post, so that it'd show up on the page Daniel and Marie Carson shared, where Cyrus—who wasn't blocked or unfriended by her parents—would see it. She'd tagged other people, too, so it wouldn't look directed at anyone in particular, and so Cyrus would assume it was only really about him. He'd see Mavis's married name, and that she was still active on social media. Just not interacting with him.

The graphic had gotten more interaction than the slapdash illustration and overwhelming typeset deserved, but Mavis wasn't surprised. By the next morning, her mother had posted a long sermon of a comment about the burden of being a parent when a child is not ready to accept their wisdom. Children are often overly sensitive, a trait which receives too much leniency given that, according to Marie Carson—who always signed her sentiments with her initials so there was no confusion about which of the Carson doctors said what—it camouflages narcissism. The woman had closed by celebrating that children grow up.

Mavis would've suffered severe morning-after regret if the post hadn't garnered the attention she'd intended. But there in her inbox was a request from Cyrus Marshall, with a short message.

Proud of you, Emme.

Mavis's abdomen had tightened. She'd felt clammy, a piercing sensation shooting between her shoulders. It hadn't been a false alarm. She'd vomited into the kitchen sink. Stared into her lackluster backyard while the faucet blasted her stomach bile away with piping hot water.

It was a week before any holes would appear in her backyard. Before the sound of metal would carve through the night. Before a man's intestines would be gored and plated on the same shovel.

She didn't have to accept the connect request to respond to his message.

Thank you.

It was all she could muster, and it was more than enough. He thought he'd snared her. That was the key. Cyrus was enlivened by the thought that all these years later, Mavis still craved his validation. That she still mourned losing him. That she didn't have the good sense to ignore his use of a nickname he must have known she'd never liked. Cyrus wasn't going to simply slink back into memory. He was going to see how far she'd follow. How susceptible she was to suggestion.

I had lunch with your father not long ago. It was after nine holes and completely unplanned, but there are no coincidences.

Mavis hadn't known. Cyrus had been deemed an idol, an addiction, a battleground for Mavis, so neither Daniel nor Marie Carson thought it necessary to tell their daughter that they were still in touch with the man. She'd only found out when she searched for his profile and saw that they had mutual connections.

She didn't ask what the significance of Cyrus un-coincidentally having lunch with her father might be. It was language meant to imply gravity. Ordainment. Even when the desired outcome was sin.

Congratulations on seven years of marriage, Mrs. Dwyer. I hope it's not too early to assume you've beaten the odds.

That time, Mavis had known exactly what he meant. Cyrus

had spent years informing her that the seven-year itch was inevitable. That it was more than restless infidelity. That until a wife had the discipline to guard her appearance, conduct, emotions, thought life—until she could confidently and honestly say that she was a devout wife on a daily basis—it was blame-shifting to focus more on the reactionary sin of the husband than the thousands of his wife's daily sins that triggered it.

The problem was that Cyrus had been right. As soon as Mavis heard Djidji's voice, visualized the diminutive woman propped on Jerrod's desk while she called another woman's husband "babe," she'd felt Cyrus under her knee, telling her through a still-intact grin that he was the man she'd married after all. The dream had been prophetic, she'd just been too optimistic and naive to accept it.

She'd convinced herself that Jerrod's imperfections were his saving grace. That the congregation vow she'd expressly rejected and he'd reinstated was proof that there wasn't any pedestal from which Jerrod would inevitably tumble. But realizing he'd fallen—from any height—proved devastating, and the taloned thoughts terrorized her. They raced and multiplied, a thousand sharp edges slicing back and forth until her head ached and her nose bled. Every time she thought she didn't have the stomach for another one of Cyrus's now constant messages, a flurry of hysterical thoughts assaulted her.

Jerrod was having an affair.

Jerrod was going to leave her. Or worse, Mavis wasn't going to be able to stay. Stay still. Stay quiet.

She wasn't as disciplined as Stephany Leonard.

She wasn't as strong as Havilah Greene.

Mavis would never leave, but she was going to be completely undone by her husband's infidelity. She wouldn't be able to hide it. She was going to erupt. The pressure was going to cause more than nosebleeds. It was going to expose the unworthiness Cyrus had seen in her years before, when he'd chosen someone else and all eyes and opinions had been on Mavis.

Cyrus was right. A wife had to be more than Mavis was capable of to keep a husband at home. Jerrod wanted to be a better man, and maybe he was. In every way but this, he'd made Cyrus seem a terrible exception. What had been normal to Mavis slowly became outlandish. Unacceptable. Evidence that she'd been failed not just by Cyrus, but by an entire community who seemed to see every one of her imperfections, and none of Cyrus's psychopathy. Then Djidji's voice cut through the rose tint, and Mavis realized that it had been seven years.

Nothing had been disproved after all. It just hadn't happened till now.

There was one way to mute the thoughts. To soften their talons and dull the impact, Mavis needed insurance. A way to keep Jerrod's betrayal from unraveling her completely. A reason to keep quiet. Look away. Smile and agree when her mother reminded her how blessed she was to be Jerrod's wife. A way to assure Jerrod she wasn't too fragile to survive his betrayal. That he needn't turn away from her for her own sake.

Mavis needed a sin of her own.

It took too long, and not long at all. Two days of messages. A dropped reminder of the café where the two used to meet, Cyrus still supposedly working behind his laptop, Mavis welcome to quietly observe for hours at a time. There'd been a pastry Mavis loved until Cyrus suggested outings were too thin a veil to dress up gluttony. Five days before the accident, he dangled an invitation under the guise of finally trying the pastry himself, and Mavis drove across town.

He was handsome. Sickeningly so. Nothing about his interior ugliness or time apart had changed that.

"You're looking well," Mavis had told him after responding to Cyrus's open arms and crooked brow by extending her hand.

It only made him smile wider. He enveloped her hand in two of his. They were warm. Suffocating. Caressing, but only enough to make a woman wonder if she were reading into things.

"Marriage agrees with me," Cyrus had answered. Mavis saw and instantly remembered his trademark near-wink. The way he'd lock gazes before narrowing one of his eyes, making sure not to close it completely. At the beginning of their courtship, she'd gone back and forth with herself. Had he winked? Was she imagining it? Was he interested in her? The end result being the way she trained her eyes on his, prompting her mother and sometimes others in the congregation to advise her against being so forward.

Cyrus was enjoying this. He was comfortable. Too comfortable for it to be his first time. The fact that it was Mavis meant something. The fact that it was Mavis doing the seducing never occurred to him. He'd made contact first. He'd sent three messages for every one of hers. The fact that her replies were never more than one sentence—and never more than four words long—pleased him. It meant she was uncomfortable. Unsure. Unfamiliar with the terrain. It meant she didn't have a Jezebel spirit. No one had successfully enticed her before. His conquest would be a singular achievement, and he'd confirm what he'd known when he put her down years before: that Mavis would never recover from him.

She knew all of this, and it mattered. It mattered that it was Cyrus Marshall, for so many reasons.

He was impatient. There would be no drawn-out courtship, no complex web of dates and arrangements to keep from Jerrod.

He was a predator. She had only to cross his sight, merely suggest that she'd accepted his version of past events, and he would do the rest.

She despised him. She wanted insurance, and unfaithfulness was the necessary sin, but she didn't want to enjoy it. She didn't want to be tempted, to complicate her life with confusing desires. She just wanted to survive Jerrod's infidelity, marriage intact.

It had to be Cyrus. It had to be someone who would act quickly and then discard her. Catch and release her, without regard for her feelings or circumstances.

"I have to show you something," he'd said when there was a table between them, and on it were two pastries that neither had any intention of consuming. Cyrus dug his phone out of his pocket and grinned at the screen, thumb swiping quickly before he turned the device and offered it to Mavis.

Her stomach had lurched, a bitter taste leaping from her esophagus into the back of her mouth. She looked from the phone to Cyrus, who was still smiling encouragingly. He didn't seem to remember the discussion around the device and her attempts to look at it. The tirades she'd endured.

Mavis had swallowed the bile and accepted his phone. She didn't have a chance to wonder what Cyrus could possibly *have to* show her before she saw his wedding picture.

"You were right about the cobalt blue."

"Golden brown belt and wingtips," she'd said, both describing the styling choices pictured and repeating a preference she'd voiced years before. "No tie."

"Renee bought me one. It was gorgeous, actually, but I couldn't do it." Cyrus had paused for effect. "Mavis's orders."

He'd framed it as though she'd done more than waxed in pathetic detail about her own imaginary wedding. Not to mention the insinuation that she'd been on his mind on his wedding day. That he'd made a decision with her in mind, in direct defiance of his chosen bride.

If she'd been lovesick, Cyrus's trap would've snapped shut. She would've thought his message clear—that she could usurp Mrs. Marshall. That she already had. Perhaps it'd been a cruel necessity in securing other dalliances, but Mavis would've preferred Cyrus leave his wife out of it.

Later on, when Cyrus snuck his fingers up her cap sleeves, hooking her bra straps before sliding them off both her shoulders, Mavis saw Renee Marshall. She wondered if Cyrus took his wife's bra before she'd removed her shirt the way he always had with her. She wondered whether or not Renee Marshall felt rushed. Whether or not her breasts brushing against the material, swaying when Cyrus put both hands around her waist and twisted her back and forth, was unnerving for the woman. It'd always made Mavis's skin crawl, but she hadn't said so. She hadn't told Cyrus that taking her clothes off out of order made it feel like he'd made the decision for her. That after her bra was gone, her shirt was a mere formality. That it would've been silly to resist by then.

"I remember these." Cyrus's voice was husky with desire, his mouth an oven.

Renee Marshall's chest was smaller than Mavis's. It'd allowed her to wear a minimalist satin gown with a plunging neckline and still look elegantly modest.

Mavis's guts roiled.

"You didn't ruin them breastfeeding," he said, ten fingertips sinking into Mavis's flesh while he tilted and turned her under his mouth. "Tell your husband I said you're welcome."

It was easier to think of Jerrod. It settled her stomach, and her resolve. When she thought of Jerrod, the pressure of Cyrus's touch became relaxing, the heat medicinal. Cyrus's voice muffled. The furnished one-bedroom condo he maintained melted away, her rhetorical questions about whether it was a marital asset or a philanderer's secret fading with it.

When she thought of Jerrod, Mavis replaced Renee Marshall in an A-line wedding dress that pooled beautifully on the church steps with Djidji Patton in her Christmas party dress. Propped on Jerrod's desk. Hair bouffanted. Nails as long as her stiletto heels.

She pictured herself folded on the dimpled sofa in her bridal suite, her wedding dress fileted, her back exposed. Mavis visualized subtly re-creating the image in some pastor-counselor's office while Jerrod confessed what she'd long known. She imagined gripping her chest with one hand as though to rend her heart through her flesh, while knowing the pain was manageable because she'd suffered Cyrus. She saw her husband's tear-streaked face, heard his distraught voice repenting, rededicating, renewing, and Mavis's body moved automatically.

She engaged.

For what would not be the last time, Mavis saved herself.

When it was finished, she was done.

"Hey." Cyrus caught her by the elbow when she was almost to the front door. "What's your rush?"

If she hadn't been desperate to leave, he would've been.

"Don't touch me," Mavis hissed, and he laughed.

"It's a little late for that, Emme." Cyrus spun her toward him, and kissed her neck when she turned her face. "Tell me you haven't dreamt of this. Say you haven't wanted this for years and I'll let you go."

Mavis locked eyes with him.

"I have never wanted you," she told him. "Not even when I begged."

The side of his mouth twitched, but the smile didn't manifest. He squinted with both eyes, stepped back without releasing her as though destabilized. He managed to steady himself, but his eyes darted. His lips parted, a narrow gash at first, and then a wondering gape.

"Don't." Mavis had passed the wisdom along. "Don't ask questions you don't want answered."

Cyrus's pretty face curled into a sneer.

"All right. You never wanted me. I'm sure that'll be cold comfort for the man you vowed you did."

His words had talons, too. They began to sink and shred the moment they were released. Mavis stood too long in the entry of Cyrus's love nest, frozen by the frenzy in her head, and he found his smile. He chuckled as he opened the front door before traipsing back toward the kitchen and leaving Mavis there.

She was still in a petrified state when she entered the intersection of Ross and 15th.

XII

Mavis wept.

Cyrus had been stoned. Buried to his neck and stoned.

Perhaps not to death, she'd thought at first. The video disappeared once viewed. She couldn't watch it again. She couldn't study the footage so perhaps she hadn't really seen the last moments of his life. In the end, it was the cold echo of the hospital bathroom that forced Mavis to accept reality. Knees drawn up, elbows pinned close to her body as though she had no choice but to fit in the narrow space between the toilet and the wall, she'd accepted his death because the video existed at all. Because the video had been sent to her. Because Cyrus had been surrounded. Because someone had come to his home, disabled him, and carried him into his own garden. They'd put him in the ground and disfigured his head and face.

His threats hadn't deterred them. His blood hadn't dissuaded them.

They'd come to watch him die, and they wouldn't have stopped until it was done.

Cyrus was dead because they'd come for her, too. They'd

come into her home, tried to disable her, and it'd taken deadly force to fight them off.

They'd come for them both.

Her and Cyrus.

Mavis Dwyer. And Cyrus Marshall.

There was only one thing they had in common. One sin for which someone might think the penalty should be death by stoning.

Two people they'd offended, who might have orchestrated the punishment. Watched as it was carried out. Recorded and delivered it.

Jerrod Dwyer or Renee Marshall.

A sound escaped Mavis. A whimper seeped from her sealed lips and ricocheted off the toilet before expanding in the open space of the walk-in shower. She closed her eyes as though to mute the sound but it had already escaped.

Don't.

Mavis breathed. A talon pricked.

Don't.

She felt Jerrod's crushing barricade, the way he'd pressed her behind him, against the hardware store shelves.

Saw him blur through her vision as he barreled into the man she would send through the Palladian window and down onto the pavers.

Felt him pull her into his arms in the back of the ambulance.

For the first time, the talons receded without goring. Before they could shred her psyche, convince her that her husband was responsible for all the terrible things that'd befallen her—that he was responsible for *any* of them—the talons shrank back.

Mavis opened her eyes.

Her husband had put his body between the intruders and

Mavis. Jerrod Dwyer was lying in a hospital bed on the other side of the bathroom door because he hadn't stayed in the guest bedroom.

But where was Renee Marshall? Where was Cyrus's oft-betrayed and perhaps not so long-suffering bride? The woman had clearly found her; now Mavis would return the favor.

Renee's page was right there, connected to Cyrus's by their relationship status, and by the fact that she reacted positively to every single thing he posted. Vague investment advice emblazoned across a picture of some dapper gentleman who had no idea what his image was promoting. Video reels of podcast snippets wherein a man broke down for a woman why she did the things she did, while the woman bickered halfheartedly and for entertainment purposes before recognizing the host's wisdom. Confusing infographics with no citations, mostly about Black capital and the nuclear family. Renee Marshall's stamp of approval was on all of them—or else the engagement served some other purpose. Perhaps Renee Marshall was simply making her presence known. Perhaps she knew she needed to.

All Mavis knew of Renee was that she'd said yes to Cyrus's proposal. That Cyrus had proposed in the first place. When he'd simultaneously broken up with Mavis after five years and excitedly announced his prophesied bride to her, holding one of Mavis's hands tight as though she would be equally bowled over, she hadn't recognized the woman's name. The women had never met, and Renee didn't attend their church—though ostensibly she would from then on. At the time, Mavis had exploded. She'd hysterically demanded how *Cyrus* knew her, and for how long, and why he would be blessed when he'd destroyed Mavis's life.

She'd gotten no answers then, and Renee Marshall's page was private now. Mavis should've guessed that.

She needed access. Once again, her parents had it.

They shared one page, though anyone unfamiliar with the habits of an advanced middle-aged conservative couple might just assume it belonged to a man named Daniel Marie Carson. Marie was not his middle name, and Mavis would've staked her life on the fact that her father had never laid eyes on the site. It didn't make her feel any better that her father perhaps hadn't interceded with Cyrus on her behalf only to befriend the woman her ex had married instead.

It hurt a bit less now that Cyrus was dead. She'd known for less than half an hour, but Mavis was startled to find that her parents' persistent relationship with the man was a bit less galling now that it was settled: Cyrus wasn't above the law. He wasn't an unquenchable star, a furious, unstable orb incapable of being contained or held accountable. Burning through spirit and flesh without changing. Without hesitation. His death meant two things: that her parents had been wrong, and that Cyrus had been exactly who she'd said he was.

Mavis straightened her back against the bathroom wall and signed into the Carson account. She'd never betrayed their trust before. She'd been accused of it, informed that some failure was more than just a mistake, but a sin against them. When during a family dinner she'd confessed the extent of her and Cyrus's intimacy, for example, they'd asked her to leave. She'd been dumbstruck, but they hadn't reconsidered. Her parents had insisted she vacate their home. She'd done so, meal untouched, and she hadn't known what to do next but rush directly back into Cyrus's arms. Only later—once Jerrod's interest had begun mending her reputation—did Mavis understand how every error being a sin against her parents had robbed her of the virtue of personal disappointment. Of having wanted better from herself, for herself.

There was too much at stake on the outside for her interior to factor in. Until she had to confess her premarital intimacy to Jerrod, immediately desperate to know how he felt, and he'd responded by asking how it made her feel. Like that mattered, too.

Now, when she infiltrated her parents' social media account to gain access to Renee Marshall's, Mavis found that she felt fine. Perhaps guilt would've needled her if she'd spent more than a moment guessing their password. TheDoctorsCarson had been the name of their internet network and the password to their home security ever since her mother's ThD had been conferred. It proved to be the password for their page, as well, and Mavis presumed, a number of their other accounts.

Renee Marshall's page was private because her life was not. As soon as Mavis could see it, she felt like she should look away. From the background photo she'd already seen on Cyrus's phone to the daily picture diary of Renee's disciplined diet, Mavis felt like she could reasonably piece together the woman's day-to-day. No detail was too mundane, and none too private. Every morning, Renee found a reason to show proof of her "quiet time," whether that was to share an insight from her study or to make a brief POV video in which she prepared some seasonal beverage in an immaculately tidy kitchen. When last week Renee had suffered a nightmare involving someone from her childhood, she'd posted a video in which she detailed not only the dream but also the other person's childhood trauma. Earlier in the month, she'd solicited wisdom from her women elders about the appropriate response when a husband's and wife's libidos are out of sync. To be fair, she hadn't divulged whose was outpacing the other's, and she'd made an all-caps plea for men and young people to avert their eyes before outlining her wonders and worries.

Mavis had been consuming Renee's page in wide-eyed gulps

for what felt like an infinite moment. It could have been ten minutes or ninety, she couldn't begin to estimate. The spell was only disrupted when Mavis heard Jerrod toss in the hospital bed. She seized, her fingertips tightening around her phone so suddenly that she heard the screen protector gap.

Jerrod had fallen asleep. She could tell by the familiar sound of his heavy adjustments and by the moans and whimpers that accompanied them. The ones she teased him about and mimicked when he asked her how she'd slept.

Mavis's eyes crept to the door, but they itched. They were unsated. Unsatisfied when there was so much more to see. As soon as Jerrod quieted, Mavis gorged, her held breath escaping her nostrils in bursts.

And just like he promised, Mr. Marshall gave me a home.

That's what Renee had posted several years before, along with a slideshow. First, a photo of her manicured hand delicately pinching a gold keychain from which a single key dangled. After that, the house itself—complete with the For Sale lawn sign and a freshly added red sash advertising that the house was sold—followed by a series of photos of a color-coordinated Cyrus and Renee. With open-mouthed glee, they embraced in front of the house, then Cyrus carried his wife over the threshold, and finally they shared a kiss just inside the house as Cyrus appeared to push the door closed.

There were more than one hundred comments, people exclaiming congratulations unanimously. And then there was Marie Carson.

He gave you a house, now you must give him a home! -MC

Mavis's mother's comment had accrued the most approval, and a reply.

I can't wait!

When her mother'd told Mavis what she owed her husband for his provision, she'd argued. Or at least, she'd countered that a home was something Jerrod wanted to make *with* her. It was an admission that she didn't think herself capable of the job, Mavis was informed. It was an indictment of her absence from her childhood congregation.

Renee Marshall had responded to Marie Carson with deference and aplomb. Now Mavis felt something like guilt. Except that it was claustrophobic. Like shame. It tightened the air around her, like a crowd observing, and Mavis felt her shoulders bunch. She felt her eyes lose focus. Every few seconds, they ticked away from the screen, glancing up at some other empty corner of the bathroom, as though she'd find someone there.

Mavis felt her own life pull back around her. She felt the wounds and bruises she'd sustained flicker back into the foreground, her phone and everything it displayed getting farther and farther away despite how close she held it.

The connection was lost. She couldn't get back inside Renee Marshall's life. She was just an intruder, scrolling through moments and memories she hadn't been invited to share.

So she'd intrude.

Mavis took a screenshot of the outside of the Marshall house and fed it to a reverse search engine.

It spat out a cached listing on the website of the Realtor Renee and Cyrus must have used.

An address, and so much more. A purchase price, and a date, and a bevy of listing photos. Mavis could move throughout the home, take a 3D tour, see an imperfection in the stairwell. Get a lay of the couple's bedroom, their two walk-in closets, and their spa bathroom. She could imagine which sink was his and which hers by the slight difference in square inches of counter space.

Cyrus's razor always sat erect in a stylish charging dock; he'd need the larger side if the rest of his products weren't going to be crowded. It was a matter of clutter.

There was no way to tour the Marshalls' fenced backyard. No satellite photos as recent as last night, and no way to see a head buried behind a row of rosebushes.

Mavis would have to go herself.

Her heartbeat fluttered into her throat.

Mavis would have to see Renee Marshall in the flesh to know whether or not the woman was the architect of her curse. To know whether or not she'd have to plant Cyrus's wife beside him to end it.

Her phone clattered against the bathroom floor.

"Mavis?" Jerrod's groggy voice slipped beneath the door.

"Yeah?"

She hadn't meant to respond. Her shaky voice had rattled free before she could collect herself.

It hadn't been a taloned thought. It hadn't been a harrowing threat designed to send Mavis into hysterics, to send her mind reeling. Mavis dropped her phone because when the thought of burying Renee Marshall occurred to her, she'd felt calm. The thought was still, and small. And true.

Before she slipped out of the bathroom and called a rideshare, Mavis took the dose of pain medication still in the paper cup on his tray and waited for Jerrod to settle back to sleep.

It was a quiet neighborhood. Even a midnight murder hadn't startled it into a frenzy. When Mavis crept around the last corner and the Marshall home was in sight, there was nothing out of the ordinary. No patrol vehicles or antennaed vans. There was no one there to investigate or report—at least not in an official capacity. There was only Mavis and the notably full driveway of the Marshall residence, as though Cyrus was the only husband on the block still at home.

Mavis briefly regretted taking the rideshare from the hospital to home to collect her husband's car. Someone might recognize it. Remember its presence later. But the only alternative was having someone drive her here and drop her off. No means of escape. No fortress from which to surveil before approaching. If she could even devise a strategy.

Now that she was here, parked across the street and one house over from the Marshalls', nothing seemed as doable. She'd defended herself the night before; that didn't mean Mavis could convincingly confront someone, let alone overpower them.

She was scared. Right this minute, and as a default state. Mavis had been afraid before a single accident or attack—she just had tangible reasons now. It wasn't in her head. Her fear was justified these days, and it was almost a relief.

That was what she'd give Renee. A reason. If life with Cyrus Marshall meant suspicion and denial and destabilizing doubt the way it had for Mavis, she'd give Renee a reason for her fear.

Mavis took out her phone. After zooming in on the house number, she recorded the front door, careful to crop her driver's side window out of the frame so that no make, model, or color details could be gleaned from close inspection of the video.

When a woman came out the front door and quick-stepped toward the driveway, Mavis gasped, throwing herself over the passenger seat. She'd have to edit the dive out of the video, but she couldn't risk being seen. Face buried in her shoulder, legs seized and tangled like a dead spider, brain reminding her of every bruise, Mavis waited.

Whoever came out of the house, it hadn't been Renee. Mavis just had to give them a chance to leave. She listened for a car to start, to reverse, to pull away. After that, she'd sit up and start again. Her heart was racing, but it was adrenaline. It was becoming familiar. It would pass and Mavis would regain composure. Her mind would clear, un-taloned thoughts reorganizing to decide her next move.

She was still stretching across the seats, face hidden, when the pounding started. Mavis's car rocked to one side and by the time she'd whirled around to face her window, a fist was drumming against it.

"Who are you!" and then the fist against the window again.

Mavis gasped and then made a series of harried exclamations while she tried to escape. She was a marionette on some invisible string, her hands and knees jumping against her will. She grabbed the wheel with one hand, sent the other shooting toward the ignition—only this was Jerrod's car, not Mavis's. There was no key or opening, only a button, and her foot had to be on the brake to start the car.

"Who are you! Why are you watching my sister's house!"

"I'm—I'm sorry," Mavis sputtered, tried to synchronize her hands and feet to start the engine, but the woman jerked open her door.

Mavis hadn't locked it. The door was open, and now the hand that'd beaten against her window reached inside. For a moment, she saw the pink walls her deployed airbags had created, but there was no such barricade now. She heard a scream and didn't know whether it was a memory of metal changing shape or whether it was coming from her.

She flinched away, the way she hadn't had a chance to in the intersection. The way she hadn't known to when Jerrod pulled her out of the way at the hardware store. It was happening again, and this time it was Mavis's fault. She'd come to Cyrus's home despite what they'd done to him, and the attack was starting again.

"Are you one of his whores?" a woman's voice screeched. "Who are you?"

This was something different. Her attackers hadn't spoken before. In the hardware store, and when they descended on her in her own bedroom, the people terrorizing Mavis hadn't said a word—unless or until they were hurt. It was a disturbing thing to realize, but it was true. Whatever it meant.

This woman was no more prepared for the altercation than Mavis. She reached into the car, as though to keep Mavis from leaving, but her hands were easily swatted away. She retracted them each time they made contact, though she didn't stop her verbal assault.

"He's married, did he tell you that?"

There was a reason she kept retreating. Every time Mavis touched her, the woman pulled her arm around her pregnant belly and turned it slightly away.

Mavis stopped. Held up her hands.

The woman's hands stopped, too.

Her chest heaved, her mouth buttoned shut despite that she was uncomfortably out of breath. She stepped back, arms criss-crossing a torso that hung low and heavy. There was no way she should've been fighting in the street at her late stage of pregnancy.

The Marshalls' front door opened.

"I'm fine," the woman called after a moment without turning to look.

Even from a distance, Renee was not the woman Mavis had

been watching in the posts and videos. She couldn't be. Her hair always looked expertly straightened before being barrel curled into soft beach waves. It was always full and glossy, a testament to the heat-protecting polish she routinely recommended to her complimenters. In the doorway, despite that it was afternoon, Renee Marshall was still wearing a large satin bonnet, and without her lashes and mascara, her eyes were too small for Mavis to see.

"Who are you?"

Now Mavis recognized the pregnant woman's small eyes. She recognized the tall forehead that ran in their family.

"You're with Cyrus, aren't you?" Renee's sister pressed. "He's at your house, and he sent you for his things. You think I'm going to let you waltz into my sister's house so he doesn't have to face her?"

The woman was vacillating between nodding and shaking her head, between being on the verge of tears and throwing her fists despite her belly.

"That's his wife!" She thrust her finger toward the house, at her sister still in the doorway, looking lost. "You think he's gonna do better by you than he's doing by her?!"

"I'm not with Cyrus," Mavis said, at last. Her mind had been racing, distracted by being caught, by the intrusive memories of past attacks, and then by all the information volunteered. She needed to talk to Renee directly, to see if she'd authored this story about Cyrus running off—or whether she believed it.

"He's been sleeping with my client." Mavis stretched her neck, pressed her shoulders down and elongated it before unbuckling and stepping out of the car.

Renee's sister was quiet. One hand absently rubbed her belly, her eyebrows crunched so that her forehead seemed even larger.

“I’m a private investigator, and it sounds like she was right to suspect Cyrus. Apparently, he *is* married.”

“Yeah,” the woman replied through a slight groan, the heel of her palm pressing into her abdomen.

“You shouldn’t be out here,” Mavis told her. “Can I help you inside?”

“Do you have proof?” the woman demanded.

Mavis felt her mouth gape and forced her lips into a small o, letting out a narrow stream of air to buy time. She hoped the expression was misleading, or at least difficult to immediately read. She hadn’t considered what kind of ID would be expected, what verification a private investigator might carry.

“That he’s a cheater?” Renee’s sister finished. “Do you have proof?”

Mavis’s lips settled together and then she nodded.

“Ironclad.”

XIII

Rebekah Sheryl led Mavis across the street and toward the Marshall house. Toward Renee Marshall shrinking away from the door.

She didn't look like a maestro. Renee kept tightening the arms crossed over her chest. She kept tucking her lips into her mouth, lifting her chin as though some invisible schoolmarm was instructing her.

When her toe connected with a small divot in the street and she teetered momentarily, Mavis felt her conviction do the same.

Renee didn't look like she'd selected and directed the players, sent them into the world—not to mention her own backyard—and waited for justice to prevail by force.

Renee Marshall looked like a woman whose husband hadn't come home.

"That's his car in the driveway," Mavis said, upspeaking so that it could be interpreted as a question.

Cyrus's widow was avoiding eye contact with her, but it had nothing to do with recognizing Mavis. The woman was threatening to collapse into herself. She was doing everything in her power to beat back a very particular fear. Mavis couldn't tell which one—it was impossible to know what anyone's personal worst-case scenario entailed—but she knew it must be Renee's bogeyman. To identify it, Mavis would have to know the deepest parts of Renee. She'd have to know what ugliness Renee would put up with to have her husband climb out of the hole in their backyard and dust himself off. She'd have to know whether having orchestrated something bloody and brutal, Renee would be tortured more by the loss of a man she'd clearly loved—or by the prospect of being found out.

Renee's sister, Rebekah, returned from the kitchen with water bottles on an oblong serving tray. The fact that Mavis recognized it made her briefly sick to her stomach. It'd been in several of Renee's videos, a decorative slab of natural wood, the varying colors rustically charming, and the polished metal handles a perfect match for the Marshalls' cabinet hardware. Now sitting in the home—invited, but only because the sisters were too distracted by their own trauma to properly assess her—Mavis felt a damp chill at the small of her back. She ached despite the generous dose she'd stolen from Jerrod's hospital tray.

This place was familiar, and it shouldn't be. She shouldn't know what metal matched what hardware, or the layout of a kitchen she hadn't set foot in. Someone had trespassed into Mavis's home the night before, and now she was the monster in Renee's.

"Here, honey," Rebekah whispered, coaxing her sister to take one of the bottles. "Drink something."

The water bottle sank into Renee's lap along with her thin hands. She was looking toward the hall as though she'd heard something. Or wanted to.

Mavis's heartbeat fluttered in her throat.

Renee didn't share Mavis's pear-hourglass figure. She had only the slightest curve where hips should be. Childbearing wasn't going to ruin Renee Marshall, and as far as Mavis could tell, she'd require no exorbitant devotion to keep trim. Which is why Mavis couldn't stop glancing at the woman's hands. Face-to-face, Renee was more slight than she'd appeared on her profile. Her knuckles and joints, in particular, were knobs, absurd baubles between frail lines.

"Yes, that's his car." Rebekah lowered herself into an armchair. "It doesn't mean anything."

"I'm sorry?" Mavis asked. She was starting to feel the scratchy cloudiness caused by the drugs in her system. She sat up straighter. Willed her mind to clear, at least enough to maintain her cover.

"That doesn't mean he didn't leave," Rebekah continued. "Obviously."

Mavis's attention pulled back to Renee, still looking toward the hall.

"He's left his car before, at his office or a parking lot." Rebekah drained half a bottle of water and then panted, dropped her head back like she needed to expand her airway.

"Are you sure you're okay?" Mavis asked.

"Yep." The woman smacked her lips and caught her breath before continuing. "Renee was terrified. She thought he'd been kidnapped. I told her he's not important enough to ransom. He was just with some woman. Again."

"How did she find out?" Mavis asked Rebekah, but Renee spoke at last.

"I went to surprise him for lunch." Her eyes fixed on the hallway, a tear slid down her cheek as though she was beginning to realize she could not manifest her husband's presence.

Mavis felt herself relax. She stopped fighting the repetitive tic she felt in her brow. Her head could swivel 360 degrees on her shoulders and Renee Marshall would be none the wiser.

"He hadn't known to wait," the widow continued. "He'd just gone to lunch."

"He lied, Renee," Rebekah insisted. "You know that because he isn't subtle. He doesn't care if you know."

If she saw her sister's tears, Rebekah Sheryl didn't soften. She didn't give in. They must have been through this before, and she must have decided it was better to let her sister cry than to watch her retreat back into delusion.

"But he was home when you fell asleep last night?" Mavis asked. How had Renee survived the home invasion that no doubt preceded Cyrus's stoning? Jerrod almost hadn't.

"I was with Rebekah." Renee's face crumpled. She didn't turn her head, but she gave up on the hallway at last, closing her eyes as she wept. "We thought the baby was coming."

A sheet of tears washed down Renee's face. She couldn't know how like her husband she looked, except that her sheet did not discolor. It didn't surge through wounds, reflecting a galloping pulse.

"Braxton Hicks," Renee's sister said through a wince. "Again. By the time this child finally drops, I'm gonna hate his guts."

Even slightly off-kilter from the meds, Mavis nearly chastised Rebekah as a reflex. She heard Marie Carson in her head and Mavis almost told the stranger that a child is a blessing. It was a refrain she'd heard a number of times, always as a stop sign when a young mother expressed exhaustion or annoyance or regret.

Thankfully, right this minute, Mavis was not her mother's daughter. As far as the Sheryl sisters knew, she was a private investigator charged with proving Cyrus Marshall a philanderer.

As far as Mavis was concerned, she was a woman trying to solve her own haunting. She had no use for propriety. Etiquette. She wasn't here to save Rebekah Sheryl's soul; she was here to save herself.

"When I got home this morning, the bed wasn't made," Renee recalled without looking at Mavis.

"Not that Cyrus does housework," Rebekah mumbled.

The bed. At its mention, Mavis felt herself rock like a buoy on the water. Felt what she hadn't realized were the intruders turning her body one way and then the other while they wrapped her in her own bedding.

"Was it just unmade?" she asked.

When both sisters paused, Mavis replayed the question in her head, listened to the conversation's progression from their perspective, without the memory of her own home invasion in between.

It sounded like nonsense.

"What do you mean?" Rebekah asked as though to confirm Mavis's concern.

Mavis straightened. She tightened her posture, lifted her chin as though to communicate that this line of questioning, though confusing to the layperson, was pertinent to her investigation of Cyrus's conduct. The sisters didn't have to understand; she just had to be convincing.

"You said the bed wasn't made," she said to Renee. "But everything was there? The fitted sheet, top sheet, comforter?"

The widow's brow curled.

"I guess so . . ."

"But you're not sure," Mavis said gently. "Can we check?"

"What would that matter?" Rebekah demanded, her misplaced

agitation evident in the force she applied to her pregnant belly, eyes closed.

"You wanted ironclad proof," Mavis replied. "If there's linen or a comforter missing and it's at Cyrus's love nest—"

Renee burst out of her seat. Mavis jumped, her palms and a knee leaping up to shield herself, but Renee rushed in the opposite direction. Away from Mavis, and out of the room.

"Renee!" Rebekah called after her sister, and then struggled to escape her own seat.

In the kitchen, Renee stood facing a window. Rosebushes bloomed in the yard, and at the sight, Mavis staggered, her hand still at Rebekah Sheryl's back in assistance.

The bushes were only a few yards away, Cyrus planted between them. He was the dark orb visible between their canes.

Mavis heard a choked gurgle escape her gaping mouth.

Renee was looking directly where his misshapen and broken head sprouted from the ground. Like she knew he was there. Like she was revisiting the scene, excited by the possibility that Mavis knew.

That's what Mavis thought until Rebekah grabbed her sister's shoulder and spun the woman around.

Renee's eyes were shut, sealed with a hot seam of tears. She hadn't been looking. She was holding her phone to her ear with one hand and covering it with the other like she didn't want it taken away. Like her sister had discouraged her from calling. After Cyrus hadn't answered her first dozen calls, perhaps Rebekah Sheryl had demanded her sister show some restraint. Perform some dignity.

The way Renee was protecting the phone from being snatched

away—the way the phone had been left in the other room—Mavis could tell the sisters were nothing alike. Rebekah couldn't understand. She didn't know what it was like, loving someone like Cyrus. Loving anyone who eroded her self-esteem. Overrode her self-preservation.

"Please," Renee prayed into the phone while the other two women looked on. Whatever dignity her sister had charged her to reclaim, she was giving it up. "Baby, I just want to know you're okay. I don't care who you're with." She was rushing, speed-talking in case Rebekah wrestled the phone from her. "Please, Cyrus. I'm so afraid something's wrong."

Her mouth hung open after the words ran out. No one took the phone away. Renee ran out of adrenaline and her hand fell. The phone dangled until her sister took the device gently and ended the call.

Mavis could see him. Through the kitchen window, she could see Cyrus at the base of the rosebushes, but she couldn't have identified him. If she didn't already know a human body was buried neck-deep, she wouldn't have given the dark silhouette a second glance. It could've been anything.

A ball lost to the neighbors on the other side of the fence.

A fallen hive, too heavy with honeycomb for the tree the bees had chosen.

Mavis wouldn't have been able to tell that the blanket she was certain was missing from the couple's bed was cinching Cyrus tight. That it had been used to carry him down the staircase and into his own backyard.

The pain in her head was sharp and familiar. Any minute, her nose might bleed.

She released a breath, long and low. A taloned thought swiped at her brain and she breathed again. Stayed calm while a tremor shuddered down the length of her neck.

For once the talons were salvation. She would've said too much, lubricated by Jerrod's pain medication.

No more questions.

Renee was no mastermind. She was looking for her husband, praying he'd return. It meant she'd make a report. As soon as she'd waited the required number of frantic hours, Renee Marshall would defy her sister and start the search in earnest. Mavis couldn't afford to be any more memorable than she already was.

Cyrus was a monster. Mavis knew that as well as anyone. Now she knew that his wife wasn't to blame for the haunting Mavis was suffering—but that didn't mean he hadn't been. He had a wandering eye, and a designated den in which to satisfy it. He'd committed himself and a significant portion of his livelihood to his transgressions. Whatever curse had befallen Cyrus Marshall was well deserved; Mavis had just happened to get herself entangled.

She felt the talons recede. Her mind was clear.

It had been horrible. Terrifying. But it was done. Cyrus's debt was paid. He was buried steps away from where his wife stood. At least Mavis could do her some good. She wasn't to blame for the deep hopelessness draped across Renee Marshall's shoulders. Not really. She wasn't Cyrus's accomplice or Renee's abuser. She'd *been* Renee. She'd been a beach the tide had fled. It'd dragged pieces of her out to sea, but she'd survived it. Renee could, too. The worst days of Renee's life were over, she just didn't know it yet. Mavis could show her. Mavis could make it so that when Renee finally found her husband, a busted gourd between the rosebushes, she'd know to be relieved.

At the mention of a love nest, the woman had fled because Renee Marshall subscribed to a familiar wisdom. Don't. She already knew what she refused to accept.

"Your sister's right about him," Mavis said. "Cyrus is a cheater."

She felt a prick of guilt, and shook her head as though to dislodge a talon. The sharpness next attacked her side, and Mavis filled her lungs. This wasn't about what she'd done to save herself; this was about saving Renee. Her mouth was filling with a bitter taste, but she swallowed the warm swell of it and spoke.

"You already know about Cyrus's property on the north side of town," she stated.

"We have a rental property." Renee's shoulders wilted, but she repeated the lie anyway. "We've had it for years. We have tenants."

"Is that true?" Rebekah asked Mavis.

"Not exactly. My client was there. Recently. With Cyrus." Mavis felt the pool re-accumulating on her tongue, and if she hadn't been in the Marshalls' pristine kitchen, this time she would've spat it out. "He keeps a wardrobe there. If anyone's renting it from you, it's an alias. It's him."

"But you don't know personally?" Rebekah anticipated her sister's defense.

"I went myself," Mavis told them, accepting the necessary risk of a partial truth so that they'd believe her. "He opened the door."

Renee sank into a stool at the kitchen island, a moan coming up through her chest, her arms falling around her sister's belly when Rebekah pulled her close.

"I'm sorry, Renee," Mavis whispered. "I truly am."

"I never accused him," Renee said, her voice weak and muffled by her sister's side even as she pleaded her case. "You can't just accuse someone of that. You can't trust your imagination more than the man you married."

"She told me that once, too."

Mavis hadn't meant to speak it aloud. She hadn't meant to tell the two women to whom she was a stranger that those were the words of Marie Carson. That her mother having dispensed the same wisdom to both women curdled Mavis's guts. It soured more at the thought that her mother knew Cyrus was a cheater by the time she repeated it to Renee Marshall.

Mavis was grimacing. She didn't feel it until the silence grew heavy. Until she realized both sisters were staring at her, their faces variations of confusion. It was the start of suspicion, and at first Mavis couldn't think what to say. She felt herself edging toward panic and resisted.

They'd believe their suspicion was misdirected, that it was overflow from what rightfully belonged to Cyrus, as long as she didn't shy away now.

"I know that particular brand of premarital counseling," she said through a sigh.

Renee's head bobbed, her lips slightly parted as though she was still undecided. Maybe she was recognizing the traces of Marie Carson in her daughter's face the way Mavis had seen the sisters' small eyes and tall foreheads.

"Something tells me they didn't caution your husband the same way?"

Rebekah snorted, and her eyes cut away. The tension broke.

"If you had the kind of counseling Renee and Cyrus had, then you already know they didn't," Rebekah said, punctuating the statement with a second snort.

"I would never be unfaithful to Cyrus," Renee interjected. She was depleted again, so spent she rocked despite that she was sitting down. "He knows that. Everyone does."

Everyone probably included Daniel and Marie Carson. Bill

and Rose Spencer. Any number of other people who'd known Mavis when she was hopelessly devoted to the man who hadn't received any cautions on her behalf either.

"Maybe you should've been." Rebekah's eyes darted as soon as the woman realized she'd said it aloud. One day soon she'd blame it on pregnancy brain, if need be, but she didn't take it back.

"What?" Two tears leapt free and pelted Renee's lap. "Maybe I should've been what?"

Rebekah wasn't willing to say the words again.

"Maybe you should've been unfaithful," Mavis answered in her place, and then she softened. "It isn't just about lust," Mavis reassured her. She stepped into Renee, touched her for the first time. Rubbed the length of the woman's forearm. "Sometimes repaying betrayal with betrayal is self-preservation. It's armor. We deserve some, too."

"You can't protect yourself with sin . . ." Renee's brow ribboned.

The frail woman didn't know better, but Mavis did. Mavis could feel the wooden staff of the shovel in her hand. She could feel the rough grain against her palm, smell the coppery fragrance and the almost earthy scent of human intestines when she gored them out of the man's abdomen.

"No one else is going to protect you," she said, her voice too calm to give away that, in her mind, she was somewhere else entirely. "You said everyone knows you, Renee. They know Cyrus, too. They've known all along."

Mavis squeezed the woman's arm to bring herself back to the present, to the Marshalls' kitchen. She relinquished the visceral memory of carving a man, of hollowing him. He was dead. She'd defended herself. She was trying to teach Renee how. To transmit the grievance she'd voiced to her mother years ago but still hadn't made conviction until now. Her skin was warming at the back of her neck, pain coagulating into anger over the one offense that could've been so easily avoided.

"You're terrified. Abandoned. And none of them are here, Renee." Mavis tightened and relaxed her hold on the woman's arm as though to give Renee a new pulse. To resuscitate her. Rebekah Sheryl stood by, stalemated between her protectiveness over her sister and the fact that she agreed with Mavis. "Everyone who stood up at your wedding and vowed to love and support the two of you? Where are they when you're hurting? Why haven't they intervened? What was the ritual for?"

The sisters answered her with silence for the second time.

"You've been through this yourself," Rebekah said. "I knew it as soon as you showed up. It's why you're doing this."

Mavis tensed—but Rebekah meant private investigation.

"You had a congregation vow?" Renee asked, a nostalgic expression spreading across her face, nudging her distress aside.

"Didn't you?" Mavis asked, some of her bluster leaking out when the sisters shook their heads.

A small talon of fear sank deep.

She retreated, releasing Renee's arm and taking an uneven step back. Then another. She moved backward through her memory, too, to the day Jerrod had given in to his mother's wishes. To the altar where Mavis stood with him, after exchanging their vows but before sealing it with a kiss. Back to Bill and Rose Spencer standing, along with a company of others, while the minister outlined their duty.

Did they promise to protect?

Did they promise to uphold?

Did they promise to help safeguard the promise Jerrod and Mavis made, one to the other?

Did they, the gathered congregation, promise to snatch back the one who wandered from the truth and so save their soul?

Mavis went back to the moment when, as one chorus, their mouths had fallen open and they'd made a vow.

A curse.

We do.

If Mavis's face went ashen, neither of the sisters let on.

"Congregation vows," Rebekah said, and dug a fist into her side as though to dislodge her unborn child from a vital organ. "I didn't know people did that anymore."

XIV

As a child, Mavis took dozens of vows. They weren't all the imaginary kind she whispered to a phantom groom when she strode down the middle aisle after church service. The daughter of faith community pillars who moonlighted as marriage counselors, Mavis attended weddings on a very regular basis, and between the ages of eight and eighteen, she participated in several dozen.

She was most requested during primary school, and couldn't recall the number of times she'd been one of three young girls to light a trio of candles. Often, she'd garnished the aisle with fragrant rose petals, paying such close attention to the instructed tempo that she accidentally mouthed the metronome to keep from walking too fast. On another occasion, she'd worn a crown of baby's breath and ribbon to recite a scripture, and on another, she'd worn her first square heel to perform a solo despite having never sung in public. Mavis had tearfully begged her parents not to make her do it, Daniel and Marie Carson very nearly declining their daughter's involvement that time—but not because she'd been terrified. Twelve years old was a fraught time in a young girl's life, full of temptations and pitfalls. It was the season during which the telltale signs of promiscuity would likely surface, and the couple were appropriately hesitant. In the end, they'd relented. It'd meant so much to the bride, to have the Carsons's daughter take part, to honor Daniel and Marie in some small way. It was the same reason Mavis had been requested every time, and the same reason her involvement was promised long before she knew another fitting was on the horizon.

Mavis's reward was not just the painful constipation that started in earnest at the rehearsal and lasted hours after the ceremony was done. The girl known for wistfully performing her bridal entrance over and over also received a pageant-worthy wardrobe. That made it worthwhile. At home, once the gut-seizing anxiety subsided, the obligation fulfilled, she was free to choreograph her own elaborate first dance in a plethora of beautiful gowns. She had tulle in soft pink, cerulean, and honey gold. She had two ankle-length dresses with crinoline underneath, one in lavender, the other in ivory. One dress she'd loved so much it'd sent a flutter through her chest—until the big day came and she actually wore the sky-blue satin. It was sleeveless, the fabric hugging her sides so that she didn't feel the saucers of perspiration accumulating as she stood onstage. Church mothers had chuckled soon enough, one motioning to young Mavis that she should fan her underarms. It was an action captured by the photographer, and chastised by Marie Carson, who spoke her daughter's name from the congregation loud enough to stop her.

Every wedding had involved a congregation vow.

At every wedding, Mavis had answered, "We do." She'd promised her watchful eye and her ready counsel with the same conviction as the adults around her, even when she was eight years old. And despite that, more than once, she'd never seen the newlyweds again.

Mavis hadn't thought much of it. The vow was something

performed and fulfilled, it seemed, in the professing. It was a promise kept simply by being made.

It was a well-wishing. An expression of approval. A kind of permission to complete the couple's vow.

Until Antonia and Quincy Bryant's divorce.

Confusion came first, for Mavis, long before scrutiny. When she was thirteen years old, Antonia came back to visit, and the sanctuary—or at least the first several rows of seats unofficially claimed by the Carsons, the Spencers, and other mainstays—erupted in joyous reunion. Antonia could hardly answer one greeting before another cheerful interruption.

She had been missed.

The family was incomplete without hers.

Where was her darling husband?

Antonia had drawn in a breath then, tightened her smile to keep it from falling. When she began nibbling her lip, Mavis unintentionally mimicked her.

Mavis thought the woman briefly entertained a lie. An easily misinterpreted vaguery, at least.

In the wait, the uproar quieted. Silence expanded, slowly pooling in the space where Antonia's answer should be.

"Quincy and I separated," the woman confessed at last. "We're getting a divorce."

The hands that had cupped her arms and elbows and rested against her back, that had squeezed intermittently to draw Antonia's attention or communicate enthusiasm, went still. Some went slack. One withdrew.

Antonia's eyes were welling, and Mavis heard someone's sympathetic moan. She saw, too, the glances, pairs of eyes turning toward her mother and resting there or falling to the wood laminate floor.

"We'll talk," Marie Carson had assured both Antonia and the congregation. "Come to lunch after service. We'll talk."

Weak smiles returned, none more fragile than Antonia's.

She wasn't looking forward to it. Mavis knew immediately. When they sat at the Carson dining table, Mavis also knew that Antonia did not want to discuss her divorce in front of the young girl. They'd prepared lunch together—Marie Carson, Rose Spencer, Antonia, Mavis, and several other women moving about the kitchen in confusingly irrelevant conversation. If anyone acknowledged or shared Antonia's tension, it was only Mavis. Everyone else seemed perfectly at ease postponing the difficult topic over which the lunch had been planned, and it reminded Mavis of how often her parents seemed to intentionally prolong her discomfort by postponing an inevitable punishment.

At the dining table, Antonia Bryant and the other women took small bites. No one wanted their mouths full when the interstitial bit of theater concluded, and Marie Carson began the real discussion.

"I'm so very disappointed," Mavis's mother said in the middle of someone else's trifling anecdote. The intrusion was to great effect, somehow catching the group off guard despite that they'd been bound in anticipation. "I never expected this from you and Quincy."

"You don't know what's happened, Marie," Antonia said bravely.

"I don't need to know what either of you did to know what you didn't do." Marie silenced the woman. "You came into the sanctuary for the first time since the two of you moved away, and it was also the first time any of us heard a word about trouble. When you'd already failed."

Rose Spencer took a deep breath, as though relieved to have someone speak words so true.

"That's not right," Marie concluded. "You know it isn't."

"Marie, I'm living the most painful experience of my life and it feels like you're upset because I didn't include you sooner."

"How dare you." The room was stripped of sound. The women drew in their breaths as though for safekeeping. "This isn't a henhouse, Antonia. We're not angry over late gossip."

"With all due respect, what right do you have to be angry at all?"

Marie Carson and Antonia Bryant were locked in each other's gaze.

"I'm having to rewrite the entirety of my life story. Every plan, and hope, and . . ." The woman trailed off.

"And all because you didn't take your vow seriously enough to ask for help," Marie replied. "We're a family—"

"Then why didn't you know we needed it?"

Mavis's mouth fell open. Inside her chest, a frantic race echoed the whirlwind in her head.

"How seriously did any of you take *your* vow?" Antonia was heaving. Her nervous system was in a state of emergency. Her hands rattled against the table before she hid them underneath, but her breath came in gusts, and her shoulders jerked uncontrollably. "We moved less than an hour away, Marie, and that was far enough to be out of sight, out of mind. *That's* not right. And you know it."

Mavis couldn't make sense of it—someone having a response for her mother. A retort. An accusation in return. Antonia Bryant had seemed as reverent and docile as anyone else; there was nothing in Mavis's memory of the young woman to explain this behavior.

Perhaps something had happened in the years between, an hour away. Something terrible but fortifying. Fortifying perhaps *because* it had happened an hour away from Marie Carson.

The thought might have radicalized young Mavis were it not interrupted. Before she could inspect it fully, one of the other church mothers beside her began to cry. It erupted out of the woman like spontaneous worship. She shook her head and tears sprang free, raining across her neighbors' colorful salad.

If Mavis hadn't known better, the outburst might have seemed outrageous. A grown woman bursting into tears over someone else's disagreement might have seemed like a ridiculous spectacle, but Mavis knew it couldn't be when the crying woman began to explain why she was so overcome.

It was the disrespect. The crying woman couldn't abide seeing Marie Carson so mistreated, not after everything the matriarch had done, everything she'd given.

"I don't mean any disrespect," Antonia answered when it seemed clear no one wanted her to. "Your guidance meant everything to me, Marie. When Quincy and I announced our engagement and during our counseling, and even the day we got married, I felt so full. It was hard to accept that you weren't going to do any of the things you'd promised." A shock snapped across Mavis's skin, but Antonia persisted. "You were never going to be there. No one was."

Rose Spencer clucked before pursing her lips.

"You wanted someone else to fulfill your vow," Rose said.

Disappointment had eroded into grave disgust over the course of one brief conversation, and Mavis felt her confusion resurface.

"No," Antonia said. "I didn't expect anyone to fulfill my part. I wanted someone to fulfill theirs. But I got over that. I wouldn't have come to visit if I hadn't."

The crying woman left the table, attended by one, and then trailed by another.

Mavis couldn't follow. She couldn't move except to look between Antonia and her mother as their audience dispersed, an uncomfortable static crackling between her ears.

They'd done it again.

They'd done what they'd just denied.

Rose Spencer and the others had abandoned Antonia, and now they were congregating in a whispering cluster one room over.

Mavis's mother drank in a deep breath with unflappable calm.

"Better to live on the corner of a roof," she said, "than share a house with a quarrelsome wife."

Antonia flinched, a tear waiting a moment before streaking her face, like blood hesitant to flow from a new wound.

Marie Carson did not seem at all concerned by the fact that her daughter had heard her. It was all the confirmation Mavis needed. By thirteen, she knew how to spot sinner and saint. She knew how atrocious guilt and unholiness felt, and she knew the way it made her act. How weak, sometimes pitiful and sometimes petulant.

Her mother's conviction didn't waver.

Without a word or a glance in Antonia's direction, Mavis left the table and joined the women in the other room.

She'd never upheld a congregation vow. That's why when she left Renee Marshall unaware of her husband's head growing in the garden, Mavis intended to finally see her parents. They'd returned from their sabbatical after news of Rose and Bill Spencer's tragic accident. She hadn't reached out when she saw their social media update, and they hadn't either—but now Mavis had no choice.

She'd taken part in the vows for most of her life, and she didn't believe she'd ever enforced one. She'd never hurt anyone, not even in a fugue state. There hadn't been any home invasions, no violent attacks visited on the couples she'd witnessed. She'd never heard about a haunting like hers at all, and why should she have?

The vow wasn't to kill.

It was to protect. To uphold. To safeguard. To snatch back.

There was no instruction to harm. No call to violence or vengeance. It took a ruthless interpretation to account for what was happening to her.

None of those other marriages had been without blemish. It wasn't possible that everyone had gotten it right but her. Antonia Bryant was proof of that, and proof that the congregation vow was meaningless. No one did their part—until Mavis and Jerrod.

"But." A whisper escaped her barely parted lips.

But maybe that wasn't what was happening at all. Maybe there was no divinely orchestrated retribution.

Maybe there was some other explanation for the last four days of Mavis's life.

She hadn't tried to identify the man at the hardware store. Even after talking to Dr. Moore, Mavis had avoided any news about the tragedy. Maybe this was why.

If she couldn't place that man at her wedding, this couldn't be her fault.

And she couldn't. She hadn't recognized him.

Mavis tightened numb fingers around the steering wheel. She was parked on an unfamiliar side street between the Marshall home and her parents'. Everything was strangely quiet, the silence pulsing like her heartbeat. There was one thought in her head, and it was too devastating to be interrupted.

She couldn't place him because she hadn't *tried*.

Mavis retrieved her phone, and then froze. She lowered it onto her lap, and then brought it level again. She moaned as though wounded and began to type. She searched the date of the hardware store attack and the location, and it spat out a face. She still didn't recognize him.

Her eyes traced the name.

Glen Reynolds.

Mavis shook her head.

This wasn't fair.

For four days people had been trying to kill her, and somehow the onus was on her not just to survive but to investigate their evil. To search for a way to blame herself for their behavior. It was the story of her life.

Glen Reynolds.

Glen.

"Glen and I wish you . . ."

Mavis yelped, short and sharp, her eyes squeezed shut while she forcefully shook her head.

It wasn't fair.

"Glen and I wish you the sweetest bliss on your union."

She screamed now, this time full and piercing. It vibrated against her windshield and windows, frantic to escape the small space. It was seeping out, she was sure. A muted version of it must be traveling through the neighborhood, infiltrating strange houses, the inhabitants pausing to place the sound.

There'd been a message in one of the guest books, it didn't matter from whom. Someone named Glen had been their plus one. She'd written his name in a thank-you card.

Three times.

It'd been late in the hours-long process of fulfilling her mother's assignment, and on the first try she'd made a mistake on the cursive loop of the letter g.

After that, she'd realized her spelling mistake too late. It was Glen with one n.

Three tries to perfect a four-letter word.

Mavis didn't have the energy to pretend it was someone else.

Glen Reynolds had been at the wedding. His behavior at the hardware store was the proof.

There were no talons more piercing or painful. There was no scenario worse than this one. She hadn't wanted the vow. Something Mavis hadn't wanted had been imposed on her, and it was going to get her killed. A ceremonial promise twisted by wicked interpretation had taken on meaning this time, and Mavis didn't know why.

Her parents would.

Mavis couldn't help that she believed it. She always had. Her parents were the last word in so many people's lives, it was impossible that they wouldn't know better than their own daughter. No matter how it felt to be bare, to be raw before them—sometimes against her will—it was a blessed place into which many would've traded.

Mavis started the car and pulled away from the curb. She swallowed, tried to lubricate her tender throat.

Daniel and Marie Carson were right because they always were; she was wrong because she was Mavis.

It was time to submit. She could live with that if they could tell her how to make this stop.

"I'll tell them everything," she spoke aloud to herself, turning the wheel deliberately, hand over hand. There was no one behind her, no fellow motorist to rush her when a handful of blocks from her childhood home, Mavis reduced her speed. Now she crept around the last corner, promising herself, instructing herself, demanding from herself what must be done. What she would do. "I'll tell them everything, and it will hurt. And they'll despise me. But it will end."

The car whined as she eased to a stop. The brakes were fine; Mavis could only assume they sensed and echoed her reluctance.

Mavis always parked on the street. It gave her a last reprieve before facing home, not being able to see much from the driver's seat but the ground-level retaining wall of the Carsons' sloping gardens. She would have to ascend the steep hillside that had been carved into four flights of zigzagging steps, each tier of their bordering gardens accented with a few orange alabaster tiles, into which the sunlight sank and from which it radiated beautifully. The orange was stunning against the deeper bricks of brown and burnt sienna, the placements painstakingly arranged because alabaster was too soft to use too often.

The gabled house—which Mavis could not see from her car and never looked toward while she climbed—was perched high above. It was a remarkable feat, the way the home at first looked inviting and by its elegant landscape proved otherwise. Visibility was no promise of accessibility.

When Mavis got out of the car, she looked across the street instead of toward home. Directly opposite, there was another hill turned steep staircase, and on the plateau positioned at the halfway point, Mrs. Frederick had created a charming terrace of bright white stone. She'd redesigned her outdoor spaces after the first of many trips to the Mediterranean when Mavis was a teenager, after which the woman had spent many an afternoon in one of the white loungers, shaded by a trio of brightly colored kites and surrounded by potted Italian cypress.

"Is that little Mavis?" Mrs. Frederick called. She waved a hand high above her head, which only made maneuvering out of the lounger more difficult.

Mavis took a worried step in Mrs. Frederick's direction. The woman had fallen last year, tripping over uneven sidewalk and badly bruising her jaw and wrist. Now, she was descending the second half of her long set of steps, one hand sliding down the rail she'd since installed. She glanced up at Mavis at odd intervals.

"Oh, it's been so long! Where's that handsome husband of yours?"

"Hi Mrs. Frederick," Mavis called back as she started across the street. "It's okay, I'll come to you."

"Child, I'm already on my way."

Mrs. Frederick's last word was strangely clipped.

She stopped. Her knee was bent, her foot hovering, but the older woman didn't finish her step.

She was staring at Mavis, her grip still tight on the railing. And then it loosened.

Her affably animated smile froze into an off-putting grimace and then fell.

"Mrs. Frederick?" Mavis called to her, but she didn't advance any farther.

The woman's foot met the step.

She released the rail.

Came down another step.

"Ma'am . . ."

Mavis wanted to turn and look behind her. She wanted to

confirm her parents' home was there now. That it loomed close. She didn't dare.

Mrs. Frederick's body moved differently. There was no hint of hesitance or clumsiness. Whatever faculties had begun eroding the year before, something had gifted them back to her. Her posture erect, she seemed elongated. She looked the way she had when Mavis was in junior high, and the woman still taught dance. Supple, lean muscle, and fluid motion.

It wasn't right anymore.

Mavis had gotten as far as Mrs. Frederick's curb, and now she set one foot behind her.

The older woman stopped.

"It's me. It's Mavis."

Mrs. Frederick dropped her chin. Her gaze locked.

"I came to see my parents," Mavis spoke through a shiver. She buried one hand in the pocket where she kept the key fob, clicking the right button twice to remotely start the car's engine. "Are they home?"

Nothing registered. There were no alterations to Mrs. Frederick's demeanor. She couldn't hear Mavis; no amount of appealing to their long history or mention of her parents' recent sabbatical to the woman's favorite corner of the world was going to bring her back to herself.

Mrs. Frederick reached the sidewalk.

"Please." Mavis's voice quivered. "Don't."

This wasn't a hardware store, or a tool-equipped garage. They weren't motorists wielding cars like weapons. If she attacked, Mavis could defend herself, whether Mrs. Frederick's posture had improved or not. She just didn't want to.

She opened her mouth to say so, the words catching when Mrs. Frederick reached out and laid a hand on her mailbox.

She finally broke eye contact with Mavis to turn and look at the black cast aluminum and its accompanying pillar and decorative metal scrolls. The woman bent at the waist, ran her hand down the length of it, her fingertips tracing the outline where it met the concrete.

"Mrs. Frederick . . ."

The woman stood and turned to her right. Began moving away from Mavis.

Perhaps this was something else.

"Mrs. Frederick? Are you all right?" Mavis didn't follow the woman, but she didn't make a getaway. She wasn't under attack. The woman wasn't threatening her—in fact she'd moved farther away. This was an altered state, without question, but perhaps the woman needed help.

Mrs. Frederick was standing beside her neighbor's mailbox, this one a simple black container on a wooden post staked into the lawn. Again, Mrs. Frederick ran her hand down the length of it, Mavis wincing at the possibility of splinters. She took a step in the woman's direction, and Mrs. Frederick stood upright.

The mailbox and its wooden post effortlessly unstaked, the woman held it in one hand.

"No, ma'am." Mavis's shoulders sank.

When Mrs. Frederick's limbs moved even slightly, Mavis ran. She doubled back toward her car, ripping the driver's door open and closing herself inside. The doors locked when she put the car in gear, and Mavis tore away from the curb.

She didn't look back. She didn't check to see how the newly agile body of the older woman bounded after her, or whether or not the rush of wind she felt had been the mailbox narrowly missing the back of her head. There were no grunts or growls, as when a monster bears down on its prey.

Mavis didn't hear anything until the wooden post crashed through her rear windshield. She swerved, her tires squealing against the asphalt as they marked a serpentine across both lanes, but she didn't scream. Glass shards pelted seatbacks, sprayed her shoulders, and embedded in her hair.

Mavis accelerated. She tore out of her parents' neighborhood, someone's mailbox protruding from her rear window like a javelin, expertly launched.

XV

Mavis was alone. She'd pulled behind a grocery store and struggled with the mailbox until the rear windshield buckled noisily and finally released. She'd been sweating by then, a humid musk trapped between her sweater and her skin, the band of her bra damp and irritating as she jogged to a pair of commercial dumpsters. They were padlocked, but one was too engorged with bulky garbage for the lid to close completely. After a fruitless attempt to discard the thing whole, Mavis glanced around before beating the mailbox against the concrete slab stretching from beneath the containers. The head broke free and she easily sank it into the gaping lid, tossing the wooden post between the dumpsters before rushing back to the safety of Jerrod's car.

Now she was hiding, scrunched down in the driver's seat with her shoulders by her ears and her knees pinned against the steering wheel. She'd backed as close to the grocery store's rear wall as she could, rendering the hole in the rear window inaccessible to anyone who didn't climb on the hood of the vehicle first. A bank of delivery bays sat beside her, each secured with a closed roll-up door except the one where an unmanned delivery truck was parked. Mavis had tucked herself on the eighteen-wheeler's far side in the hopes that no one else would venture this far.

She hadn't wanted to stop. She wanted to speed back to the hospital, get Jerrod, and escape. The congregation vow was the cause of all this, and it could only be dangerous where the congregation might find her. Outside the town where they'd been married, she could rest. Think. Plan. She'd only stopped because she couldn't do any of that with a mailbox protruding out of her back window, unless she wanted to be pulled over. There would be no explanation but the incredulous truth, and it would send even a curious skeptic to Mrs. Frederick's house asking questions the old woman wouldn't know how to answer.

Havilah Greene didn't recall or believe that she'd been digging in the Dwyers' backyard.

The hardware store assailant had refused to accept he'd been the perpetrator.

The intruder Mavis blinded had been afraid and confused, forgetting her own violent intentions.

By now, Mrs. Frederick would have forgotten her impressive javelin throw.

When the stupor subsided, they had no idea what they'd done. They could attack and maim—they could kill—and they would return to themselves, their conscience clear. Even if their lives were ruined.

Now Mavis was huddled in her hidden car because her parents would have descended on her, given the chance. As soon as the vow had taken hold, they would have overpowered her. Childhood relics would've become implements of destruction in their hands, and nothing would have stopped them but Mavis returning evil for evil. If they failed, it would've been because she'd hurt them first. If her parents had succeeded, the carnage would have been waiting for them when they came to.

Mavis covered her ears, a distressed hum radiating from her throat as though to cover the almost audible raking of talons.

She would never have come back down the hillside steps. Her parents wouldn't have taken her confession; they would've taken her life.

Buckled further in her seat, the damp cotton of her sweater rough against her skin, Mavis couldn't decide how her mother would respond to finding her daughter's mangled body at her feet—but no parent deserved that test of faith. No one could be expected to survive it, no matter what they were like. Not even Daniel and Marie Carson.

Mavis jumped when the car became an echo chamber. Panic coursed through her until she recognized the sound. Her phone must've paired with Jerrod's CarPlay, a generic ringtone bleating loudly all around her.

It wasn't Jerrod. He had an assigned tone; a romantic few measures of harp music to let Mavis know it was her husband.

It might be the hospital, a nurse calling to tell her that Jerrod was asking for her.

Or that he had suffered some unexpected malady.

A blood clot.

A ruptured aneurysm.

In the bright moonlight cascading through her still-intact Palladian window, Mavis saw the intruder standing over a crumpled Jerrod all over again. The man repeatedly stomped and kicked her husband before Mavis had the presence of mind to core his abdomen. But maybe he'd been hit more times than she'd realized, sustained more damage than the medical staff could tell.

The hospital was calling to say that what had killed Jerrod

had been slow. Too slow to be observed. Slow enough to let him wake, and hunger, and ask his wife if she'd known the man she'd killed. Slow enough to let Mavis believe she'd saved his life, and then to be distracted. By a video. By a stoning. And then by Renee Marshall.

The hospital was going to say that, in his last hours, Jerrod had been alone. That when he'd passed, Jerrod's wife hadn't been there.

Soon, everyone would know.

The rhythmic thud of the ringtone finally punched through Mavis's taloned thoughts, and she stabbed a button on the steering wheel with a shaky finger.

"Mavis, I raised you better."

She glanced at the central display. "Mom?"

Marie Carson.

Mavis sat up straight.

They'd seen her parked in front of their home. They'd seen her leave without coming up.

But then they must have seen Mrs. Frederick, too. They must have seen their neighbor's remarkable feat of strength, and their daughter flee in fear for her life.

"Please do not interrupt me. If the both of you can show such respect to *his* parents, you can spare a modicum for me." Mavis's mother paused as though to test her daughter's obedience.

Mavis didn't speak. There had been no salutation because this was not going to be a conversation. Whatever this was about, it had nothing to do with the attack she'd just survived.

"The Dwyers are petty people," Marie Carson declared, as though for the first or final time. "They begrudge your father's and my accomplishments. I'd know that without the gift of discerning, so it's galling that you pretend not to see it."

Jerrod was fine. A tickle danced along Mavis's skin. Her shoulders relaxed.

"If you had children, you'd know that the easiest thing a parent can be is available. It's remarkably simple when you've got nothing going on, no one else dependent on you. Where else would you possibly be?"

It was strange. Mavis knew exactly how she was meant to feel, how she usually felt when blindsided by her mother's disapproval. She knew precisely when guilt was meant to spawn. Where frenzy should take hold. Whenever her mother spoke accusingly, not specifying an accusation, Mavis's mind frayed. She raced between recent memories—jostled and disjointed as soon as she tried to study them—to identify her fault. If she knew what upset Marie Carson, she'd know how best to demonstrate that she'd made amends. She could convey to her mother that repentance had taken place, that wisdom had already been acquired.

Today Mavis felt none of the normal responses. Despite that this ambush was the conclusion of a particularly long dry spell, it didn't shake her to shattering. Mavis hadn't seen or heard from her parents for weeks prior to the accident at Ross and 15th; she should be a wreck. But she already was.

There was no more space for alarm. She'd reached the canopy of her fear.

Mavis's breath came steady.

She made an acknowledging sound to let her mother know she was still listening. It was automatic, the timing based on a lifetime of experience. She found that she could likewise go through the emotions, assigning a placeholder where things like guilt and shame should be. When she did, the unwieldiness of the ongoing haunting dissipated; its frightful edges softened.

When Mavis responded to her mother the way she normally would, a calm settled over her.

She felt better.

Safe.

"The Dwyers don't have your father's and my calling or myriad obligations, that's why they've done their darndest to suggest that presence is as valuable as spiritual guidance. They'd have to believe that." Marie Carson was suppressing a scoff, and probably tossing her phantom hair. She'd cut it shoulder-length years before, but hadn't broken the long-haired habits and mannerisms.

Mavis's mother was incensed by truths she'd divined years ago. By now, Mavis knew the woman wasn't just upset about the Dwyers being present for Mavis and Jerrod; Marie Carson was upset at the insinuation that *she* should be.

Mavis fell against the headrest.

Jerrod wasn't okay. He was hurt and alone. She'd left the hospital without telling him why, and hadn't called or texted since. He'd called his parents—or else the hospital had—because Mavis should have. Hours ago. The home invasion didn't need hiding. News of it wouldn't lead to questions or accusations against her, or her marriage, and Jerrod deserved to have someone beside him. Even if it meant that someone would ask Mavis where she'd gone.

Jerrod had called his parents from the hospital, and then his mother had called hers.

"What's worse is you allowing Deborah Dwyer to tell us that there was a break-in last night, and that your husband is in the hospital."

Mavis's stomach cinched. When her intestines seemed to spontaneously knot, an earthy aroma wafted out of her memory.

The recently acquired knowledge of a human interior's coppery smell billowed from her imagination and decorated the car.

Marie Carson didn't mention that a man's bowels had sloshed out in front of her daughter, his blood slick and black in the dark study. She didn't say that he'd crashed through her child's picturesque window and landed on the pavers in the couple's backyard.

She would have, if she knew.

"I should've heard it from my daughter," she concluded. "Now. Is there anything else *you* want to tell me?"

Marie knew something else. If she was going to force Mavis to confess, it was only on the slight chance that her daughter would accidentally divulge more.

This was when Mavis's thoughts were meant to tornado. She was meant to tumble over herself, desperate to find a suitable offering. In her husband's car, where an outside breeze could still breach a rear window opening as she sat behind a grocery store, sheltered by an unattended rig, Mavis paused the appropriate number of moments.

She pretended to search. Let her mouth fall open so her mother could hear the hollow.

She already knew Jerrod had told his parents some sanitized version of how he'd gotten hurt. She knew what he *hadn't* said. The only other thing the Dwyers knew was the only thing the Carsons might take offense to.

Deborah would've told Marie about the last time she'd rushed to the children's side and found the Doctors Carson weren't there.

"I was in a car accident," Mavis said, after which her mother made a condemnatory sound. Clearly, she already knew. "It wasn't long ago. I'm sorry I didn't tell you sooner, Mom. I didn't think it was serious enough to ruin your sabbatical."

"I accept your apology," Marie Carson was saying through a weighty sigh. "And we appreciate that. I just hope Jerrod informed his mother why you didn't disrupt our sorely needed leave."

"He would've," Mavis answered. "I certainly will."

Marie Carson had given the exact phrasing she wanted delivered and now sighed again, satisfied.

Mavis had promised to tell her parents everything; she couldn't imagine it now. It'd been a fear response, and now that the woman was on the phone, Mavis feeling less at her mother's mercy than she'd ever felt, it seemed ridiculous.

If Marie Carson had brutalized her only child while in a stupor, the woman would've forgotten both the act and the why. If Mavis confessed what she'd done—that she'd broken her wedding vow, and that she'd done so with Cyrus—her mother would remember it.

Always.

Often.

Even if this nightmare ended, another one would begin.

"Are you on your way now?" Mavis asked.

The question slipped out easily. It sounded eager, and it was meant to.

Mavis knew her parents weren't at the hospital. If they'd gone—hurried uncharacteristically to Jerrod's bedside as soon as they heard about the attack on their son-in-law—they'd know their daughter wasn't there. It would've been the second topic of this one-sided conversation. *In sickness* meant nothing if not *in hospitalization,* she would've been scolded.

The Doctors Carsons weren't coming. Despite her mother's

tantrum, one little hospital stay didn't rise to the level of priority when there was always so much work to be done. Whatever that may be.

Mavis sank deeper into the comfortable leather cocoon of the driver's seat, anticipating the excuse. Whatever the scenario, however troubling it should be in principle, knowing its outcome was proving to be the difference between chaos and peace.

"I'm sure by now you've heard of Bill's passing," Marie Carson said, taking on a mournful tone.

Mavis imagined chastising her mother for not informing her personally. Had she not been in the same accident that killed him—if she hadn't been the reason Bill Spencer drove headlong into her—she would have learned online. On the church page, shared by mutual friends she otherwise hadn't interacted with in years.

Sister Rose didn't remember seeing Mavis at the hospital the day her husband died, or Marie Carson would know about that, too. Her parents' complete lack of curiosity about the unpunishable details of Mavis's life meant that no one had put together that she and the Spencers had been in the same accident. The Doctors Carson had come home and fallen like a hedge of protection around the Spencer family, yet they'd offered *her* nothing.

Mavis's tongue felt warm in her mouth. A smile tickled her cheek. She would've delighted in clucking her tongue at Daniel and Marie for once, certainly, but Mavis sobered. Satisfied with the possibility, she reeled herself in before peace could make her reckless.

"I've been with Rose and the kids since your dad and I got home, helping with the funeral arrangements," her mother was saying. "They need us desperately right now."

Mavis made an appropriate hum.

"They'll need you, too, when we lay Bill to rest."

Mavis couldn't remember the names of Rose and Bill Spencer's adult children, all of whom had their own families and networks, and certainly did not seem to have need of her.

And it couldn't happen. The Spencer funeral would be a death sentence.

"Mom, my husband's in the hospital. I'm afraid we won't be able to attend."

Silence.

Mavis resisted speaking again, and, in a few moments, heard a familiar shuffle. She knew what had happened before she heard his voice.

"May, it's your father."

"Hi Daddy." Mavis's voice came out small and tinny. She felt her shoulders creep.

"I missed your condolences when Bill passed," he told her. "It's been a difficult loss for everyone, and it would have made all the difference to hear from you both. The Spencers were very generous to the both of you. As a man, I expect Jerrod to rally to pay his respects."

"To rally?" she asked.

"It'd be different if it'd been the other way around," Daniel Carson continued. There was almost a sport to the way her father could respond to Mavis while seeming to refuse to answer his daughter. He was an expert at expounding without acknowledging. "A young man like Jerrod can rebound from physical hurt when he needs to. If he wants to."

Mavis felt her calm melting off. The air that had seemed to circulate into the broken rear window stagnated. It stiffened.

"You don't even know how badly he was hurt," she chirped, a fiercely rapid heartbeat tightening her throat. "Neither of you have even asked."

Her parents hadn't asked about her either, but that hardly seemed worth mentioning. It would be self-centered. Attention-seeking. She was allowed to take offense on behalf of her husband.

"First the car accident, and now this attack. On our home!" Mavis involuntarily gasped. She shuddered, shoved back against the once comfortable seat. "You have no idea what we've been through lately!"

She could feel the panic amassing, the astonishment. She'd felt the same way when her parents blamed her for Cyrus not proposing. She'd felt the same icy claustrophobia before she'd exploded, demanded that they demonstrate the influence they claimed to wield. That they *do* something, that they help her for once. It was one of the single most humiliating memories of Mavis's life. She didn't want to repeat it.

"So tell us," her father said.

Mavis closed her eyes, willing herself not to breathe so quickly. She'd been through worse now. There was something worse than the constant emotional upheaval that came with being so far beneath her parents' expectations. Psychic damage had met its match in real, physical assault.

Busted lamps pierced skin.

Fingers gored eyes.

Shovels loosed entrails.

Even airbags drew blood.

She could survive Daniel and Marie Carson.

"Unless you're too proud," her father said.

"I shouldn't have told you anything," Mavis bit back. "Why

would I tell you more when you don't have the slightest sympathy for what you already know?"

"Your mother and I are not surprised that you're under spiritual attack."

Mavis froze.

"I won't presume to know what it's about, May, but you're my daughter. I just hope Jerrod's up to his task. I want him to come by the house when he's discharged, and pick up one of my handguns. If he's feeling vulnerable enough to miss a funeral, he'll need help protecting his family. I just hope this passiveness doesn't become catastrophic."

A sharp tear began in Mavis's gut. The dark of the study flashed over the daylight in Jerrod's car. For a moment, she was holding the shovel again—but it was her own stomach she was carving it into. She felt a bilious gust billow up her throat, a copper earthy smell seep out from her memory again.

She was coming apart.

"You never once doubted Cyrus," she spat. "Nothing he did to me made you worry he wasn't up to the task."

"May—"

"Nothing about his unfaithfulness or his manipulation or his coercion were *catastrophic*!" Mavis bellowed the last word. "The only thing Jerrod could have possibly done to be lower in your eyes than *Cyrus* is marry me!"

If she were in their home with them, she could've fought back, at last. Mavis wished she hadn't fled Mrs. Frederick. She wished she'd fled up the hillside steps to her parents' house. She wished they'd hurt her for real so she could hurt them back.

Daniel Carson had taken the phone from his ear. Mavis knew because when he returned, the soft bristles of his beard scuffed against it.

"You're blessed beyond measure, Mavis," her father said.

A cascade of tears broke free and splattered Mavis's lap, but she didn't make a sound.

"I've always left it between the two of you—the way you've always been sensitive—but you are blessed beyond measure to have Marie for a mother."

Mavis sank back against the seat.

"Something's going wrong in your life, and you have to be willing to humble yourself. Your mother's wisdom, her goodness. Mavis, whatever you're going through, she's your best hope."

"How lucky for you, Dad. That Marie Carson is my best hope." Mavis's words dragged. She recalled during her pubescent years when her father remarked relievedly that he'd gotten the easy burden by having a daughter. He didn't have as many responsibilities as if she'd been a son. "Or did you mean that my hope is *in* Marie Carson?"

Daniel Carson didn't respond verbally. He made a gruff throat-clearing that Mavis took as a withdrawal. He couldn't tell her to put her hope in her mother. Not after the character flogging she'd endured for making an idol of a man.

"Is your hope in Marie Carson, Dad?" she asked her father. "It would certainly explain a lot."

With three loud pulses, the call dropped.

XVI

The alluring click of a woman's mouth moving around her teeth vibrated into the quiet hallway, and Mavis stumbled to a stop. She'd been hurrying down the ward to Jerrod's hospital room when she detected the familiar voice.

"Home yet, babe?"

The salutation Mavis had heard over speakerphone replayed. Not for the first time.

Djidji Patton was somewhere on the ward.

Which meant she was in Jerrod's hospital room.

The small woman was hypnotic, but she wasn't psychic. She couldn't know Jerrod was there unless he'd told her. Unless he'd beckoned her.

Jerrod had reached for Djidji. Again. Mavis had left in hopes of finding an end to this nightmare, and her husband had brought in a spare. Yes, she'd left him bruised and alone—and safer than he'd been while she was there—but it had only taken a matter of hours for him to call on the woman whose voice had set catastrophe in motion.

Don't.

The word was inadequate. Stephany Leonard's warning was

no match for this moment, not after the marathon of destabilizing moments that had come before. *Don't* was too flimsy a directive to withstand the many slings and arrows—the talons—of married life. Mavis should've known it sooner. Women weren't given real weapons, and they weren't allowed shields. Mavis—and Stephany and Renee Marshall, for that matter—was meant to survive by sheer obedience. Because she was told to. It was her one responsibility, this nesting doll of obligation into which a million invisible tasks and requirements fit. What Mavis didn't know—had never known—was how her mother managed to thrive.

The plucking of a harp. A small vibration at her hip.

Still in the hall, Mavis fished out her phone.

A text from Jerrod.

Just now? In the brief gap between the deep rumble of his voice and Djidji's glossy enunciations?

Told Mom and Dad you went home to get me something, in case they ask you later, he'd written. *All clear when you're ready to come back, baby.*

Djidji Patton was *all clear.* Or else Mavis's husband did not expect her to return. The texts were for a narrative. Perhaps to assuage guilt.

Her phone vibrated in her hand.

I hate this.

Mavis felt her jaw soften.

Djidji's voice still seeped through the wall, changing as she moved about the hospital room, rising when the sound of water echoed around it—but Jerrod's messages followed each other closely.

I want to get up and come find you, and I can't.

I shouldn't have let you leave. I shouldn't have fallen asleep.

He didn't ask where she'd gone. He didn't say anything about the fact that Mavis's location was still turned off, as it had been since the last day she'd seen Cyrus alive.

I just want to know you're safe, and okay.

Mavis went to him. She came through the open doorway and seconds later, her arms were laced around his neck. She felt his own encircle her body, heard him breathe while she pressed her face to his, neither of them speaking.

She didn't acknowledge Djidji. She hadn't glanced in the woman's direction upon entering and now she closed her eyes to breathe in Jerrod's scent. To isolate the feeling of being in his arms, the way she'd done in the ambulance.

Until Mavis felt a hand on her back.

Her eyes opened.

Small and warm, the open palm rubbed a gentle circle. Djidji hummed. It was heavy with consolation, sounding almost like a precursor to prayer, though if the woman petitioned anyone on the Dwyers' behalf, she did so silently.

Finally, Mavis turned, twisting her body so that she sidled close to Jerrod, perched herself precariously on the available sliver of bed. He opened up so that she could tuck into him, her eyes finally landing on Djidji while her husband kissed her forehead.

The other woman smiled pitifully.

"Djidji brought us flowers," Jerrod said close to Mavis's ear, and the woman's eyes widened. Djidji turned on her heel and gracefully heaved a stunning bouquet from the table before swiveling back.

"They're beautiful," Mavis offered. But they were garish. Overlarge. Unquestionably expensive, and obviously not from the gift shop.

"My father was in and out of the hospital for two years before he passed," Djidji answered. "Mostly in."

It startled Mavis, the immediacy of the overshare when all she'd done was compliment some flowers, and she straightened her neck. It felt awkward, but her body insisted on reacting, on making some nonverbal indication that Djidji's non sequitur of an anecdote was unwelcome.

"Nobody should have their whole world replaced with one room, especially not rooms like this. You start to think living—getting back to the life you used to live—is impossible, like it's a miracle."

Neither Mavis nor Jerrod said a word—but Jerrod's posture relaxed. Mavis felt his hand slide down her arm. She knew the look he must be wearing.

He understood. He appreciated Djidji's self-centering story. It made sense to him, how she'd gotten there, how a hospital room could be triggering.

Encouraged, the woman kept on.

"I mean, it *is* a miracle. But it's always been a miracle, you know? Every single day." Now she cast her eyes aside, like self-consciousness had finally caught up to her. It wasn't the taloned kind, the intrusive brand of vicious anxiety that made Mavis's nose bleed. Djidji's was voluntary. A natural sequence in her presentation. A gentle finale that ensured her audience would raise her up. "I guess," she said more quietly, "you just don't think about it until someone tells you your odds."

Her performance complete, Djidji looked down at the massive bouquet. And though she held it easily, her naked biceps comfortable in a practiced flex, it looked to Mavis like she didn't hold it at all. The arrangement seemed to explode from the woman's diminutive body. Surely the baby's breath had been made pink by passing through Djidji's soft and supple lungs, the carnations red because of the blood. The sharp green leaves of butcher's-broom pierced the air, searching for something else to impale, unsatisfied with having erupted from Djidji's chest cavity.

"I'm sorry about your father, Djidji," Jerrod said. He still pronounced her name perfectly. Fluently. Like it was at home on his tongue. "No one's giving me odds, thanks to Mavis. She saved my life. Really, I'm fine! I could walk out of here if my wife and Dr. Moore would let me."

Djidji nodded vigorously, the corners of her eyes stippled with tears. She smiled, giggling, and swatted at them.

For Mavis's part, she felt caught between her husband's praise and his resistance to seeming vulnerable in front of this woman. Mavis hadn't known he was fine, that he was well enough to be discharged. She'd come back to the hospital with the intention of pleading with him to do just that. Now, she wondered why it was important that Djidji see his resilience. Whether this was the display of manliness her father had demanded—and what it meant that Jerrod was making it now.

For someone else.

The visit was brief—at least after Mavis's return. She escorted Djidji to the door, laying her hand against the frame so the woman knew she wouldn't be accompanying her any farther. Instead of leaving, the small woman riffled through her purse for a moment, and then leaned toward Mavis without offering what she'd retrieved. Djidji held a card to her chest as though to draw Mavis's attention to the way modest necklines only accentuated her bust.

"You should have my number," Djidji said, hushedly, while Mavis's brow crunched. "In case you need anything."

Mavis blinked at the woman's large eyes, still swollen with ready tears.

"Jerrod already has it." Mavis felt the sharpness of her retort, imagined it piercing Djidji's ample breast like impaling butcher's-broom. She almost never thought of the perfect reply while there was time to deliver it. It was hours later, after some verbal assault had caused her to shrink, that she rewrote the interaction in her mind. It was always the Imaginary Mavis who got to level her eyes at someone, deliver a deadpan dressing-down to her parents. Only Imaginary Mavis had filled Rose Spencer with shame for suggesting to a twelve-year-old that she should begin tracking her weight. But it wasn't Imaginary Mavis looking back at the woman who called her husband "babe." It was Mavis letting Djidji know she knew about the phone calls.

"And we both just heard him claim he's indestructible," Djidji whispered before kissing her teeth as though Mavis's retort hadn't broken the skin. "Anyway, I said if *you* need anything, Mavis."

What would she need beside Djidji's disappearance? This was a strange way to trick Mavis into inviting her closer, to make it Mavis's fault the next time . . .

While the talons began to sink, Djidji draped one arm around Mavis's neck. She slipped the other around Mavis's waist, tightening both until her lips were crushed against Mavis's shoulder.

"An eye is fixed on you," Djidji said into Mavis's body. She didn't feel Mavis go rigid; her hug stayed warm and steady, her small hand rubbing another circle into Mavis's back. "But you're gonna be okay. I lit a candle. I'm praying for you both."

Jerrod didn't resist. At Mavis's request, he signed himself out of the hospital against medical advice, and during the ninety-minute drive, he didn't ask his wife about the hole in the back windshield, or about the dingy sheet she'd salvaged from the grocery store dumpster. She'd closed it in the back doors, wrapping the sheet around the outside of the car to shield them from the elements. Luckily, he also didn't ask where they were going.

She couldn't have told him; the destination wasn't specific. All Mavis knew was that there was a distance they had to go to be safe. A line they had to cross.

Mavis's faith wavered at the county line. She'd told herself the vow couldn't reach them this far from where they'd been wed, but her body dissented. The scab on her pierced shin cinched tight. Bruises she hadn't felt for hours throbbed. Talons teased. They tapped along her cranium, threatening a migraine.

Mavis drove on, but now she recognized Jerrod's vigilant watching. She saw the way his eyes scanned, and the number of times he glanced over his shoulder. His hand hovered over her lap whenever a motorist's maneuver might escalate into an intentional collision.

She hadn't made her confession at the hospital, had begun waffling even before she'd twice been touched by Djidji Patton. She'd almost convinced herself that there was another way—or at least that admission would only make things worse. That it would end the vow she'd *wanted*. But something about Jerrod's fear—something about its familiarness—rekindled Mavis's guilt. Whatever her husband had done, *her* unfaithfulness had been a reaction. She hadn't been overcome by passion; lustful desire hadn't gotten the better of her. Mavis had chosen something and someone she didn't even want. She knew it had been a form of self-defense, but in someone else's framing, it might seem more like vengeance. It might seem mean-spirited in a way that meant she was a ruined woman who shouldn't be forgiven. Mavis had to be the one to tell Jerrod what she'd done, and why.

They rocked, the car's suspension managing a roadside motel's uneven driveway. There were faint lines where the asphalt was still intact and Mavis parked between a mismatched pair.

"This place is nice," Jerrod said.

"It's postapocalypse chic."

"You almost never see paint this deteriorated." He nodded toward the motel office. "Look at that artisanal cracking."

"That's not the *paint* cracking, silly," Mavis said, shaking her head. "It's the *wall.* You pay more for detail like that. I just hope the room is musty."

"Oh, you don't have to hope," Jerrod said over Mavis's laughter. "If we're very lucky, it'll be rancid." He was still looking out the front windshield, but his hand had found its way to Mavis's thigh. "I think I can survive it, with you."

It broke her. The talons suggested perhaps that was the point. Perhaps Jerrod was being this way to eviscerate her, to multiply her guilt and shame, and remind her that she had never deserved to be a wife.

"Baby," he whispered, wiping tears from Mavis's face.

"Mrs. Frederick," she hiccupped out. Or at least she tried. She didn't enunciate, her mouth unable to close around the hard consonants of the old woman's name.

"Baby," Jerrod said again. "Baby, breathe."

Everything was catching up to her. Every emotion and reaction that would've made escape or self-defense impossible during the attacks fell over her now. Jerrod reached for her again, and Mavis jumped. She felt herself scream, heard the tearful outburst ricochet off the car windows and come barreling back. She collapsed lower in the driver's seat, shielding her face and screaming back at the memories, the sensations flashing through her body.

Repent.

Marie Carson's voice broke through the panic attack.

Repent, and be saved.

Her mother's voice neutralized electrified nerves. Settled flailing limbs and shaky breathing.

Repent.

They weren't her mother's original words, but that didn't matter. It was Marie's authority that convinced Mavis once again what she had to do.

She didn't straighten her posture or regain her composure. She just began.

"It isn't a curse. It's the vow," she told him. "That's why all of this is happening."

Something pinched at the center of Mavis's forehead. Sharp, and sudden.

It wasn't a lie. The violence *was* because of the vow Jerrod had organized with his mother—but it wouldn't have started if she hadn't broken theirs.

Repent.

Mavis's mouth felt thick. Her already heavy tongue seemed ready to expand, a slab of concrete wide enough to seal a tomb.

The panic began to seep back in.

"I watched Mrs. Frederick change," Mavis said. "I went to

my parents' and when she saw me, this ailing old woman who's known me my entire life tried to kill me. She would've. They all will. Because of our vow, and what the congregation promised."

She was trembling again, a cold sickness creeping from the pit of her stomach back up her esophagus.

She still wasn't telling the truth.

It was so much harder to tell Jerrod than it had been to sleep with Cyrus. Mavis was equipped for that. She'd learned to leave her body a long time ago, to suffer through what someone else was doing to her, physical or otherwise. In time, it was dangerously close to comfortable, the complete knowledge that she was a victim of someone else's wrongdoing. That she had neither chosen nor could she change whatever was happening.

Confessing that she'd orchestrated it, that she'd contacted a man who'd seemed to have thoroughly forgotten her, and that, despite several opportunities to stop, she hadn't—that felt like Mavis was to blame. It felt like she was the bogeyman she'd feared.

Jerrod sniffed and Mavis heard the crackle of spontaneous congestion. He was crying. She hadn't noticed.

"I know," he said, quietly. Tears ribboned down his face, the lines throbbing and alive. "I let the congregation make that vow . . . and then I failed you."

Mavis didn't hold her breath; it stopped, as though her body was in stasis.

"You didn't even want it." Jerrod held his head in his hands for a moment, and then righted himself again. He turned toward his wife, herself a pillar. "Mavis. I'm so sorry. I know why this has been happening, and I should've told you before they came inside our home. I could've ended it, but I was so afraid to tell you what I'd done . . ."

Mavis was dizzy.

"Djidji," Jerrod said, and Mavis's chest swelled. Her eyes quivered as though trying to contain all her anticipation. She felt them gape, hungrily, desperate for Jerrod to tell her what she needed to hear.

What he'd done first.

Why she'd done anything at all.

"Mavis, baby, I'm so sorry. I'm sorry I thought it was harmless. I'm sorry I thought that as long as we never touched, it was something else."

A talon pierced.

"You had an affair," Mavis said, squinting around the pain, clawing the confession away from him to inspect it. "You had an affair with Djidji."

"Not—"

Jerrod struggled, his mouth opening and changing shape, his brow crashing down.

"I don't know how to say it was just emotional without—I'm not trying to downplay it. I know. I just mean I would never have slept with her, with anyone—"

The talon sank deep. Soon, a trickle of blood would settle on the rim of Mavis's upper lip.

"All of these attacks—I know it wasn't harmless. I know it's punishment, that you could have been hurt or killed, and Mavis, I would die before I let anything hurt you."

She wasn't moving. She wasn't looking at the split in the motel wall, even though she'd turned to face it.

She was feeling her bra fall away beneath her blouse. The fabric of the top grazing her skin, and a nasty tingle shooting through her breasts. She was feeling the way her body had turned involuntary arousal into the threat of sickness. She was feeling warm breath on her skin, hot hands. She almost screamed—but then the stone collided with Cyrus's head.

Mavis breathed.

There was a cracking sound that hadn't been captured on the silent video, and Cyrus's teeth bowed.

And again.

Crack.

A sheet of blood veiled a bludgeoned face before Mavis felt her husband's hand encircle hers.

"I'm sorry, Mavis. I'm sorry I forced the vow on you in the first place, and I'm sorry it's what's hurting you now. I'll do whatever it takes."

It was impossible to see inside the split in the motel's wall, to see how deep it went. Mavis stared at it now, and imagined seeing past the obvious dark. Surely there was only a dank, unkempt room on the other side. Nothing worth shielding from the elements, except out of habit. She'd feel safer inside that room than she felt outdoors for the same reason—habit. Tradition. Because it had always been believed so.

"Mavis," Jerrod spoke again, stroking her arm as though to rouse her from sleep. "Just tell me what to do, baby."

Daniel Carson would snap his newspaper. Without a word or the benefit of his undivided attention, he would communicate unequivocally that Jerrod was doing something wrong. It was never what Mavis thought, never the offense that seemed most egregious. It wouldn't have been the emotional affair with Djidji Patton, but rather the certainly unnecessary confession of it. It would've been sitting quietly while his troubled wife steered him in the opposite direction of home. It would've been ignoring that she'd disappeared from the hospital and that he'd never asked where she'd been. Now, it would've been his passive plea for Mavis to instruct him on what to do next.

"We have to start over," Mavis said. She turned to face Jerrod, thumbed the wet streak that had curled beneath his chin. "That's what we have to do. That's how we end it."

He nodded, quickly.

"We'll end that vow and make another. We'll start again."

Relief collapsed across Jerrod's shoulders, and he took hold of Mavis, his hand steadying the back of her neck as he nodded again.

"We'll start again," he whispered, almost hoarse, before he kissed her.

XVII

Antonia Bryant was the reason Mavis had stopped going to her parents' church.

By the time Mavis and Jerrod were married, it had been years since Antonia's divorce announcement and luncheon ambush. It might have been a distant, if distinct, memory—except for how often the woman had been discussed since. Whatever spark Mavis had felt as a child, realizing it was possible to disagree with Marie Carson, it was still Antonia who'd been easily cropped out of the picture. It was Antonia who was alone and astray. Antonia who had been deceived by the world, and by the promise of choice. Mavis learned that spouses and church families were not all that different. Once committed, they were irreplaceable. Irreplicable by design. No second marriage or membership could be valid, let alone trusted. Otherwise, there was no such thing as obligation, no imperative to compromise, to die to self. There was no possibility of real love, if mistakes weren't fatal.

It was confusing, then, when a newly married Mavis learned that Antonia hadn't given up on a faith family altogether. That she'd been part of a different congregation for quite some time.

Remarried herself, Antonia Bryant was Antonia Reese when she sent Mavis a friend request.

"I rebuke that," Marie Carson had remarked almost before Mavis finished mentioning the request in passing. "I rebuke that attack on my house. We won't be giving the slightest toehold. Absolutely not."

Mavis hadn't known it was about her mother. She was a decade or so younger than Antonia, true, but she'd been in the woman's first wedding. She'd sat with Antonia through many an evening event, helped her plate at more than one women's breakfast early on a Saturday morning. It hadn't seemed out of the realm of possibility that Antonia was curious to see what had become of Mavis.

"Why would she be curious about you?" It was rhetorical, if the quizzical lines threading Marie's forehead were any indication. "Discerning is seeing an attack even when it's dressed up as friendship. Humility is accepting that a woman who publicly disrespected your mother needs to reconcile with *her,* not you."

Any response would've immediately indicted Mavis as lacking one or both of those virtues, so the friend request went unanswered—but it didn't stop Mavis studying Antonia Reese's profile.

Social media could be misleading, but Antonia Reese *seemed* happy. She seemed connected, grounded and surrounded by people who traded long, thoughtful, sometimes playful comments back and forth. For the second time, Mavis found herself astonished by this woman seemingly escaping—though perhaps not unscathed—from the only world Mavis knew.

And then she came to a post cross-shared between Antonia's profile and one of the woman's fellowship groups.

If it weren't for grace . . . the post began.

If mercy wasn't new every morning . . .

Mavis's throat had tightened around her heartbeat, her eyes jumping between phrases. She was trying to slow down, to follow Antonia's words in some sort of order, but Mavis couldn't stop jumping ahead.

. . . recognizing that there were ways I'd *failed in that marriage . . .*

. . . paranoia . . .

. . . emotional immaturity . . .

. . . a liar . . .

She only gleaned fragments, stray words in Antonia Reese's testimony—but they were terrifying. Mavis didn't know why. She didn't understand why Antonia Reese's confessions threatened to choke *her*. Unless there was some manner of blackmail unbeknownst to Mavis, the post—and its intentional broadcast on multiple pages—hadn't been made under duress. Antonia was sharing faults and flaws of her own volition—ostensibly—so why were stinging tears pricking Mavis's eyes?

Mavis realized she'd heard several of the more painful details of Antonia's post before.

"*She had a lying spirit,*" someone recalled.

"*Antonia always resisted correction . . .*"

It'd turned out that many a church member had noticed hints of young Antonia's inevitable demise in seemingly innocuous traits and behaviors. Once she was gone—once Antonia's divorce was known—it had been necessary to impart to an even younger Mavis where those well-observed missteps had led. The criticism *had* been in love, however relentless and nitpicking it might have seemed at the time, and it was her own apparently characteristic defiance that had required Antonia to suffer needlessly.

After the friend request, Mavis had slowly withdrawn her own church attendance. She and Jerrod let weeks pass between appearances. She'd alternate where they sat so that when missed, people might assume they simply hadn't seen her.

Her parents would not search. They'd always required a certain amount of space to fulfill their many obligations and would go on assuming their daughter was where they expected her to be—despite that they'd long since stopped checking.

Mavis strategized a quiet exit rather than have loving criticism constantly foretell future failures. She knew from painful, talon-producing experience how sharp the double edge of intimacy felt. How deeply it cut to be too clearly and constantly seen. How impossible it had proved to satisfy scrutinous gazes, and how exhausting to make the attempt only to be blindsided by another necessary reproof.

Mavis was too flawed to survive community. At least, people would say when they noticed her absence that she hadn't dared look for it elsewhere.

However happy Antonia Reese's ever-after seemed with her second marriage and congregation, she'd paid a lofty price—and everyone knew it. Assuming the happiness was real at all. Mavis would've been a fool to trust a curated profile and her solitary interpretation of it.

Not far from the dilapidated motel where she and Jerrod had spent the night, Mavis couldn't help but wonder where Antonia Reese was now—and how many last names she'd accrued.

Mavis was on her way to a church she'd never heard of, one she'd found online. She hadn't bothered reading their statement of faith, or the pastoral staff biographies. She wasn't looking for community. She just needed an aisle. Maybe an altar call. A quiet moment that looked like prayer or worship so that she and Jerrod could renew their wedding vow and end this nightmare. So that Mavis could repent without having to cross-post it.

"We don't know the whole congregation," Jerrod said, both hands on the steering wheel. He was being as uncharacteristically vigilant as he'd been the night before, when Mavis sped away from the hospital. Her promise of renewing their vow and starting again had bought him a brief respite, but a handful of hours of turbulent sleep in a bed neither Mavis nor Jerrod felt comfortable being undressed in had undone it. Her husband might survive with Mavis beside him, but her presence apparently offered little else.

"That's the point, baby," Mavis answered, laying her hand on his leg. "We'll be safe there."

"No," Jerrod said. "I mean, we don't know *our* congregation. We don't know every person who took the vow."

"Oh." She watched a pasture out the window. "Yeah."

"This might've been going on before we even knew about it. People might've been trying to get close to us, trying to attack us, and we never knew because we didn't recognize them."

Mavis was sure about when it'd begun. The crash at Ross and 15th. She'd crossed paths with Rose and Bill Spencer immediately after her infidelity, and they'd tried to kill her. Looking back, it had been very unambiguous. She couldn't imagine an attack going unnoticed, but one almost had. Jerrod had already been proven right.

"Like the hardware store," she said, only watching her husband out of the corner of her eye.

Jerrod's face was contorting. It melted, one corner of his mouth drooping as though in the throes of a slow-motion stroke, and she looked away.

"He was a plus one," Mavis confirmed quietly, as though to the passenger window. "We never even met."

Dr. Moore said the man had been inconsolable. That he'd been involuntarily confined because he wouldn't accept that he was the perpetrator of such violence, refused to listen to a re-counting of what he'd done.

Like his victims, the attacker's life was over. Like his victims, he would never know why. His tragedy would unfurl for the rest of his waking life, his confusion and fervent denial only sealing an asylum fate.

"I hadn't thought about . . ."

When Jerrod trailed off, Mavis resisted letting her eyes drift to him.

"How many vict—" He stopped again. "How many people I . . ."

She relented, turning in time to see the realization drain Jerrod's brown skin of luster. His eyes glistened with a new sheen.

"Don't," she pleaded.

Jerrod didn't move, he didn't even blink, and still a series of tears fell in quick succession.

"It isn't your fault. They were trying to kill us."

"Because of me," he said, his voice a rumbling whisper. "They're dead because of me. And the worst part—it would've ended if you hadn't saved me."

Mavis bit through her bottom lip. She drew a sharp breath, her hand leaping from his lap for a moment, her eyes wide.

"That man would be alive if you'd let him kill me first," Jerrod finished.

"Don't!" she cried before she'd recovered, felt blood spread across her teeth. "It isn't fair! People break vows all the time and nothing happens! Nobody gets hurt . . ."

"People always get hurt," he said.

Deep colors plumed over his chest and across his back. Mavis couldn't see them right now, beneath his clothes, but she knew they were there. A ribbon of blood sutured busted lips and a pair of stitch strips held the brow above his right eye.

"They don't always die," she told him.

"Mavis," he began.

"No, Jerrod, it isn't fair. This can't be all your fault just because *this* vow suddenly mattered." She pulled the broken skin between her teeth when the sharp taste softened. "Would you want me to blame myself?"

She watched him, scanned her husband's face for the slightest shift.

There was a business park up ahead, on the opposite side of the road. She could see it in her periphery. In one of those tall, angular buildings with more windows than walls, there would be a church. There would be an aisle, and salvation, and no need to torture herself.

But Mavis had never learned that skill.

"If the roles were reversed," she asked. "And they were coming after me. Because of something *I'd* done. Would you want me dead?"

Her heart was palpitating. Racing uncomfortably. Churning her blood in her chest.

"I don't know," Jerrod answered.

Mavis's heart stopped.

"It's an impossible question, baby. I can't imagine it." Jerrod parked and then put his hands back on the steering wheel.

"Jerrod." She was pleading again. "You just suggested that I live without you if that's what it took to end this."

He wouldn't look at her.

"Could you live without me? If this were my fault? And it would end?"

"It's not the same—"

"How? How isn't it?" she insisted.

"Because, Mavis. The roles would never be reversed."

"What do you mean?"

"You'd never be unfaithful."

They fell quiet before she whispered, "How do you know?"

"Because I'm everything you have."

Don't.

Stephany Leonard's warning resurrected.

Don't.

This time it meant, don't resist. Don't deny. For once, don't make it harder than it had to be.

Don't refute her husband's love.

Don't refuse his faith.

"Baby." Jerrod reached toward Mavis, his brow creased in concern.

"What is it?" she asked, before she felt his thumb smudging warm blood above her upper lip.

Mavis's second wedding was everything the first wasn't.

Simple. Brief.

Secret.

The Doctors Carson would never have approved, but that didn't matter. Mavis was saving herself. She'd devised her own salvation and it didn't matter what her parents thought of a corporate space turned sanctuary. It didn't matter that the service was out of order, that the worship team opened with a song before a member of pastoral staff presented a scripture reading.

That nursery-aged children were coddled in their parents' arms where they might soon become disruptive. It didn't matter that congregants brought their newly procured coffee and tea with them to their seats, or that those seats were upholstered and comfortable.

None of the unfamiliarity of this disordered foreign church mattered to Mavis, but she could sense that it mattered to her husband.

When they'd first come in, Jerrod had accepted an extended hand of welcome, his bright smile automatic and warm while he exchanged pleasantries with the usher. He gregariously fielded salutations from passing parishioners who Mavis could tell didn't realize they were visitors. Which was Jerrod's fault. He was affable and easygoing; no one ever thought him a stranger.

Mavis had slipped into her church persona, too. She couldn't have helped it. Unfamiliar as this particular body of people was—however disapproving of it her parents might be—there were enough hallmarks of Sunday morning worship to usher her spirit into performance mode. Any trace of fatigue or worry melted from Mavis's face. Her posture straightened. Her soft smile answered inquiries in advance: she was unburdened, and she was blessed—as she could only be if she were doing life well. And in a congregation who could not possibly know otherwise, Mavis performed with ease. At last, among strangers, she mastered the peaceful expression attributed to righteousness. The grace she'd so envied in others. At last, Mavis understood how Antonia could defect, how she could ingratiate herself into an entirely new congregation. Mavis knew how the woman could be so happy and at peace.

She was anonymous. At last, Mavis had a choice in what people knew. She had a choice in who she would be. Today, she was wise and discerning. Today, she was a wife with the full confidence of her husband, trusted to bring him good.

"I think that's a pastor," Jerrod spoke directly into Mavis's ear when she'd taken a seat while others continued setting up for service. "Should we go over?"

"No, no," she replied, patting her husband's hand as though quieting a child.

He'd given her a quizzical look, glancing between his wife and the pastor, but he didn't insist. A moment more and Mavis turned, let him see the calm on her face.

"Everything's gonna be okay," she assured him before pecking him on the lips. It was a brief kiss, chaste and respectful so as not to cause others to stumble.

They hadn't spoken again until the very end of service. Jerrod shifted in his seat several times, but Mavis didn't divide her attention, even to disapprove. She was having too wonderful a time.

After a tight, thirty-minute sermon during which Mavis studiously filled in the provided worksheet, the congregation stood to their feet. The worship team had returned to the stage, leading people to sway and sing a slow, simple introspection, or else drift to the altar for prayer.

It was time. Mavis took Jerrod's hand and led him out of their aisle and toward the front. Members of the pastoral staff waited below the pulpit, but Mavis drew Jerrod far to one side, out of anyone's reach or earshot. She turned toward her husband, his dark eyes gleaming in the low light, his forehead creased.

She swayed now, offering her husband upturned hands. Jerrod only looked around.

All through the sanctuary, eyes were closed, heads were bowed. Their witnesses were responding to the invitation still being encouraged from the stage, or they were deep in personal prayer. Some huddled together, hands laid on backs or joined.

"Mavis," he said, stepping close, though his gaze still crisscrossed the room. "What are we doing?"

"We're renewing our vow," she told him. "We're ending this curse."

"Like this?" he asked. "During an altar call?"

As though to make his point, someone from the front began drifting toward them, head angled inquisitively. Their slow approach gave Mavis time to dismiss them, a discreet flutter of her fingers communicating that she had no need of their services.

"Mavis," Jerrod continued. "Without a pastor?"

"We've done that." She tried to infuse her voice with authority. "We can't involve anyone else this time, baby."

"I get that . . ."

"But?" Mavis asked.

"But this feels right to you? Crashing someone else's service to exchange vows, when they have no idea what we're doing? You'd still think this was the way . . . if you were clearheaded?"

"Am I not?"

"I don't know," he said. "You've needed to manage your pain since all this started—understandably! But I know you took my pills, too."

Jerrod wasn't searching the sanctuary anymore. Now his gaze probed his wife's. In reply, Mavis raised her chin. She let him look her fully in the face, see her eyes clear and bright so that he would know she had nothing to hide.

Repent.

Mavis's chin tucked toward her chest, and she disguised the withdrawal by clearing her throat. When she tried to resume her bold posture, she found she'd lost her nerve.

She did have something to hide. For now.

"We're the only ones we can trust," she told him. She'd shut her eyes as a reflex at the condemning sound of her mother's command, but she forced herself to hold her husband's gaze again. "Unless you don't."

"Baby," Jerrod crooned. "You know I do. With my life. And I want you to know you can trust me, Mavis. I swear. I'll do whatever you think is right."

Locked in each other's gazes, she nodded. She took her husband's hands, slowly twisted the band on his finger.

"With this ring, I thee wed."

Jerrod quietly echoed her.

"With this ring, I thee wed."

Together, they recited vows Mavis had heard throughout her childhood, vows she'd pantomimed in myriad gowns and even the occasional square heel. Jerrod repeated after his wife, line by line. It couldn't have happened any other way. He wouldn't have known what to say, if not for her.

They sealed it at the end, said, "I do," one after the other.

Jerrod kissed her softly and Mavis's heart fluttered in her chest. A tear trickled down her cheek, relief catching in her throat.

They'd exchanged new vows. A new marriage had begun, in which there was no Djidji Patton to fear, and no Cyrus Marshall to regret.

There was nothing to repent now, so Mavis could be honest.

She wasn't sorry.

She wouldn't take back the stone that'd interrupted Cyrus's angry tirade. She wouldn't take back that it shut him up, the way nothing had before. However shocking the video had been, she wasn't repentant at the memory of his disfigurement. Very quickly, it'd become comfort. Justice.

She couldn't regret the path that'd led to it.

Now, she didn't have to.

Go, her mother's voice declared, *and sin no more.*

Mavis could do that.

She pulled herself into Jerrod's arms as worship drew to a close.

She would go and sin no more.

XVIII

Mavis slept.

She didn't know she'd fallen asleep until she woke up, bewildered.

"Hey," Jerrod said, reaching for her leg while he drove. "Welcome back, sleepyhead. We'll be home soon."

The confusion receded slowly. Mavis was in the passenger seat of her husband's car. Immediately before that, she'd been at the restaurant where they'd had a newlywed lunch. She could only have slept for a little over an hour, but the sun had changed position. The temperature had dipped.

The business park church felt like a lifetime ago. The dilapidated motel, an alternate universe.

Mavis stretched her aching neck; she'd crashed into sleep too quickly to properly position herself, and she was paying for it now.

Jerrod squeezed her leg, a soft smile playing at the corner of his lips.

"I love you," he said.

"Someone's giddy," Mavis answered, still tilting her head in either direction.

"It's relief." For a moment, she thought Jerrod would sober, but he took in a long breath and broke into a full smile. "Which, we're learning, makes me giddy. And it knocks you all the way out."

He laughed so easily Mavis couldn't help but smile. Slowly, the reflex reversed.

She hadn't planned on taking a nap. She hadn't even felt tired. There was no memory of weighted eyelids, or fuzzy thoughts. One moment Jerrod was pulling out of the restaurant parking lot, asking if she was ready to head back, and the next, she was waking up to the metronome of the turn signal.

"I crashed in the hospital," Jerrod was saying. "But that was like my body gave out. We haven't had regenerative sleep in days."

"Five days," Mavis said. She felt him look at her. "The accident was five days ago."

She'd almost said only. The accident was only five days ago. The span of time felt simultaneously too short and too long.

The vow had been triggered five days ago. For five days, Mavis had been experiencing continuous trauma. She'd had numerous unsettling encounters, survived startling attacks as recently as yesterday.

Her life had been completely interrupted. Overtaken. Altered.

"You had to be exhausted," Jerrod said, his thumb moving gently back and forth on her leg.

But she hadn't felt it. It didn't feel like succumbing to exhaustion.

"What?" Jerrod asked, glancing at her while he drove.

"I don't know," she answered.

Was this a talon, this paranoia making her skeptical over something as harmless as falling asleep? Did it need to be? Wasn't sleep deprivation enough to account for it? Post-traumatic stress?

Violence changed brain chemistry, after all. It did undeniable damage, unlike other kinds of abuse that felt acute but didn't leave a mark. The quiet mundanity of neglect, or bullying, that could be denied by both the doer, and by Mavis.

After the five days she'd had, Mavis's paranoia could be the result of irreparable new damage, or evidence that words hurt as much as stick and stones—even if their purveyors were never brought to justice.

She should be able to tell the difference.

"You're scared."

Mavis didn't answer. Her eyes moved slowly, as though the search was internal.

"You're scared it's not over."

Was she?

"It's not crazy," Jerrod assured her. "This has been . . . unbelievable. In the worst way."

She heard his words strain, heard his throat tighten around them, and knew what would come next.

"I'm sorry, Mavis. And I'm gonna spend the rest of my life making sure you know how much, if that's what keeps you safe."

"No." Mavis turned in her seat. She traced his hairline around his ear, tugged his lobe. "You're not gonna spend the rest of your life apologizing. That's not how forgiveness works."

He glanced at her again, his eyes glimmering with emotion. Whatever Mavis had been feeling—whether evidence of her former weakness or a byproduct of the nightmarish past week—it subsided.

The feeling that replaced it was entirely new. It was grace, and having occasion to offer it felt divine. Mavis felt magnanimous. Strong, the way she hadn't until boring a shovel head into a grown man's torso. But this strength was quiet. Modest. It was shared and—judging by her husband's glassy eyes—it was appreciated.

It was the epitome of covenant love. Great potential, realized.

No congregation could find fault with it.

"We made a new vow." Mavis wove her arms around Jerrod's and pulled herself close enough to lay her head against his shoulder. "The old one's over. I know it is."

Her body knew it, too. That's why she'd crashed into sleep. After days of fractured, shallow slumber, of nonstop alert, her system had forced a reboot because it knew it was out of danger.

She was safe.

Everything was going to be okay.

Jerrod jabbed the ignition, quieting the engine. Afterward, he and Mavis sat in silence, eyes on their front porch, and the short stack of gardening soil that had recently been delivered.

"I don't want you hurting yourself. I mean it," Mavis said, still looking at the front of their house. She pressed on despite the way her voice wavered, as though the unsteadiness was simply from disuse. "I just need you to help me get them in the backyard, and I'll take care of the rest."

She was distracted. She'd expected a barricade of tape across the door, and in its absence, found herself worried. The investigators who'd been there when she and Jerrod were rushed to the hospital must have come and gone. Which meant they'd taken what they needed for whatever they planned to do next. It meant that in the backyard, where Mavis was anxious to be—alone—there might not be any dark stains left on the pavers. There would still be the splintered point of impact beneath a broken window, but someone might have collected or otherwise cleared away what Mavis thought had soaked into the stone.

What Mavis hoped was hers to keep.

Jerrod broke the quiet with an acknowledging hum. He was responding to his wife's suggestion, not her curiosity over the absence of tape. Whether there had been any in the first place, or whether it was some inaccurate expectation she'd gotten from TV. He was looking at the white tab protruding from the doorframe, perhaps wondering whose business card had been left—and whether it communicated an invitation or a command. Perhaps he, too, wondered whether the death of the intruder made their home an active crime scene at all.

Silence had become a sinkhole between them, and they'd both fallen in. If she wasn't careful, the sun would set before Mavis got to the backyard.

"Get some rest," she told Jerrod.

"We'll see," he answered through a deep sigh, unbuckling his seat belt, and shoving his car door open wide, feet still at the pedals. "First things first, let's go fix what's fixable."

The garden soil wasn't terribly heavy, Mavis able to follow Jerrod around the side of the house with one of the sacks half on her shoulder and the rest cradled in her arms. It wasn't exactly painless five days out from a seat belt burning her chest and a dashboard punching her knees backward into her tailbone, but it also wasn't the hardest thing she'd done since.

"Do you want to have a baby?" she asked her husband's back.

"Today? It's probably too late for that."

The hole that'd been impossible to find from the study was immediately obvious from the back gate. For one thing, there was a large concentration of upturned dirt, not quite in a pile, but something closer to a sand bar that horseshoed around the hole. The burial pit. The place where the congregation would have planted Mavis before stoning her to death—if she'd been like Cyrus, who'd argued and spat and would not have agreed to sin no more.

Jerrod dropped his sack, trying to mask any pain with stretches.

"What brought that on?" he asked, one eye winking at Mavis while he rotated his shoulder.

Mavis shrugged, still cradling her soil. She let her eyes drift across Jerrod's physique until he laughed, pulling the sack from her arms and then wrapping her in a hug.

"Of course I want to have a baby with you," he said, between kissing her hair. "Do you?"

Mavis wanted more of the divine feeling she'd had before. She wanted to wield grace, and sacrifice might provide an endless supply. With one decision, she could daily prove and perform her devotion. There was a reason she didn't deserve Cyrus's fate, and having escaped it, Mavis wanted nothing more than to do what he had never been capable of. She wanted to grow. Hips and all.

"I do," she said, smiling up at Jerrod when he playfully gasped.

"Two vows in one day." His smile dipped, the sheen returning to his eyes. "I don't deserve you. But I will."

Before the levity could evaporate completely, Jerrod released his wife and headed to the garage for gloves and tools.

The shovel was gone. From the fence at a back corner of the yard, Mavis could see no tentpole protruding from a dead man's torso. It'd been taken to a lab, tagged and ready for processing. Someone would want to confirm that the fingerprints were Mavis's and the entrails had belonged to an intruder. Again, if television was to be believed.

There must be something left.

"Baby?" Jerrod's voice had to travel. When he returned from the garage, Mavis was standing beneath the ruined Palladian window, eyes trained on the place where the man had landed.

The wedding guest.

The congregant she'd killed.

The darkness was still there. It hadn't been sopped up. It couldn't be taken from her.

Neither could the sound she imagined the stone made when it cracked against Cyrus's temple.

Or the memory of blood spilling down his face like a curtain.

Jerrod's hand lay against Mavis's back. She blinked up at him, slowly smiled.

"You all right?" he asked, his mouth curving already as though he was only prepared for one response.

"I'm perfect." Mavis beamed, kissing his nose before snatching the work gloves and jogging back to the hole in the ground. Her body screamed at the unnecessary exertion but Mavis's smile didn't waver. Jerrod was ignorant of her discomfort; it was good practice for pregnancy.

Together, they pushed the original dirt back in. Jerrod didn't notice that Mavis was taking her time, interrupting their progress to meticulously scour the grass for more upturned earth. He didn't wonder at his wife's suggestion to compress the dirt with water, or her insistence that she retrieve and attach the hose herself. He didn't ask why they should ensure the site be difficult to re-dig. He was distracted by the way his muscles were tightening the longer he stood or knelt or bent over. When he could no longer resist grimacing, Mavis became insistent.

"You have to take something," she said, stretching her own recovering body now that frailty might convince him. "I'm gonna wrap this up anyway. One bag of soil should top it off."

He wasn't resisting. He'd been attentive for days, but now he was exhausted. It was easy to revert back to old dynamics, to let Mavis excuse him from things that might cause discomfort.

"Please take your pills and soak in a hot bath?" she pleaded. "For me?"

"You're coming in?" he asked, already glancing behind him.

"I'm right behind you."

Jerrod moved slow. He wouldn't be back. He verified that his wife had her phone on her, and then retreated to the house to relax.

He didn't see Mavis reconsider.

When she returned to the garage, he didn't know it. He didn't see her collect the pruning shears, the small one with the curved blade and the large straight-bladed scissors. He didn't see her use the gardening spade to plant them handle-first deep in the dirt they'd just packed, ensuring that the blades were open and pointing dangerously up. She didn't have to explain why she stomped the spade until the handle broke into several pieces. Why she spread the shards with the looser soil they'd had delivered. That it was a form of insurance.

Jerrod was none the wiser when Mavis stood above her handiwork in silence.

It didn't take much to wake her. Mavis wasn't completely sure she'd actually fallen asleep. The guest room shadows were unfamiliar and the rarely used bed was too soft. Jerrod's mouth was gaping, a godawful series of Jurassic growls erupting at odd intervals—but it must have been anticipation that kept Mavis from dreaming.

She checked the security feed on her phone.

Nothing. But she hadn't expected to see the filled-in well at the fence line, and she hadn't expected Havilah Greene to be at the original hole in the camera's line of sight. That didn't mean the woman wasn't out there.

Mavis slipped out of bed.

Out of the house.

Into the night.

She kept her back pressed to the wall and there, she could hear them.

Someone was in her yard. In the back corner, by the fence, where Mavis had been hours before.

She hadn't heard the sound of metal piercing earth. She'd buried all the tools. It must have been the opening and closing of the gate that woke her. Now in the yard, it was the sound of them digging by hand.

It was the congregation. One of them, at least. Maybe more.

It wasn't over.

Mavis didn't scream. She didn't feel herself come undone, didn't close her eyes against a rending talon. Blood didn't move down the narrow groove above her lip.

For once in her life, she'd prepared. The worst-case scenario was unfolding, but Mavis wasn't caught unawares. There were dark figures hunched over in her backyard, but it was Mavis who waited in the shadows.

She listened to them dig through the loose dirt.

Heard the soft thud of a broken handle being tossed aside. Then another.

They wouldn't find the spade. It was beneath Jerrod, nestled between the mattress and the box spring in the guest bedroom. Whoever had come, they would have to keep digging by hand, and soon they'd finish displacing the new soil. They'd reach the water-packed and compressed dirt and have to exert themselves even more. They'd have to plunge their fingers forcefully, claw their way deeper. There was no chance of them unearthing another burial plot in one night, which meant their attention would be fixed. Like the other congregants, they would be undeterred, impervious to interruption until they finished their task—unless, like the hardware store attacker, they were physically impeded. Or unless, like Rose Spencer and the intruder Mavis had blinded, they were hurt.

Mavis took out her phone and held it. She was breathing quickly now, the back wall's stucco exterior pressing through her nightshirt and into her back.

Don't . . .

Mavis closed her eyes.

Don't move. Don't retreat. Don't lose faith.

Then, a night-rending scream.

A wild and feral howl.

"No!" Havilah Greene cried. "No, no, no, please!"

Mavis tapped a button on her phone and a flashlight beamed. She'd disabled the motion sensor on the security camera. In its absence, the light from her phone cut through the night and the shrouding darkness beneath the tree canopy. In its radius, Mavis saw Havilah in shock. The woman was sitting in the dirt, feet still shuffling in front of her as she tried to scuttle backward. She'd thrown herself on the weight of one hand. The other she was pinning to her abdomen.

Havilah was unhinged. Panicked sobs racked her body. She was babbling, praying, screaming for whatever had happened to be undone.

Mavis approached. She was camouflaged behind the light, but Havilah wasn't paying attention. The white of her shirt was changing. Blushing. A red sphere growing around her pinned hand, the material and her skin drenched in fast-flowing blood.

"Wake up!" Havilah screamed. "Wake up!" She twisted in the dirt, looked down at the wrist she seemed to be trying to gut herself with, only to close her eyes and scream again.

Havilah didn't want to see it. Could not believe it. She descended into unintelligible sobs, contorting herself to reach back toward the place she'd been digging. She seemed to want something, but couldn't reach it.

"Wake up," she cried.

It was contagious, the genuineness of total dysregulation. At any other point in Mavis's life, she wouldn't be able to contain her own tears. She'd cover her mouth, overwhelmed by mere exposure to such heartbreak.

Tonight, she wasn't moved. She watched as Havilah seemed to finally become aware of her presence, and the light. As Havilah scuttled to her feet and escaped from the backyard, still hysterical.

There was another congregant on her knees, now brightly lit. Digging despite the commotion. She, too, ignored Mavis, continuing to thrust her fingers into the dense soil.

Mavis came closer. Swept the area with her light, and saw it.

Two fingers, sliced clean through.

The shears had cut them from her hand, and Havilah Greene had run home without them.

XIX

Mavis awoke terrified. Wide eyes darting, pulse vibrating in her throat. The all-too-familiar way sleep bottomed out and she found herself in the middle of a panic already in progress.

There were fingers in her yard.

Mavis had felt strong the night before, but by daybreak she was herself again. The morning after the home invasion had been the same. No matter how fierce she became, no matter how she surprised herself, at some point in the wee hours, the promise of new horrors settled on her chest like a demon. A fresh and crushing exhaustion resurrected at the thought of needing to be that fierce again. Of having her life depend on it.

It was never going to end.

The curse was never going to end.

Mavis stared toward the ceiling without seeing, a shaky breath rattling her lungs. The soft mattress of the guest bedroom felt like quicksand beneath her. It didn't take much to imagine it slowly absorbing her body. Pulling her in, and closing around her.

At least she'd be free.

Mavis's eyesight stabilized.

Til death do us part.

The flat white ceiling of the guest room came into focus, along with something else: Jerrod had been right.

Dying in the home invasion would've ended it.

The vows were tethered. The congregation's, and their wedding vow. It couldn't be replaced, or renewed.

To end the congregation's vow, the wedding vow had to be completed.

Til death.

That was it. No redemption, and no reprieve.

Her repentance wouldn't have made a difference. Only her death.

"I was hoping to be back before you were up." Jerrod's head hovered in the doorway. If Mavis weren't weighted down, she might've jumped. "Do you need anything from upstairs before I go?"

His fingers were curled around the doorframe. Mavis couldn't see the rest of his hand, but she knew they were attached. She'd seen excised fingers now. She knew how limp and unnatural they looked. Animated—as Jerrod's were while he absently drummed them against the wood, as Havilah's had been during her many impromptu keynotes at ViV—they could be handsome. Familiar. After dissection, fingers were uniquely grotesque.

"I'm just going around the block," he told her.

"It's fine, baby. I'm fine."

"I'll get whatever you need from upstairs when I get back."

"If you can handle being in the bedroom, so can I. Really," Mavis answered, lilting her voice and raising her brow in an open, untroubled expression. When he seemed on the verge of relenting, she yawned, stretching and then resettling with a soft smile as though comfort kept her in bed. As though all was well.

Jerrod didn't know the congregation was digging again, and

he'd never known why. He didn't know what happened once the dig was complete—or how quickly Cyrus's handsome face had been disfigured. Jerrod didn't know about his wife's counterattack, or the amputated fingers in the yard. He had no reason to doubt their vow renewal. When he was gone and jogging through the neighborhood despite his promise of a gentle, limb-loosening walk, Mavis would bury Havilah's fingers. She would reset the booby trap of shears in tightly packed earth and undo the diggers' work.

Havilah Greene wasn't going to come asking for them. There was that, at least. However she explained her maimed hand and missing digits, it might involve a relapse of sleepwalking; it would not involve Mavis Dwyer, or the fact that she'd seen Havilah on her property before.

Mavis's rebound to fear and exhaustion didn't have to account for an investigation into the human remains in her yard. But eventually Cyrus's would be found.

It'd been two days since his stoning, and there was nothing saying his decomposing body hadn't already been discovered. If not by his wife—whom Mavis could believe was still fetal somewhere in the home and not strolling between the rosebushes—then by a neighbor offended by the smell or alerted by an animal with a taste for decaying flesh. Mavis wouldn't be the first person questioned, but eventually Renee Marshall would find out Mavis's real identity—and precisely how they were connected. Her husband's last steps would be retraced by people who didn't have a vested interest in *not* finding the truth.

It didn't matter that she couldn't have killed Cyrus alone. She'd lied to gain access to his home after his death. There was no universe in which that alone didn't win her an in-person conversation with someone she'd rather not speak to.

Mavis sat up like she was spring-loaded.

She couldn't be interrogated if she completed the vow.

If there were questions about the coincidence of her ex's murder and the series of unfortunate events she'd endured over the past week, she wouldn't have to answer them.

If she completed the vow—or rather, if she allowed the congregation to—she couldn't lose Jerrod. He couldn't change his mind about her.

Even Daniel and Marie Carson didn't speak ill of the dead.

Exhaustion had felt like a fog clogging her gray matter, dampening her synapses. Now it dissipated.

It shouldn't feel like such a relief, matter-of-factly considering the neat solution of ending her life. She'd never considered it before. Never through all the years of paralyzing panic and shame. Not when she was forced to show her face after chronic humiliation, and not when the reception was worse than she'd feared.

But that would've been failure. If she intentionally hurt herself, she would've been taking the coward's way out, confirming every criticism.

This was different.

This was autonomy, cleverly disguised. Not that it had to be. No one would think Mavis capable of subterfuge, and they couldn't resist thinking her a victim.

The ferocity she'd recently come to know possessed Mavis anew.

Dying now would save her marriage, and save her the trouble. More. It would enshrine her memory and reputation.

Electricity sparked, chased itself to the end of her lower extremities. Mavis twitched in the bed, her toes tingling. She threw back the covers and stood.

The guest room was too small. She needed space. In the hallway, she immediately began to expand. In a matter of moments, Mavis felt larger than she'd ever been.

All those years of struggling, of striving. Of being told she'd failed before she started. The congregation, at last, revealed the fix. A solution with the power to unburden her. To salvage every relationship in her life. To alleviate the scrutiny that made her imperfections unbearable. To elevate her to the status of Dearly Beloved.

And if it didn't, she didn't have to know. For once, it would be Mavis evading consequences. It could all be so easy—because she'd kept it from Jerrod.

After Havilah's hysterics, Mavis had gone to bed without waking him, and at first it'd made the morning panic worse. Trying to manage fear and exhaustion alone compounded it. It'd made the cold tornado through her chest more quickly.

He didn't know.

He wouldn't be ready for the next attack.

And soon, he'd figure out that his indiscretion was not to blame.

Now Mavis was relieved. If she'd told her husband the truth about their predicament, she'd have to tell him the sole solution. He would resist. He'd worry she was out of her mind. Tell her she was sleep-deprived. Drug-addled, despite that she couldn't have taken too many doses if her body still felt pain.

There was still a flurry in her chest, but now it was excitement. It sent chills coursing through her, and Mavis had to move. She strolled her hallway, fingers grazing the corners of picture frames and inspecting floating shelves as though the space was new. Or as though she was.

Mavis took in a tranquil breath.

Another act of grace, then.

She bit her lip, but not through it.

She'd do the responsible thing; she would test her resolve. For Jerrod's sake, Mavis wouldn't let the congregation take her out without giving ferocity one last chance to stick. To do that, she'd have to fashion a moment like the ones that'd given her strength. Replicate what made her powerful.

Like Cyrus's stoning. The moments of impact, and bloodletting.

Or her own hands around the shovel's handle as she carved an assailant's abdomen open.

Or watching from the shadows as Havilah Greene's shirt blushed.

It would take another act of violence to prove once and for all whether Mavis would always rebound to fear.

She knew exactly who to call.

The café belonged to her parents' church. It'd started as a pop-up, at first only operating before and after service. A brick-and-mortar location was eventually secured and—according to Marie Carson—it'd become a blessing for homeschool moms: a nonintrusive gig when their kids were old enough for organized activities. That's who Mavis was expecting to see behind the counter when she arrived. Someone she recognized, or at least someone old enough that they'd been invited to her wedding.

She'd intentionally arrived late. Driven past the café several times, waiting for Djidji to arrive, head inside, and place her order. She'd given the baristas time to notice Djidji. To change. To descend on Jerrod's mistress the way they'd descended on Cyrus.

They didn't.

The baristas were strangers. Nonmembers, judging by any number of their body decorations and at least one outrageous haircut. In the years since Mavis had stopped her weekly patronage, the homeschool mothers must have found other uses for their free time.

"I'm sorry I'm late." Mavis hustled in, hands upturned apologetically. Djidji met her halfway between her seat and the door, dismissively batting one of her hands away before pulling Mavis into a hug.

"You've got your hands full," the woman said. "I could've come to your house! You didn't have to leave Jerrod alone!"

"I needed the fresh air," Mavis replied without mentioning her husband's own morning constitutional.

"I just want to help any way I can." Djidji laid her hand over Mavis's on the table.

"I appreciate that. That's why I called."

"Tell me." The woman seemed poised to leap across the round surface and into Mavis's lap. It must've been overcompensation, this strangely aggressive enthusiasm.

"This is gonna be hard to believe because you just saw him in a hospital bed, but I think Jerrod wants to get back to work."

"That is not hard to believe," Djidji laughed. "Not in the slightest."

Mavis bared her teeth, forcing a laugh past them.

"I can't believe he survived working from home the past week!" Djidji's jovial expression froze. "What am I saying—you had your accident! Of course he was home!"

Mavis waved the other woman off.

"He was just being overprotective," she said, rolling her eyes. "Doting."

"He better!" Djidji winked.

"But when it's his own self, he's immediately restless. I think he feels isolated. Maybe he's missing the social side of going to the office?"

"Oh, I'm sure he is!"

Mavis hummed.

"We're missing him, too! Work just feels like work without him." The woman actually sulked.

"Yeah?" Mavis nodded along.

"Oh my god. Everybody loves J. He never misses a birthday lunch or celebration. He doesn't mind fraternizing with the assistants."

"Oh, do you all go out a lot?"

"Usually we order into the office, but Jerrod actually covers it. The other admin girls are always jealous; they really gotta stretch their petty cash, but my guy's a provider." The woman giggled, her head intentionally bobbling before she took a sip of her black coffee.

The dark, pungent drink didn't suit her. It felt contrarian, like a character quirk in a television show. Something meant to be provocative, unexpected, but too heavy-handed. It was wholly unbelievable. Djidji's sip was defiantly long. Afterward, she licked her pouty lips with the tip of her shockingly pink tongue.

"That's how you refer to him?" Mavis asked, half her mouth curling up into a smile. "Your guy?" She was fighting back laughter. It rumbled in her throat like phlegm while Mavis struggled to tame her lips.

"Oh, that's nothing." The other woman shook her head, crisscrossed her hands a time or two as though to cancel a play. "You know office culture."

Mavis's eyes still twinkled jovially when she fixed them on Djidji's.

“I don’t actually. I’ve never worked outside the home.”

“Oh, that’s right! I knew that.”

“My guy’s a provider,” Mavis said, shrugging one shoulder.

She didn’t mind that the mothers had abandoned the café. That there were no congregants to condemn Djidji the way they’d condemned Cyrus. It didn’t matter whether or not they would’ve recognized her had they been there. Whether Jerrod was only getting hurt because of his proximity to Mavis and not because of what he’d confessed to. It was all right that—left to their own devices—the congregation would’ve let Djidji go completely unpunished.

Everything was going to be okay.

The ferocity was swelling in Mavis’s chest. She felt it throbbing down her arms, sparking in her fingertips. It pulsed at the back of her head. Soon she would be lightheaded.

“How often did you have lunch with my guy?” Mavis asked. “On your own, I mean? Outside of office culture?”

Djidji’s expression cleared. It didn’t fall. That would’ve betrayed some measure of surprise. That she’d been taken aback. She wasn’t. The playful, daffy-sweet charade was simply no longer necessary.

“And you don’t call him your guy. At least, that’s not all you call him. Right? Babe?”

Djidji narrowly avoided rolling her eyes; Mavis could tell by the way the overlarge orbs instead momentarily bulged. As though Djidji was impatient. Unamused. Mavis was confronting her, and Djidji looked like she couldn’t be bothered—but she didn’t speak.

“You are bold.” Mavis labored the words. “I always thought that was a compliment, but it isn’t. I thought women like you were strong, and sexy, and desirable, but . . . that’s not it. You’ve just got nothing to lose. Nothing of value. Just envy for what other women worked for. Didn't you say an eye is on me?"

Djidji still didn't speak. She offered no defense. Facade discarded, her face was unreadable now.

"You don't have to confess. Jerrod already did."

Djidji's brow wrinkled.

"He told me. I know you two have spent time together." For a moment, Mavis's throat cinched painfully. She swallowed hard, suffocating the taste of Cyrus's cologne. "It must've been fun, pretending he belonged to you. Letting people believe you were a real couple while he ordered your coffee."

Djidji still didn't bat an eyelash.

"But then I got hurt and reality came back into focus."

Mavis felt a fresh wave of ferocity crash over her shoulders. She'd never had a confrontation like this before. She'd never kept her composure, stopped short of screaming or kept her anger from devolving into a tantrum. She couldn't tell whether Djidji was quiet with disgrace or whether it was a familiar disregard. Both her parents had at times let Mavis exhaust herself mounting a defense or imploring them to do it for her, only to abruptly twist the upper hand. At the end of it all, they'd say something simple but devastating. They would put Mavis firmly in her place, or else they'd deny her. They would leave her without response. It would be like she hadn't said a word.

This would be different. She'd make certain of it.

"Everything that's happened this past week," she said. "The accidents and turmoil, the awful chaos he brought on us—he apologized for all of it."

Djidji's eyes swept from one side to the other, but Mavis didn't care.

"You're not his babe, or his work wife. You're his regret."

"Forgive me," Djidji said, but her tone was strange. It wasn't repentant; it was skeptical. Mockingly so. "Jerrod thinks a couple of coffees and one or two games of footsie at the office *caused* something?"

A sharpness hit Mavis between the eyes.

"I'm sorry," Djidji said again, but this time she was guffawing. "It didn't even cause an affair, but he thinks we're the reason you were in that accident? Actual intruders broke into your house in the middle of the night because I massage his neck?"

Mavis went cold. If this woman weren't sitting directly across from her, an incredulous sneer plastered on her pretty face, Mavis would have snatched at her own shoulders, searching for the ferocity as though for a slipped cloak.

"He's a silly man, I'll give him that." Djidji seemed to have recovered now. Her eyes rolled freely, and she reached for her coffee. "I knew he wasn't bright—I mean, a grown man that's that uncurious is a huge red flag for *me*—but that's . . ."

She trailed off, but her eyes drifted back to Mavis.

"I flirted with your husband. I know that's not okay. But these things—bad things, one after the other?" Djidji kissed her teeth. "He's a fool if he doesn't at least consider that somebody else did something much worse. I mean . . . you did get hurt first."

Djidji brought the cup to her full lips.

"He really didn't ask what *you* did?"

XX

Mavis had been practically comatose by the time she got to Whitley Owens's card. Her mother's edict at the wedding reception had been strictly observed, and immediately following brunch the next morning, Marie Carson had instructed her daughter to fulfill her obligation. Mavis had spent four of the first twenty-four hours of her married life opening, reading, and then recording the names and addresses of her guests, before preparing handwritten replies.

She'd met Whitley during her temp-work years. At the end of Whitley's first week, when the young woman's first temporary position led to full-time employment, she'd wondered aloud how Mavis had managed to remain a temp for so long.

"I hope that's not rude," Whitley had blurted, apologetically. And, of course, Mavis had reassured her it wasn't, before giving herself a chance to decide how she felt.

"I get it all the time," Mavis had told her, shrugging as though the repetitiveness had dulled the question's edges. "It's just personal; I don't want to do a disservice to the employer, investing in a career I know I'm leaving."

"Ah." Whitley'd nodded, certain she understood. "You're going back to school?"

"Oh, I mean when I get married." Mavis's smile had fit snug, like an expression held too long for a picture. By now it must have looked plastic, but that didn't mean it wasn't genuine. It'd held even while Whitley's eyes flicked down toward Mavis's left hand. "Not engaged yet!" Mavis had raised her hand and wiggled her unadorned fingers for some reason, laughing as naturally as she could. "Just don't want to get comfortable!"

Whitley had matched Mavis's open-mouth smile and awkward breath-holding. She was a nice girl, and hadn't meant to imply anything by her confusion. She didn't ask any more questions, and a year later, she said nothing about the dozen temporary jobs Mavis had invested in, all at which the woman was a perpetual newcomer, anxious and insecure. Whitley hadn't been the type.

Seven years later, Mavis remembered Whitley Owens's startlingly effusive congratulations on her nuptials. It'd stood out among the more sterile well-wishes and familiar blessings from her church family. Even after reading the card half a dozen times, Mavis couldn't shake the feeling that it was sincere. Whitley was emotional. She'd never made a congregation vow before, had never heard of one. She was overwhelmed and honored at having been part of the service, along with her twelve-year-old daughter, Lily.

From the comfort of Jerrod's car, Whitley Owens was easy to find. The women were still connected via social media. Parked around the corner from Djidji's rowhouse, having followed her home from the café, Mavis went directly to Whitley's page because of something she remembered seeing. Whitley was participating in a No-Buy Year. She was abstaining from purchases for a calendar year, a feat she was accomplishing through old-fashioned communal sharing and bartering. She'd become a member of a digital marketplace in order to advertise her needs, and her offerings.

It only took a few clicks for Mavis to make a profile of her own. A few clicks more to attach a picture of Djidji and input her home address. Within a matter of minutes, Mavis had identified one of Whitley's biggest asks. She wanted a fourteen-cup food processor, and was certain she was being delusionally optimistic about the possibility of actually bartering for one.

Mavis searched images of food processors, filtering out manufacturer photos and selecting several from a series taken for an already expired auction.

In her message to Whitley on the marketplace, Mavis disclosed two almost imperceptible cosmetic imperfections and suggested that for a single mom, she would be willing to part with the appliance for free—as long as it was picked up that day. Mavis didn't know Whitley's status. She didn't have time to scour the woman's socials to confirm or deny the presence of a partner. Dangling her most coveted line item for free dependent on her fitting a very specific demographic would reduce the possibility of Whitley sending a romantic partner who had not been at Mavis's wedding.

Whitley must have had her notifications on. She responded to the bait almost immediately, gushing gratitude and promising to come within the hour.

Mavis was impatient.

Something's just come up. Any chance you can be here sooner?

Now there was a pause. Whitley was brainstorming. Or she was skeptical. Small flaws or not, she was recognizing the improbability of the offer. She was considering her safety, or else playing out scenarios to ensure this wasn't some type of new scam. But Mavis was offering a free appliance to a woman on a forum devoted to mutual care and radical consideration.

She should press.

Imply there were other takers.

Don't.

Mavis culled a breath into her lungs. She waited.

On my way! Whitley responded.

Mavis got out of the car.

As soon as Djidji answered the door, Mavis rushed forward.

"I'm so sorry, can I use your restroom?" She was frantic, impatient, one hand a knotted fist against her pelvis as she pressed into the other woman's space.

Djidji's own hand instinctively rose to protect herself, the door closing slightly to bar entry.

"Mavis?" Djidji's defensive posture relaxed, but her pretty face crinkled in dismay as she stepped back. "What are you doing?"

"I thought I could make it home, but I'm about to burst—may I?"

Mavis pushed past the woman and into her home.

"How do you know where I live?"

Mavis rushed toward a nearby door and yanked it open to find a small closet.

"That's not—it's just down the hall," Djidji said, still frazzled from the ambush, but permissive.

Mavis opened a second door and disappeared behind it. Enclosed in the small water closet, she shed her frenzy.

She closed her eyes as though ending a scene.

Rolled her shoulders forward and back.

Djidji was permissive. She'd asked how Mavis knew where she lived—but she hadn't demanded. She hadn't insisted on being answered, as anyone with a true concern would've. That meant there was a reasonable explanation for Mavis's knowledge. One that didn't involve stalking.

It meant Jerrod knew where Djidji lived. That Djidji had considered that the details of her address had been shared during a privileged conversation between husband and wife.

Perhaps Jerrod had been in this bathroom before. Smelled the palo santo that clung to the air and knew where it emanated from.

Mavis opened her eyes. Calmly looked around the small, but lovely, space.

The oval bowl on top of the mirrored tray. It was filigreed gold, on four delicate stems. Mavis leaned toward it, inhaling deep. Yes. The musky, warm fragrance was housed inside.

Mavis unbuckled her pants and sat on Djidji's pristine toilet to wait, humming absently. She hadn't had anything to drink at the café, but she needed to kill time.

There was shuffling just outside the bathroom door. Djidji was leaning close.

Mavis bared down and was happily rewarded with an audible stream. She took to humming again.

Of course, Djidji was listening, but it didn't matter. She'd let Mavis in. Actions had consequences. Even for a couple of games of footsie and shoulder massages.

Djidji was going to learn that some doors should never be opened.

Tap, tap, tap.

"Mavis?"

"Hm?" she answered pleasantly, unfurling a length of thick tissue paper and tearing along its perforated edge. She didn't bother replicating the arrow fold.

"Should I call Jerrod?"

Mavis hummed thoughtfully before flushing the toilet. She moved to the sink and washed her hands.

"Mavis."

She dispensed a dollop of scented lotion into the palm of her hand, lifted it to her nose. It was like mulled cider, spicy with tones of citrus. Far too strong for a guest bathroom lotion. Too bold when paired with palo santo—but very on-brand for the performative Djidji Patton, who teetered on tall heels and drank black coffee for shock value.

"I'm calling Jerrod."

Mavis opened the door and flicked off the light.

Djidji was standing exactly where Mavis imagined. Now the woman put a hand on her hip. It was much more affectual than crossing her arms over her balloon chest would've been. It was a gesture that—at her small stature—could still be taken seriously.

"That didn't sound like an emergency, Mavis."

She didn't respond, only smelled the back of her hand. Outside the scented bathroom, the mulled aroma was growing on her.

"I understand that you're upset," Djidji was saying. "But this is wildly inappropriate. This is my home."

"Jerrod is my husband," Mavis replied.

"That's right. Which means your aught is with him, if you insist on making something out of absolutely nothing."

She wasn't yelling. She wasn't insisting Mavis leave. The woman must have felt Mavis's behavior was warranted, because she entertained her imposition at all. She didn't think herself as innocent as she pretended.

"And you wouldn't be upset, if our roles were reversed?" Mavis asked. There was still time to fill.

"Our roles would never be reversed."

It was a familiar refrain. Jerrod had said the same thing.

No one ever thought Mavis capable of hurting them the way they hurt her.

"I would never choose a man like Jerrod," Djidji went on. "Let alone fight over him. I'm not saying that to be disrespectful, it's just the truth."

"But you'd massage his shoulders and call him babe."

"My god, do you not know the difference between a pet and a man?"

The doorbell chimed.

Mavis's eyes flicked toward the front of the home. Djidji's didn't.

"Jerrod isn't going anywhere, girl," the woman said.

The conversation was important enough to resist interruption. Or maybe it was part of living alone as a single woman. Maybe Djidji didn't answer the door. Maybe she expected deliveries to be left. Worse, maybe she depended on some sort of camera before answering. Mavis had rushed the entry too quickly to recall.

"He doesn't have the spine to leave." Djidji's eyes settled at half-mast, her chin making a small circle as though to emphasize her condemnation. "And he doesn't have the stomach for a real affair. If the worst thing you have to worry about is flirting, and him airing his little gripes at the office, you got off easy."

"Gripes?" Mavis blurted. She hadn't meant to. She wanted Djidji to answer the door. To let Whitley in.

But Jerrod had gripes, according to the woman he'd be disappointed to know had meant nothing by their affectionate interactions—and she knew them.

Jerrod had spoken ill of his wife. Complained about her to another woman. At least.

He hadn't swallowed his frustrations. Hadn't assumed that he was to blame for his dissatisfaction.

Jerrod had identified Mavis as the source, and been certain enough to entertain strangers with the details of his wife's failures.

Mavis's phone vibrated in her pocket.

Whitley didn't want to miss out on her food processor. She would wait.

"Every man has them," Djidji answered, dismissively. "If you dressed like me, he'd think it was too much, but since you don't, he thinks you're a frump."

Mavis winced, startled by the suddenness. There'd been no hesitation, no warning for the attack.

"You're boring, you lack passion, you're fragile . . ." Djidji rattled them off. It seemed automated, the criticisms leapt to mind and out of her mouth so easily. Like she'd heard them many times over. Enough to effortlessly commit a series of them to memory.

Jerrod had freely given this woman an arsenal, and he'd thought nothing of it.

But they were just words to Djidji. They were benign. Meaningless. The woman didn't seem to recognize that every accusation was a blade. Every utterance was a pointed attack and Mavis felt them in her chest. "Coming from J, that's all pretty rich."

The fact that Mavis didn't collapse into cardiac arrest made it worse. She felt like she was hemorrhaging, but no one could tell. They didn't have to. It was all happening inside of her, in secret. Someone could deal a death blow and carry on like they'd done nothing wrong.

She wanted scars. Evidence. No more talons and invisible torture.

Mavis wanted blood.

The doorbell chimed as though to answer.

Mavis fished her phone out of her pocket and looked at it, then tilted her head.

"You called him."

"Who?" Djidji's small face crinkled. "Jerrod? No, I didn't."

"How does calling my husband make this better?"

"I didn't call him."

"Open the door." Mavis crossed her arms defiantly, but made sure to nibble her lip. "We can have this conversation together."

Djidji turned back toward the entry.

"It's not Jerrod," she was saying as she walked.

Mavis let a distance grow between them before she followed.

The sunlight spilled in through the open door.

"Hi!" a voice sparkled politely.

"Hi." Djidji's reply was more reserved. She was waiting for the woman to justify her presence.

The voice from the porch wasn't right. It'd sounded enthusiastic but timid. Young.

Mavis stepped around the corner of wall that was obscuring her view of the entry, and her heart lodged in her throat.

It wasn't Whitley at the door.

"Lily?" Mavis asked, and the young girl's eyes leapt to her.

"Yes! Did . . . my mom—she asked me to pick it up, I didn't know she let you know—"

Djidji turned half around to look quizzically at Mavis.

Don't.

Don't move. Don't turn back.

Don't be fragile.

Lily had been at the wedding, but it made sense that she didn't remember Mavis. She'd been in middle school at the time. But she'd taken the vow. That was what mattered. She was only nineteen now, but if Mavis gave it time, the curse would still take. Lily would do exactly what her mother would've done. If Mavis wasn't fragile, ferocity would catch. It would carry her through, keep her composure so she was careful to keep Djidji between them until it was too late to change course.

"Mavis, do you know—"

She ignored Djidji.

"Lily," Mavis said instead. She locked eyes with the young woman, whose increasing nervousness made her rock back on her heels as though considering escape.

Mavis didn't blink.

"Okay, whatever this is, this is done."

Djidji moved to close the front door, and Lily caught it with a hard slap of her hand.

Mavis smiled.

Lily's eyes were clear of confusion now. She was gone. Whomever the bubbly nineteen-year-old was in her right mind, now there was only the vow. She wore a softball jersey—either from a high school team or perhaps she was a rising college athlete with aspirations—but that was the past. That life was over. After today, nothing would be the same for any of them. Mavis would have to live with that—until she didn't. Until the vow took her, too.

Mavis felt stronger than fierce. She felt powerful. When Lily came into the house, intending to attack Mavis, and Djidji defended her home, Lily turned on the small woman. All it took was an understandable resistance, a raised hand and a sidestep to bar the young woman from entry. The same kind of interception that had saved Mavis at the hardware store and cost strangers their lives.

"Mavis!" Djidji cried, panic chasing out the scream too

forcefully. Her voice sounded immediately raw. She was cowering away from Lily, backing through the entryway. She was giving Mavis a chance to intervene. To catch the young woman when she passed her. To save Djidji. But Mavis was saving herself. Her marriage.

"Jerrod didn't wonder, by the way," she said, Djidji already deeper in the house, Lily passing Mavis now without a glance. "He didn't ask me what I'd done."

Djidji wasn't paying attention. Her pouty lips were parted, her eyes dewy and quivering—but she stopped retreating. She raised her hand to Lily's chest. She was standing her ground.

The nineteen-year-old's hand snapped shut around Djidji's wrist, and then she twisted. Fast. Perhaps like she was pitching a curveball; Mavis wasn't versed in the sport. She knew, however, that softballs did not have bones. They were not intricately connected, with joints and tendons and a network of nerves. When Lily wrenched Djidji's wrist, the small woman's hand bent back toward her body, her fingers nearly touching her own forearm. It was disturbingly noisy, a cacophony of unnatural snaps and pops.

Djidji's big eyes swelled. She set them on Lily as though it would make a difference. Men must've been weak at the sight of Djidji's beautiful features contorted in sadness. They must have folded around her, with coos and comfort, promising to make things right. Why else would the woman have despaired so prettily?

Lily wasn't moved. She couldn't be. She was a congregant now, and Djidji had come between her and the upholding of the vow. Whatever she would do to Mavis given the chance, what Lily did now was in service of Mavis and Jerrod's marriage. It was part of the promise to support and protect. Djidji had repeatedly interfered. Regardless of her justifications, her callous dismissals, the woman was guilty. There had been innocent victims of this curse; Djidji was not one of them.

Mavis followed them away from the front door. She heard Djidji's panicked breathing as the woman's mind split over the pain of her broken wrist and the search for her phone. She heard Lily rip a heavy sconce from the wall with one fluid motion.

Mavis stepped into the open kitchen in time to see Djidji retrieve a knife. When the small woman whirled back toward her assailant, Lily wore the gold decor like oversized knuckles, her fingers curling through its scrolling flourishes and closing in a fist.

Lily punched Djidji in the face, and the smaller woman bounced against a counter before she crumpled to the floor, wheezing.

The sconce was not molded plastic. Mavis should've guessed. Djidji's taste was so expensive and excessive. The sconce was metal, now kissed with a bright red seal, and still intact on Lily's hand.

There was a clicking, not unlike the sound Mavis had heard in the hall on her way back to Jerrod's hospital room. This one was less alluring, though once she'd placed it, Mavis found it much more attractive. It was coming from the back of Djidji's throat, her tongue pulsing, blocking and unclogging her airway repeatedly. Her eyes were still open, but only slightly. Only enough for Mavis to spot a sliver of brown so deep it seemed black.

Djidji wasn't unconscious; she was convulsing. After one blow—not counting the collateral assault of the counter's edge—the bold woman was incapacitated. She survived skyscraper heels and body-sculpting garments daily. Hours-long salon visits several times a month, if Mavis had to guess. All to sustain a level and intensity of attention to which Mavis was unaccustomed. But Djidji was a lightweight. She offered Lily little to no foreplay before collapsing, defenseless.

She wasn't the type to play possum, Mavis decided. One hand completely ruined, she'd gone through the trouble of grabbing a knife. Surely Djidji would've made more than one attempt to use it before resorting to elaborate theatrics and a feigned seizure.

She wasn't going to get up. She wasn't going to struggle anymore. When Lily straddled Djidji, crossing her own body with the sconce-enhanced fist and then backhanding the convulsing woman, red spray sparkled through the air before clinging to surfaces.

Mavis turned back the way she'd come. She heard Djidji's body throttled again before she reached the front door. She heard Djidji or Lily grunt with either impact or release. The last thing Mavis heard was the sound of wet splatter as she walked through the front door without pulling it closed.

XXI

Mavis crept.

She'd gotten home from Djidji's and immediately pulled Jerrod's shirt over his head. He'd laughed, stumbling out of the rest of his clothes, barely wincing when his wife's hands ran over his chest. When Mavis backed toward the staircase, he'd been uncertain.

"Are you sure?" he'd panted. "We can go back to the guest room."

"That bed is too soft," Mavis had answered between kissing and biting his lips.

"Whatever you say, Goldilocks."

"Yeah? I'm not boring you?" she asked, her voice husky with adrenaline. She was practically dragging him up the stairs.

"Nothing about this is boring."

Djidji was right. He wasn't so bright.

Jerrod let Mavis lead him into their bedroom, through the study door, and then onto the daybed sofa in front of a broken Palladian window.

Glass had still been scattered around the room, surely. A breeze had flowed in and out of the destroyed window. There'd been a dark stain on the floor, partially beneath one of the bookshelves.

It had been exhilarating.

Jerrod hadn't asked why they'd bypassed their bed, he'd just fallen on top of Mavis and roped his arm around her body. Half an hour later, he was snoring on the hardwood, not terribly far from where he'd been felled three days before.

Mavis had crept out of the study and sat on her bed to text her parents.

Days after they'd cast her out of their home, insisting she leave without having dinner, her mother had shown up at her apartment unannounced.

Thankfully, Cyrus wasn't there, though he had been the night before. He'd immediately sided with Mavis, which she hadn't expected. She'd been even more taken aback when he'd insisted to her that she was a grown woman. She hadn't needed to confess anything to them, he'd told her. It was such a welcome departure from the advice she so often received that Mavis hadn't bothered to reconcile it with Cyrus's constant infantilizing. She'd let him wrap his arms around her and she'd nodded against him when he asked if she wanted him to stay the night.

"I didn't have to tell you," an emboldened Mavis had asserted to Marie Carson. "Sin or not, it's our business, not yours."

"If he wanted any business with you, he would have spoken to your father by now." Marie shook her head. "Did he leave a ring beside the bed before he left?"

She'd waited for a reply she knew wouldn't come.

"Why would he?" the woman had said, to end the silence. "He's doing you a mercy by not leaving money."

Mavis felt herself blush. She knew when her mother had seen it because Marie Carson's chin lifted. The brown skin of her daughter's face and chest adopting a rosy glow was confirmation. It meant Marie was right, that regardless what Mavis argued, her body knew better. But her mother had never been magnanimous in victory. The humiliation was the point. Evidence of it did not mark the end of a confrontation. Instead, her mother seemed fed. Mavis had had her suspicions before, but watching Antonia's public scolding and rejection had solidified it:

Marie Carson delighted in shame.

Igniting it. Inspecting it. Prolonging it.

"Your father was devastated; do you know that?" the woman had continued. The first wave of her daughter's embarrassment always sated her appetite; now she would slow down. She would savor the moment. "He wondered how we ended up here. But *we* didn't. You are not our only child."

Plump tears streaked hot lines down Mavis's face. She couldn't hold them any longer. She shouldn't have tried. Refusing to grant her mother the spectacle of her surrender had only ever proved painful. It was a challenge, Mavis had learned, and a responsible parent would not let it go unanswered.

"You are not the litmus. You do not get to prove or disprove our success," Marie Carson declared. "We've raised up too many spiritual sons and daughters who have cleaved to us and coveted our guidance to give you that authority. *You* failed *us,* Mavis. Not the other way around."

She'd accepted Mavis's sobbing as concession. *Then* Marie Carson's arms were open—so to speak. The woman laid one hand on her daughter's bowed head, the other against the young woman's back. She'd kneaded Mavis's forehead with an oil-drenched thumb, grinding as though to burrow the liquid beneath the skin. She'd anointed the doorframes the same way, passing from one room to the next and cleansing Mavis's apartment of what the young woman had done.

She didn't explain how Mavis should endear herself to Cyrus now. She levied no critique against the man who'd implied Mavis could secure a proposal by offering her body to him in advance. If Mavis was lucky, Cyrus would someday be the head of their household, but until then she was sole custodian of their sin.

When she texted her parents years later, she offered a sacrifice she knew would be pleasing and acceptable.

I'm sorry for the loss of Brother Spencer, and that Jerrod and I weren't by your side at his homegoing.

The text was read within moments. No bubbles followed; there would be no interruption. Mavis wrote on.

I would say that we've taken your guidance and your spiritual shelter for granted, but as your daughter, Jerrod's appreciation of you begins with me.

Mavis's lip caught on one side. It was so easy to compose. Like the bait she'd posted for Cyrus. It was so simple to tell them what they wanted to hear. It didn't take an ounce of thought or cunning when they'd been so very demanding. The only marvel was the number of years Mavis had wasted being terrified when she could have played along. Her parents were redundant, their chastising and criticism always the same. Without effort, Mavis knew what was coming. It was only now she realized: she could have been fierce the entire time if only she'd made two of herself. She could have been the Mavis they expected, and another one. A freer Mavis they never saw. The one who decided for herself in her parents' absence, comfortable in the knowledge that they'd never find out. That, like Jerrod, they weren't really looking. They were never around. There had never been the slightest curiosity. Whatever Mavis hadn't broadcast, no one would've seen.

The problem had never really been Daniel and Marie Carson; it'd been fear all along. It'd only been confusing because it'd seemed singular. Specific. But with practice, Mavis's fear had metastasized. It'd grown and spread until taloned thoughts were indiscriminate. They were thorough. Eventually, Mavis was afraid all the time. But she hadn't had to be. She understood that now.

I'm committing to myself, to Jerrod, and most importantly, to you, that things will be different from now on, she wrote, glancing through the open study door to her husband's slowly respiring form. *I've asked Jerrod to accept Daddy's offer of protection, and I'm hoping you'll extend your own, Mom. Will you bring the handgun and the oil? I'd really like you both to bless the house.*

Now there were pulsing dots in reply.

Ask, Marie Carson wrote. *And you shall receive.*

She couldn't be there when her parents arrived. Mavis had to be somewhere they couldn't access. But she wanted to watch.

She knew what would happen. That if they got close enough, they would become congregants. Perhaps they would at least wake more easily—the way Deborah Dwyer had when Jerrod caught her sneaking outside the study door. The woman hadn't turned on her son. His interruption hadn't resulted in a misdirection of justice. Deborah Dwyer had immediately come back to herself at the sight of her child.

It was too much to hope that Daniel and Marie Carson would disprove decades. That it would suddenly matter that they were her parents, despite the many times they'd told her it didn't. They'd taken a surprisingly anarchic approach to child-rearing, displacing Mavis as their automatic priority, reminding her often that being born of them did not privilege her. It might've seemed incongruous with a dozen other teachings, but it was only because the girl was clingy. Predisposed to a spoiled nature. It would grow her up to earn their attention—something at which she had rarely succeeded. She'd envied other young women and men who seemed more centered in her parents' good graces, and Antonia Bryant had topped that list at one time.

In her living room, Mavis positioned her phone on a tall surface, her fingers lingering on the device.

She'd thought of Antonia's luncheon more in the past week than she had in years. Remembered how startled and invigorated she'd been, watching the young woman name her disappointment and confront the people who'd failed her. If she'd meditated on it then, Mavis might have liberated herself sooner.

Something had stopped her. It was the fact that Antonia topped the list. The fact that Mavis's mother had delighted in Antonia. The way that she'd spoken about her. The many times Marie Carson had invoked her to underline Mavis's lacking.

Mavis might have sided with Antonia that day—she might have been freer every day after—except that she was glad to see the young woman despised. She'd been relieved by Antonia's demotion. It was a strange thing to recognize, since Antonia's humiliation hadn't profited Mavis in any way.

"They'll be here any minute," Mavis called to Jerrod. He'd insisted on taking a shower before his in-laws arrived, as though they might smell or sense what he'd done with their daughter in the hours before.

"Are you sure you don't want to freshen up?" he asked, bounding down the stairs and tucking a fresh shirt into his pants.

It was more a request than a query. Jerrod wanted her to. For more than seven years, his habit of implying his wishes rather than lambasting Mavis for not divining them herself had been proof of her husband's kindness. She hadn't blamed him for the fact that the resulting anxiety felt the same. That second-guessing how often a question was, in fact, a gentle command had provoked talons. Piercing. Rending.

Djidji Patton would've kissed her teeth. She might've carried on flirting with him, but as soon as the party ended and the tab was paid, she would've scoffed to the other assistants that only a pet couldn't form a declarative sentence.

Mavis didn't want to freshen up, but it was as good a premise as any.

"I'll be right back," she replied, patting his bruised chest and kissing her husband before walking past the stairs.

At the end of the hall, she opened and closed the guest bedroom door without going inside. After a moment's pause, during which Jerrod did not peek around the corner and during which she heard the muffled audio of a video playing on his phone, Mavis escaped into the backyard.

Her parents' engine purred as they pulled into her space in the driveway.

Mavis closed the backyard gate behind her, slipping away from her house and into her neighbor's garden.

Her pulse was charging pleasantly. She was accustomed to the quick transitions of her nervous system, the way mundane stimuli could spontaneously hijack her day. It'd always felt like frenzy. Blood coursing through her limbs, energy amassing in her body.

Now she felt strong.

Fierce.

Mavis let herself into her neighbor's solarium. The Windsors were a gregarious couple, often away from home, and they left it unlocked in the very likely event that their cat, Kelvin, was seen wandering the neighborhood. It was most often Mavis who escorted him home, sometimes sitting in the solarium awhile to keep the furry nomad company.

Today Mavis sat with her legs pulled up on a floral sofa, clucking her tongue until Kelvin appeared. He leapt up beside her, bowing his back and forcing her fingers through his tortoiseshell coat before collapsing in the small space that remained.

"Our secret," she whispered, nodding when Kelvin spared a glance. "Good."

Mavis wasn't wearing her watch; she was holding it. It was easier to look at that way. She scrolled through the watch's apps and selected the remote viewfinder. After a moment, her living room appeared, the high angle making the entire room visible.

She was getting good at this. Planning, and executing. Deciding outcomes for herself. The talons had seemed to dictate so much, or someone else had. Mavis had spent her entire life feeling like a passenger, her destination out of her control.

It wasn't so hard, getting her way. Maybe that had been the point of all of it—making sure Mavis never found that out.

Her parents were talking to Jerrod in her living room. The three were standing in the center of the room, her father the most animated. It was an interesting phenomenon to watch clandestinely, when no one in the room knew they were being viewed. Her mother having done the lion's share of interacting with Mavis ever since she could remember, it'd been startling and not a little painful to watch Daniel Carson enthusiastically engage with Jerrod and other men. At least now she could dispel the taloned accusation that the man did it expressly to upset his daughter. Mavis wasn't anywhere to be seen, and he was still more social with his son-in-law.

Whatever Daniel Carson was telling Jerrod, it was a seemingly innocuous anecdote that had not yet transitioned into the inevitable lesson. For now, one of her father's hands was in his pocket, the other holding a firearm case at his side while he swayed from his heels to the balls of his feet. For his part, Jerrod listened jovially, his smile vacillating between a hint and something fuller. He didn't seem to know where the conversation was headed, even though he should've. There had never been an interaction with his in-laws that did not conclude with a series of imperatives. The Carsons were milder with their son-in-law—at least *to* him—but he'd witnessed the impressive maneuvers employed on Mavis countless times. He'd learned not to intervene. Or rather, Mavis had advised him after the post-wedding-brunch incident. It didn't help. Of course, Jerrod hadn't insisted. He hadn't told her he could not sit idly by while she was treated roughly. He hadn't strategized a response that *was* helpful. He'd simply learned to follow Daniel Carson's lead, and left Mavis to the care and conduct of her mother.

Mavis tugged at Kelvin's dark coat with her free hand, and the cat purred, approvingly.

She couldn't see her mother's face. Marie Carson's back was to the phone.

Until it wasn't.

While Daniel and Jerrod laughed, her father's features relaxed and natural while her husband's mirrored them pathetically, Marie Carson turned her head.

The woman's face was something close to slack. It lacked the tension of someone in control, had become the blank slate of an avatar. A congregant.

Mavis took her hand back despite Kelvin's dissent, and held the shutter button on the remote camera app.

She needed video of this.

She had to rely on her memory to relive Cyrus's stoning. The intruder's fall, and the way the shovel nearly dissected him against the pavers. She wanted proof that being her mother's daughter *did* matter, even if she didn't have long to enjoy it. Because there was no other reason Marie Carson should have been overcome by the vow at this distance.

Jerrod glanced at his mother-in-law but quickly returned his attention to Mavis's father. He didn't look again, even when the woman turned and began walking as though unaware of the living room wall.

In the neighbor's solarium, Mavis stood, Kelvin jumping to the floor as though to escape a landslide. While the cat dashed away, Mavis took a step to her right. On her watch, she saw her mother's chin tick slightly to the left.

A clipped gurgle escaped Mavis's throat.

There was a wall and a property line, a fence and the curved windowed perimeter of the Windsors' solarium between them, but Marie Carson was locked on her daughter. For once, Mavis had the woman's undivided attention. Her mother had no choice.

Daniel offered the hardcase to Jerrod, who took it and promptly left the room to secure it as he'd no doubt been instructed. When he was gone, Mavis's father turned to look at his wife, and his shoulders squared.

Mavis involuntarily hummed a note.

Like mother, like father.

Daniel Carson's posture sharpened. In two large strides, he met his wife at their daughter's living room wall, and standing side by side, they stared as though seeing through it. As though looking directly at Mavis.

Her mouth gaped. It was dry, but that was because she'd taken her Percocet before inviting Djidji to the café.

The cold in the center of her chest was because of her parents.

Mavis kept her finger on the watch. Stepped from one side to the other just to see her parents' focus shift. They matched her movements, however slight.

As long as she was on the other side, the Doctors Carson would stand facing Mavis's living room wall. While they were congregants, there was no one more in need, more deserving of their attention.

Mavis trembled. They were serpents, and she was their charmer.

Jerrod returned without the gun case, and found his in-laws bewitched by the pearlescent finish of the warm neutral paint. Later, when Mavis retrieved her phone and played back the video, she'd hear what he said to them. It wasn't much. When neither Dr. Carson responded, Jerrod backed out of frame. Within moments, Mavis's watch vibrated. Jerrod was calling.

Mavis smiled, but it had nothing to do with him. She'd silenced her phone before positioning it.

She was getting good at this.

XXII

Ferocity stuck.

When Mavis woke the morning after barging in on Djidji Patton, she wasn't afraid. The talons hadn't returned. Her mind wasn't being fileted by the thought of all the ways her life was indelibly changed, by how relentless the vow had been.

Mavis wasn't terrified—but she wasn't stupid either. She'd spent her entire life on edge, anxious and afraid.

Only the vow had provoked a change in her.

The vow had paled her familiar fears by comparison, shrunk them. It was ruthless and vicious, and it had forced Mavis into a kind of clarity. She'd figured out how to survive.

Mavis's transformation was tied to the vow. To its violence. When it ended, her clarity would, too. She had to end with it.

Jerrod's infidelity might not have been the cause, but he didn't know that. And still, seven days after her car accident, when Mavis woke up and asked him to go back to work, her husband kept a secret.

"I just need things like they were," she told him. Jerrod had found her in the study, in front of the translucent tarp keeping out the elements. He'd sidled up behind her at the ruined window, wrapping his arms around her torso, and she'd let her head fall back against his shoulder. She'd covered his hands with hers. "I need to feel like everything's okay again, you know?"

Jerrod's face sank into her shoulder and Mavis felt him hold his breath.

He was thinking about her parents. The way they'd stood with their noses almost touching the living room wall. The way they hadn't responded to the sound of his voice.

Mavis had watched the video all night. She'd only slept for partial hours at a time, reaching for her phone before her eyes reopened. She hadn't been awoken by any congregants, either in her house or outside of it. It was just the pull of the recording, the insatiable desire to watch her parents stand at attention. The knowledge that they were helpless beneath the spell of the vow.

The congregation had certainly been in her yard. Someone else's fingers might have been dismembered by the booby trap. They might've cried out, suddenly awake and in anguish near the fence line, struggling in vain to decipher where they were, and how they'd gotten there in the middle of the night. Maybe their hands were intact. Maybe the congregation had started a new hole somewhere else, the way Havilah Greene had after Jerrod installed the security camera.

Whatever the case, the vow wasn't complete. Jerrod was burying his face in his wife's shoulder because he knew that. He had to know. At the strange sight of Daniel and Marie Carson, he'd retreated from the living room and not come back into view during the hour the couple was there. He'd stayed away even after the Doctors Carson awoke.

Mavis had watched their entire stupor from the Windsors' home. She'd tested her control of her parents at various distances, backing through the solarium, eyes locked on her watch's image. When she'd crossed the threshold into the neighbor's galley kitchen, her father's shoulders sloped. Her mother's chin ticked sharply to one side and back. Stepping back into the solarium, Mavis had watched them straighten.

She toyed with them. Mavis couldn't help it. All of a sudden, her absence mattered. Distance mattered. Whether she drew closer or moved farther away, it changed them.

She could've kept it up for hours, if she knew exactly when the Windsors would return.

Relenting, Mavis had gone back into the kitchen and stayed there. After a few moments, her parents looked around her living room, as though waking from a trance. They'd blinked as though to loose blinding scales from their eyes. They were still searching for their daughter, only now they were awake.

"Mavis?" Marie Carson had called. Mavis didn't need to hear the audio to know that. She'd watched her mother call again, and wait, the woman's hand slowly drifting up, fingers spreading. After a moment of stillness, this time because Marie couldn't shake the feeling that her daughter had been close and was now suddenly gone, the woman had visibly shuddered. She'd looked up at her equally bothered husband and shaken her head. Made a nonverbal utterance of disapproval. Marie Carson did not play with demons. She'd stormed out of Mavis and Jerrod's house without blessing a single room.

Jerrod still hadn't come back into frame, and when Mavis saw her parents' car pull away, she'd gone home. She'd retrieved her phone, confirming the videos she'd captured before looking for her husband.

He hadn't realized he'd locked the guest bedroom door, he'd told her, and he hadn't mentioned her parents' behavior. Now, arms wrapped around her, face buried in her shoulder, he still didn't. He'd dressed for work, let her prepare his coffee. He'd already put on his suit jacket before finding her in front of the Palladian window.

"I can stay," he said, at last, kissing her neck after. "If you're uncomfortable being left alone."

At least he was tortured. If he was going to leave her there in front of a busted-up window, in the room where she'd saved his life, at least he couldn't look her in the eye.

"You can't stay every day," Mavis cooed, tilting her cheek so that they were skin to skin. "I've got to get used to it, don't I?"

Mavis turned in his arms, wrapped hers around his neck.

"And it's over, isn't it?"

Jerrod could've confessed then. He could have told her what she already knew—that the congregation was still a threat.

He swept the tip of his nose against hers. Kissed Mavis like it could be the last time.

He was trying to scare her. Wordlessly instill a niggling fear, a hesitation that she might voice herself.

His hand was holding the base of her neck, tenderly massaging between her hairline and her shoulders.

He couldn't know that the talons couldn't reach her anymore. That she was free of them.

He was trying to make her fragile, the way he'd told Djidji Patton she was. All so that he didn't have to confess that his repentance hadn't worked, that he didn't know how to protect Mavis. That he was not too good to be true.

He shouldn't be able to leave. A good husband couldn't. But Mavis had her own plans. She'd devised her own protection, so she told Jerrod what he needed to hear.

"They only ever came at night, remember?" she whispered.

Jerrod's forehead fell gently against hers. He drank in her

scent, nodding against her and tightening his embrace. A moan escaped him, his eyes closed.

Mavis's eyes were open.

She watched her husband do everything but confess, and then she watched him leave for work.

Djidji Patton wouldn't be there, but Mavis didn't imagine Jerrod would tell her that either. He'd probably be relieved, at least today. By the time anyone had cause for concern, all of this would be over.

Mavis reclined on the daybed sofa in the study. A breeze pressed the tarp taut before releasing, so that the room—the window—seemed alive. It respired the way Jerrod had when he'd fallen asleep on the floor. The way he had the night of the home invasion, when the man Mavis killed had left her husband in a broken but breathing heap.

Mavis didn't expect there to be news. Not about Djidji, not yet. After checking the delivery status of an order she'd made the night before, she looked, not expecting to find anything of interest on the social media accounts associated with her local news stations.

When Lily Owens appeared, Mavis sat up.

The girl was pictured in the same softball jersey Mavis had seen her wearing the day before. Her honey-blond hair was in a ponytail, the curly length of which was draped over one of her shoulders. Reddish-brown dots stippled the young woman's tawny skin. Mavis wouldn't have known what it was if she hadn't watched Djidji's blood splatter the day before. There was a more obvious smudge crossing one of Lily's cheekbones and smearing into her hairline.

It was the girl's eyes that ground Mavis's breath to a halt.

They were puffy and red, wild and pleading.

From her mug shot, Lily was looking out at Mavis in incredulous confusion.

The article said she'd placed two calls. The first had been to her mother. Lily told Whitley Owens that the victim was dead and—thinking that her daughter had discovered the aftermath of someone else's violent attack—her mother had advised the teen to call 911. That was Lily's second call.

An audio file was embedded in the post.

Heart pounding, Mavis pressed play.

911, what's your emergency?

The same young voice Mavis had heard the day before replied.

There's a woman here and I think she's dead.

Okay, where are you?

There was fractured breathing, and Lily's mouth must have brushed the phone. She was looking around Djidji Patton's home. It must have seemed completely unfamiliar.

I—I don't know. I don't know where we are.

Lily was crying.

We're in a kitchen.

Have you taken any substances?

No—I don't know.

What's your name?

Lily.

Mavis could almost hear the girl deflate. Something was sinking in, some understanding at least of how the scene would look was beginning to take hold.

My name is Lily Owens.

The clip ended, the seek bar jumping back to the beginning, and the pause icon transforming back into a play button.

Mavis tapped it, and listened to the audio again.

The article said that when first responders arrived, their worst suspicions were confirmed. The caller was also the killer—even if she didn't seem to know it.

There was mention of a barter forum, and the promise of a food processor, but none had been found at the scene. Authorities speculated that perhaps the dead woman had given it to someone else, and that was Lily's motive. The nineteen-year-old softball star, sent on an errand for her mother, had flown into a dysregulated rage over someone else's used appliance.

It was nonsensical. If it didn't involve more than two shattered lives, it'd be laughable.

Mavis enlarged Lily's mug shot again.

It didn't matter how outlandish the speculation was. They had the killer, apprehended with blood on her hands—and her face. There wasn't any reason to look further.

Mavis felt her insides clench, audibly churning like a rock tumbler. Her guts were moving, alerting her to the sudden need for relief. She'd experienced it a hundred times before, her bowels surging into activity when sudden stress overwhelmed her. But this was different. The flurry in her intestines was accompanied by a giddiness. Excitement.

There'd been no rubber-band effect. Her fear hadn't crept over her in bed the morning after. Mavis had been fierce, but it was more than that. She'd done more than defend herself, though she'd done that, too.

Mavis had taken control. Not just of herself, not of something small. She'd gone out into the world and made something happen. She'd choreographed something in her mind, cast unaware people and gotten them to play their parts because she'd anticipated their behaviors and reactions.

It was a feat she'd always thought reserved for villains. For callous masterminds. Either that wasn't true, or Mavis had become one herself. She couldn't decide which explanation she liked more.

This was how her mother thrived. Mavis might've understood sooner, but she'd been too fragile to notice. She'd been sensitive. Reactive. Bludgeoned by the impact, she hadn't marveled at the way Marie Carson took hold of what might've otherwise hurt herself, and turned it outward.

Mavis had always flinched when she should have deflected; she'd hidden from what she could've harnessed. She knew better now.

Her phone vibrated with a delivery notification.

She was going to need every hour of Jerrod's absence.

Mavis set to work.

XXIII

When he thought Mavis was asleep, Jerrod kissed her. He softly set his lips against hers, drawing his hand along her silhouette. He stopped at her hip, squeezing the way he always did.

"I'm sorry, baby," he whispered, before kissing her again. "I love you."

Mavis kept her eyes closed when she felt him get out of bed. She didn't say anything when she heard the bedroom door open. Jerrod wasn't going to the bathroom, or into the study.

Mavis opened her eyes at the sound of her husband slowly plodding down the stairs. She listened to him move through the downstairs hall and go into the guest bedroom.

That's where he'd put her father's gun. It wasn't there anymore, but Jerrod didn't know that.

When Mavis had taken her father's hardcase out of the guest bedroom closet and removed the gun, it wasn't because she planned to pull the trigger. Mavis could no more shoot herself than she could walk on water—but having it close by would embolden her. She'd only asked for it to lure and test her parents, to see if once again they'd place an obligation above their only child. Once the gun was in her possession, Mavis understood that it was armor as much as armory. It meant she had a choice. That she wasn't helpless. Having her father's gun would make submitting to the congregation a greater show of strength.

She hadn't expected Jerrod to get out of bed in the middle of the night. She didn't know he might go to find it.

Mavis replayed Lily Owens ripping the heavy sconce from Djidji's wall.

Everything was a weapon now. Death included.

Jerrod had left her alone and Mavis didn't know why.

He would never hurt himself. She was certain. That wasn't why Mavis had moved the firearm. She'd wondered why he'd put it so far from their bedroom, except that neither of them had ever felt comfortable with a weapon in the house.

He'd heard about Djidji today, surely. An arrest had been made, the woman's employer and loved ones must have been informed. Mavis had been right; her husband hadn't said a word. He'd been glassy-eyed after work. Clingy and, some might say, fragile. It was an understandable response to a colleague's murder, paramour or not.

But the congregation came at night, and Jerrod had gone downstairs, leaving Mavis to wait for them on her own.

It was unbearable. At first, Mavis forced herself to stay in bed. She thought she needed to pee, but what did that matter? By morning, there wouldn't be any signals traveling between her bladder and her brain.

The minutes crept by. She'd think she was ready, that she wasn't afraid, and then Mavis would try to close her eyes and almost choke on her pulse. Her eyes would frantically scan her darkened bedroom for the shadowy figures who'd come for her once before.

Mavis exploded out of bed and ran to the restroom, closing herself inside without turning on the light. She began to hyperventilate in the dark. Palms pressed against the wall and the counter, the toilet in between. Bright colors burst in front of her eyes. Her mouth gaped and she drank in air like a whale pulling krill.

"This is how," she panted, spit dangling from one corner of her mouth. "This is how I save my marriage. This is how I save myself."

Her shoulders quivered until they collapsed, Mavis letting out two panicked sobs before she balled her fists.

She wasn't this person anymore.

She was fierce.

She could be fierce for one more hour, if it meant she'd never have to be again.

When Mavis came back into her bedroom, she forced herself to stand at the window. Underneath it, a half-blind woman had cowered because of what Mavis had done. Now she looked out over the still-empty backyard.

She'd left the back light on so that the congregants would see the new burial well she'd dug while Jerrod was at work. It was closer to the house, bathed in light, so that Mavis didn't have to shiver in the dark. So that the stones didn't catch her off guard when thrown. So that she could find the gun she wouldn't use. So that the congregants could see her face, in case it made any difference.

They hadn't come. Not yet.

They would.

Perhaps Jerrod could hear his wife moving above his head. Maybe he knew she was awake, if he still was. Locked in the guest bedroom again.

Jerrod was not too good to be true, but it didn't matter. Neither was she, and the longer they were married, the more likely he was to find that out.

Mavis made her marital bed. Beneath the skylight she'd always loved, she swelled and then smoothed the sheet. Straightened the comforter the congregation would wrap her in a second time.

Mavis laid on top. At first her arms lay limp beside her, her legs straight. Tense.

Mavis brought her hands over her heart, held one with the other. She breathed deep and closed her eyes. When tears ran toward her ears, she let them.

It wasn't cowardice to tremble.

It wasn't fragile to understand the gravity of what she was going to allow.

What she was going to do. Because she deserved to own this.

This was a decision, and it came at a great sacrifice. Whether or not it simplified things, whether or not it spared her, what had made her life unlivable didn't change that.

An earthquake could not have shaken Mavis's body more than she shook now.

She hadn't considered the pain.

She remembered the wails from the hardware store, from the bedroom, from the backyard. The way people had panicked at the realization that something had been broken, violently destroyed, and it had forced them back into their right mind only to shatter it.

She remembered Djidji Patton seizing after the first blow.

But those attacks had been different. They'd been interruptions. Hers wouldn't be like that; hers would have ritual. Ceremony.

Mavis was going into the ground, the same way Cyrus had.

The first stone had stunned him. It'd hit him so hard it interrupted his tirade. From the looks of it, he'd gone immediately into shock. If he was lucky, that meant it hadn't hurt too badly.

Maybe it wouldn't hurt for Mavis either.

Before she could lay hold of the thought, Mavis heard a faint creaking sound.

Her heart galloped.

Maybe she'd imagined it, and the backyard gate was still closed.

She was hyperventilating all over again—but that was okay. She didn't have to be calm. The congregation would roll her in her comforter while she trembled. They would carry her down the stairs without noticing her tears. She didn't have to be stoic. Fierce didn't have to be fearless.

Mavis closed her eyes and finally took a deep breath.

She was strong.

This was strength, and it would still be if she couldn't face the stones. She was strong even if, in her darkest moment, she used her father's gun.

In the still-quiet house, muffled crying echoed from downstairs.

Jerrod was awake. He'd heard the same creaking. He knew the congregation had come.

They weren't together, but Mavis tried to convince herself it didn't matter. That in a short time, it would be over, and Jerrod would have seven years' worth of memories to overshadow the distance of one night. Completing the vow meant every memory would shine brighter. It meant everything about Mavis would be precious. Sacred. Beloved. Every mistake would be a heart-warming anecdote; every flaw, human.

When Mavis was no longer flesh and blood, she would be perfect.

A door opened. The congregation was coming into the house. There were footsteps in the hallway, passing the guest bedroom, starting up the stairs. There had been three the last time; now it sounded like more. The vow was ever evolving. Under its spell, the congregants adapted; they learned.

There weren't enough bullets in her father's gun to kill them all. Even if there were, the rest of the congregation would keep coming. Most of them were strangers. Spread out. She would cross paths with them without knowing, in malls, or airports, or on vacation thousands of miles away. She wouldn't always be in her own home, where deadly force could be justified. She could not kill them all. Even if she did, she wouldn't get away with it, and being arrested—imprisoned—would mean a death worse than dying.

The first set of footsteps made it to the landing.

A sound escaped Mavis, her throat pulsing.

Don't.

Don't move. Don't resist.

This was the answer.

She was good at this. She was in control.

Mavis closed her eyes as the bedroom door opened, congregants filing in and filling up the space around her bed.

They moved her gently, rocking her from one side to the other the way they had the first time, as they wrapped her blanket over her. When she sighed as though in deep slumber and bent her elbows, the congregants didn't react. She hadn't resisted. She wasn't fighting back. They simply bound the blanket tightly around her frame, bent arms and all.

Mavis's eyes sprang open at a strange but familiar touch. She closed them again quickly, the congregation paying her no mind. They continued turning her horizontally on the bed while a steady stream of tears washed over her face. It coursed around the back of her neck and behind her ears.

She *had* felt her father's hands. Daniel Carson was one of the handful of people binding her for burial. It was Mavis's father who pinned her mummied ankles between his arm and his body, pulling her slowly over the mattress edge.

Mavis felt like she might break.

Another congregant latched onto Mavis's thighs, and another onto her waist. A fourth secured her shoulders, and the procession began out of her bedroom.

"Leave her alone!" Jerrod's voice bellowed from the base of the stairs. He was holding the wall and the handrail, making a barrier of his body as though that would stop the multitude.

"Jerrod!" Mavis called down to him, her view interrupted by balusters as the congregation carried her toward the top of the stairs. "Jerrod, don't! It's okay!"

He wasn't listening. He was yelling even though he didn't have to. They were many, but the congregation didn't make a sound. They were silent. Single-minded. They had Mavis in their clutches and that was all that concerned them.

"You're here for me!" Jerrod steadied himself as the group rounded the corner and momentarily paused at the landing. "You're here because of me—"

His voice had wavered.

"Jerrod, get out of the way! Please!"

"You're not leaving here with her," he said.

A congregant stepped in front of the procession and started down the staircase toward Jerrod. If not for being held, Mavis would have collapsed.

"No!" she cried. "Jerrod, baby, please get out of their way! They won't hurt you if you move!"

"You're here for me," he said, again, as though to the person descending toward him.

It was Whitley Owens, against her will. Her daughter was behind bars for a vicious murder that neither of them could understand or explain, and Whitley had been called out of bed—if the woman could even sleep—to fulfill the vow.

She was fully dressed, unlike most of the congregation. Maybe she'd been at the police station, answering questions. Pleading her case. Demanding answers. Maybe Whitley had been crumpled in an uncomfortable interrogation chair at her wit's end, the detectives giving her a moment to collect herself. To have a drink of water. Maybe she was exhausted, until she wasn't. Until her posture straightened unnaturally and she stood, walking past a station full of people who couldn't force her to stay. Maybe she'd walked out into the night and straight to Mavis's house.

Whitley stopped on the last stair, blocking most of Jerrod from Mavis's sight.

"Jerrod, please move!"

Whitley's hand was already tightening around the square cap of the newel post. The same way her daughter had effortlessly dislodged Djidji's sconce, the same way Mrs. Frederick had unearthed a staked mailbox, Whitley Owens tore the cap from the post and wound her arm back.

"Jerrod!"

He moved. He leapt to the side and out of Whitley's reach so suddenly it looked like a glitch.

Without hesitation, the woman dropped the cap. She turned her head and started down the hall as though Jerrod had disappeared. As though, out of the way, she had no more interest in him.

"Thank you," Mavis cried, her body aching in exhaustion with every jostling step her captors took. "Thank God."

She could see her husband's face now, that it was streaked with tears. His eyes were red as though the tears weren't recent—but that wasn't what worried Mavis.

It was the way Jerrod's brow furrowed. The way his neck recoiled, his eyes searching. He was trying to make sense of this.

"I came downstairs," he said, almost under his breath. "I came downstairs so you wouldn't go up."

The procession was moving past him, following Whitley down the hall.

"Mavis," Jerrod called after them. "I came downstairs so you'd be safe."

His voice trailed after her father.

"They killed Djidji."

The back door was open, more congregants waiting on the other side.

"They killed Djidji because of what I did," Mavis heard her husband say, his certainty waning.

She wished her father would close the door behind him, that Jerrod would stay in the house until the ceremony was over. She knew they wouldn't. Jerrod was going to follow them out, once he got his bearings. He was going to stumble down the hall, his mind resistant to the one fact that would make it all make sense.

She needed him to be the man he'd been for seven years. The man who didn't see her, who didn't know her well enough to know how scared she always was. She needed him to keep believing she existed only in the spaces where he expected to find her, that she was only capable of what benefitted him.

To be fair, before the vow—before calling Djidji—Mavis had never really seen him either. Jerrod was her husband. Her proof. Her reward. Djidji's casual conversation had proven Mavis didn't know Jerrod—especially not what he thought of her.

All she wanted to do was go back. To rewind back to when their marriage had been perfect.

"Mavis!"

Jerrod hadn't stayed in the house.

At the sound of his voice, Mavis jumped in her captors' arms. Bound, she fell to the stone pavers, crashing down on one shoulder before her face smacked the ground.

Jerrod's interruption had almost made her forget her plan.

Mavis rolled, collapsing her bent elbows so that the once-tight blanket gaped around her. She had space to move her arms now, and the wrapping only loosened more.

Already dizzy from her short fall, Mavis panted as she made her break, dirt and yard detritus invading her mouth and sinuses, arms wriggling up and out of the cover.

She couldn't see where she was going, she just kept going until she couldn't.

Something collided with Mavis's torso, her body buckling in the middle but with momentum enough to continue rolling. She laced around the obstruction like ribbon, her free fingers overextending painfully as though searching for something to cling to.

It was a leg. Someone had kicked Mavis in the stomach, her mouth falling so wide that she sprayed spit across the yard. She made a sound like a hurt animal and fell back, vision blurring to black.

"Mavis!"

There was a roar like a train bearing down on her. Dull but dangerous sounds of impact, of spontaneous combat.

Jerrod was fighting. Every time hands clamored for Mavis, fingers clawing at her clothes, they were themselves wrenched away.

Her eyes still pulsed, the world impossible to properly make out as it melted and seesawed around her. She couldn't see it, but Mavis knew what was happening. Again.

She moaned but couldn't say Jerrod's name.

Mavis had taken a double dose of her pain meds, in case shock wasn't strong enough to dull a stone, but maybe hyperventilation rushed the drugs through her system, or somehow damped its effect. The congregation was going to kill her tonight, and she was going to feel it.

Unless Mavis got into the hole, Jerrod was going to die, too.

It hurt to breathe. Mavis only made it to her hands and knees with the help of several congregants heaving her up.

She let them. She didn't resist, and their clutches calmed. She let a silent Daniel Carson wrap his arm around her waist and haul her away from a dogpiled Jerrod and toward the pit she'd dug.

Her father dropped her to the ground, and Mavis dove into the hole.

"I did it," she yelled. She had to cull every ounce of strength in her body, but she cried out, "I'm in the ground!"

The torturous sounds stopped. Jerrod's attackers abandoned him on the pavers and calmly headed for the lawn.

"Jerrod? Baby?"

She could almost see again. Mavis pressed her eyes shut, willing her vision to reset.

"Jerrod, are you all right?"

He groaned in return, and Mavis collapsed a little in her burial pit as the first batch of dirt rained down over her. She tucked her head and then stood up again.

She could see him. Jerrod was on his knees, on the pavers, struggling to get to his feet.

He was hurt. She couldn't see how badly, but he was bleeding, on his head and down his arms.

"Mavis," his deep voice croaked.

"It's okay, baby," she said. His image was throbbing now,

animated by her tears and interrupted by the dirt the congregation was pushing back into the hole. "It's gonna be okay now."

"They're here for you," he said.

Mavis froze, but the dirt still fell.

The congregation worked in silence, Havilah Greene working with one free hand, the other in a cast. A half-blind woman was among the congregants gathering dirt from elsewhere in the yard, Mavis having used her newly purchased shovel to both dig her grave and to spread the earth so that the congregation could not quickly resort to stones. They were already compiling their arsenal. Marie Carson and Rose Spencer were coming through the gate, rocks in hand, followed by congregants Mavis would have sworn she'd never seen. She probably hadn't, since her mother dissuaded the wedding guests from greeting her. They were spread out, in her yard, and wandering the neighborhood, reverently preparing to uphold the vow they'd taken.

"They're here for you, aren't they?" Jerrod asked this time. He was still fighting it, searching for permission to disregard his suspicion. Desperate.

Don't, Mavis heard Stephany Leonard say. For once, it was sage advice, so Mavis relayed it as gently as she could.

"Don't," she begged, shook her head not at the dirt cascading over her, but at her husband.

"Baby," Jerrod responded. "What did you do?"

Mavis hadn't felt it in a short while, the pierce of talons. The stinging, painful sinking in of sharp and rending claws.

He knew.

Jerrod knew that the offense had been Mavis's.

He knew what she must have done; it wouldn't take long for him to deduce with whom. When Mavis was dead and gone, head busted and blooming like Cyrus's, Jerrod would go searching for answers and he would find them. He'd know that this was the way the vow was defended. This was the ritual enacted. Everything else was just opportunity or interruption. When they crossed paths with Mavis and changed on sight, they would settle for killing her quickly, but stoning was the way it was meant to be done.

Cyrus had been stoned. Djidji hadn't.

Jerrod would find that out.

He was struggling on his feet, the sclera of one eye bright crimson.

"You let me think it was my fault," he said, stumbling toward the grave. He was going to come to her. He wanted answers, to understand. Congregants were raining soil over Mavis and using her shovel to dig up more, but it would take them forever. That's what Mavis had intended; now her plan was backfiring.

There would be no Dearly Beloved. No perfect wife in Jerrod's memory. He wouldn't cling to their seven years together, wouldn't recall her fondly to her parents and the congregation. Not now.

He knew what she'd done, and before a single stone was thrown, he would force her to confess to it herself.

All her ferocity, for nothing. All her strength, moot. She was going to be disparaged in her absence, maligned when it would seem the tally was complete.

Mavis couldn't live with that.

"Say something," Jerrod bellowed.

The congregants didn't flinch.

"Baby." His voice was a whimper now, his head hanging, steps imprecise. He stumbled past Whitley Owens as she gathered upturned earth with her bare hands, pushing himself off her bowed back. The woman didn't react. Mavis was in her grave; they would entertain no distractions now.

She sank in her burial pit.

"Mavis!"

He was coming to get her out. He didn't care that the congregation would rise up and destroy them both. Jerrod wanted her confession, no matter the cost. He felt entitled to it, the way Mavis had been explicitly forbidden. She had been counseled to suffer in silence and uncertainty—but Jerrod refused.

In the loose dirt collecting around her feet, Mavis felt for the handle. Felt her finger loop through the trigger guard.

When Mavis stood, her father's gun was in her hand, tears streaking grimy trails down her dirt-showered face.

"I'm so sorry, baby," she wept.

Don't.

Don't hesitate.

Don't waver.

Don't miss.

Mavis pulled the gun clear of the ground, aimed, and fired.

Jerrod kissed his teeth, like Djidji. His brow crashed down. He laid his hand over his heart, but that wasn't where he'd been shot.

It didn't make sense. The blood had sprung from his shoulder. He shouldn't have been able to raise his arm—but he wanted Mavis to suffer. That's why he kept coming, passing between silent congregants to reach the pit his wife was in.

When he got there, Jerrod let himself collapse to one knee. Like he was proposing, or else was trying to remind Mavis of the night he had. The night he'd saved her life. The night he'd changed everyone's mind about her.

She *was* deserving.

She *was* worthy and capable and wife material.

He'd gotten on his knee and offered her everything she'd ever wanted, and now he was doing it again. One day, another man might, as well.

The gun in her outstretched hand didn't matter. The congregation kept showering her with soil, and Jerrod kept leaning close, his face pinching. Pain was overwhelming his confusion. He was going to be clearheaded in a moment.

"I'll love you for the rest of my life," she told him, and then Mavis pulled the trigger again.

The bullet sank between Jerrod's eyes and he tumbled to the side.

The shot had been so loud it took a moment before Mavis registered the quiet. The silence. As though across her yard, a dozen people had suddenly paused. There was no more digging. No footsteps. No stones falling against each other as they were compiled.

The congregants awoke.

Some trembled as though the vow had been a second skin and now they could shed it. Slowly, they noticed each other, recognized Mavis's yard—or didn't.

She was still in the ground, pointing the gun where her husband had been. Then the tremors started, and the firearm clattered down the hole to Mavis's feet.

She followed it down, her own cries not enough to drown out the sound Deborah Dwyer made when she emerged from her stupor to find her son's dead body at the edge of a grave.

EPILOGUE

Coffee wasn't usually permitted in the sanctuary, but exceptions were made. Mavis accepted a steaming cup from her father, adjusting the caution sleeve.

"They didn't have hazelnut," Daniel Carson reported. "I talked to them; they'll have it next week."

"Thank you, Daddy." Mavis didn't belabor her father's disappointment, just smelled the medium roast, lightened by a hint of vanilla creamer, and smiled gently. The next moment, she was handing it back.

Rose Spencer was approaching, the older woman's diamond cluster earrings dangling past her sleek white bob.

Mavis extended her hands, into which Rose placed her own before the two women exchanged kisses. The affection was more greeting than anything, both women careful not to leave lipstick on the other's cheek.

"How are you?" Mavis cooed, her brows laced.

"Always better when I'm here," Rose replied. "And you?"

"I'm blessed," Mavis answered through a thoughtful deep breath.

They were holding each other by the elbows, faces a delicate mix of grief and grit.

"Mavis, sweetheart." Her mother's voice swept over her shoulder and Mavis turned. "I wanted to introduce you to someone."

Mavis held her hands one atop the other, pressed delicately over her middle. It was a posture of poise, one that exuded willingness and patience. She wouldn't interject, despite being capable of introducing herself. She rarely did that anymore. Now, her mother presented her.

"Tamika, this is my daughter, Mavis Carson-Dwyer."

The young woman was all nerves. Her lips kept tucking into her mouth and reemerging, her lipstick either matte or severely distressed. It would never last through service at this rate.

"Such a pleasure to meet you," Tamika gushed, accepting Mavis's limp hand and immediately adjusting the strength of her grasp to match.

"Tamika and I were hoping you could make some time to sit with her," Marie was saying, tilting her chin to signify discretion. Mavis nodded, a sober expression cresting and then immediately receding so that her gentle smile could resurface.

She understood. Tamika was struggling. There was no ring on her left hand, but nowadays it was impossible to know what that meant.

"We'll have lunch," Mavis decided.

"Yes," Marie Carson nodded, glancing toward Rose.

"After service," Mavis specified, and several nearby women set off as though to begin preparations.

Tamika was lost among them. The young woman glanced nervously around. She didn't speak, but she didn't have to.

Mavis stepped close. She wrapped an arm around Tamika's back and led her closer to the altar, a few steps from hungry ears.

"How are you doing?" she asked, Tamika's eyes darting quickly before she replied.

"I'm blessed."

"So am I," Mavis affirmed, encouragingly. "This morning, I woke up without the man I married, but I know I'm blessed to be a blessing. The way Jerrod was a blessing to me for seven perfect years."

Tamika's eyes settled on Mavis, a yearning almost visible beyond the nervousness.

"I'm so sorry for your loss," the young woman said, head bowing. "I listen to your and Sister Marie's podcast. I know everyone does, but. It's helped so much, hearing what a beautiful covenant you had, before he—"

"If being a widow surrounded by a steadfast community of faith family is the price of loving Jerrod, I'd choose it a thousand times." Mavis let her proclamation sink in. "It's carried me—this community and his memory—through the most difficult and beautiful month of my life."

"It's so recent," Tamika exclaimed, her face immediately betraying second thoughts. "I just can't believe your husband passed a month ago, and you've juggled so much."

For a moment, Mavis only breathed deep. She nodded, her eyes drifting as though over a store of memories.

"How did you get to forgiveness?" Tamika's yearning was fully exposed now. She hadn't heard Marie Carson return, didn't see the woman standing just behind her shoulder, eyes cast down before her daughter.

The young woman could've meant any of the congregants who'd descended on Mavis's backyard. The investigation had been necessarily brief. There were no earthly explanations for what had culminated in Jerrod's death. All that had been confirmed was Mavis's right to self-defense. Any attempts to understand how the congregation had amassed, or why they couldn't explain their presence themselves, had been abandoned within days. Mavis's recollection was law. Whatever intentions she assigned to the congregants they accepted as fact, many still waiting like prisoners for her judgment—Marie Carson among them.

"All have sinned," Mavis said, her mother uttering a prayerful agreement. "I don't know that anyone has ever been through what I was called to experience. Maybe it was a path paved only for me, a testing and trial that required others to falter. What I do know is that there had to be a betrayer for redemption to come."

A soft choir of affirmations alerted Tamika to their audience.

"Come to lunch," Mavis insisted. "Listening to podcasts—even mine—is all well and good, but we have to come closer if we're going to sharpen each other."

The young woman almost flinched. It was that promise of refining that she was resisting.

Mavis took Tamika's hand again and squeezed it. Tight.

"It's dangerous alone," she said. "None of us makes it outside."

Tamika's lipstick was all but gone, only a stain remaining the next time her lips reemerged.

Mavis retracted her hand. Pulled herself in like a lure. She let a distance extend between them, let her eyes lose some of their focus. In response, Tamika's yearning flared.

"Can I bring anything?" the young woman asked, and Mavis smiled.

"Just yourself."

ACKNOWLEDGMENTS

All my love and gratitude, especially to my Paul and Ezzie, without whom this wouldn't be any fun.

Innumerable thanks to my agent, Victoria. It's really always you and me.

To my beloved readers: Amy, Elle, Jasmine, Nesta, Anna, and Elena—you help make every story better.

ABOUT THE AUTHOR

Bethany C. Morrow is a bestselling author. Her young adult work includes JLG Gold Standard Selections *A Song Below Water* (a Locus, Ignyte, and Audie Award finalist) and *So Many Beginnings*. She is editor/contributor to the young adult anthology *Take the Mic*, which won the 2020 ILA Social Justice Literature Award. Her adult novels include *Mem*, an Indies Introduce and Indie Next pick, and *Cherish Farrah*, a social horror and the April 2022 Belletrist x Book Club pick. She was the 2021 Mansfield Lecturer at Roosevelt University, and her work has been featured in the *Los Angeles Times*, *Forbes*, *Bustle*, *BuzzFeed*, and more. Morrow is also included on *USA Today*'s list of 100 Black Novelists and Fiction Writers You Should Read.